The Guadeloupe Guillotine

Larry Jeram-Croft

Front cover image: The windward coast of Martinique

Also by Larry Jeram-Croft:

The 'Jon Hunt series' about the modern Royal Navy:

Sea Skimmer
The Caspian Monster
Cocaine
Arapaho
Bog Hammer

The 'Jacaranda' books about the Caribbean of the
modern day and Nelson's time:

Jacaranda
The Guadeloupe Guillotine

Science Fiction:
Siren

Chapter 1

He sat on the stone bench with his head in his hands staring at the rough stone floor. He should have been worrying about the pain in his jaw and groin; about the loss of his friends and his real life. Maybe he should also be worrying about what would happen when the Mayor caught up with him. Hitting him over the head with the butt of a shotgun was probably not the best thing to have done bearing in mind he was the only benefactor he had. It didn't help that this prison cell belonged to the Mayor in the first place. All this was enough to burden a man down with worry, yet it was the least of his concerns.

No, what was scaring the daylights out of him now was the noise and vibration. Over recent weeks he had become so used to the monster grumbling in the mountain behind the town that it barely affected his consciousness. Over the last few hours it had steadily grown worse. So much so, that plaster was starting to rain down from the ceiling and he could feel shocks through the soles of his feet to accompany the increasingly loud and frequent explosions. He had tried to attract the attention of the guard, to ask to what was going on and beg to be let out but no one answered when he hammered at the heavy wooden door. For all he knew, everyone had already fled and he was alone in this tiny enclosed space, surrounded by emptiness.

He cursed the old friend who had put him here. He now understood why he had asked where he would be held. He clearly wanted rid of him and it was looking increasingly certain that he would be successful. However, it didn't look like revenge would be on the agenda.

Suddenly there was a crack so loud it hurt his ears. Even inside his stone tomb. A second later a continuous rumbling sound was felt as much as heard and he knew that the top of the mountain must have finally blown out. No expert on volcanoes, he nevertheless knew what was likely to happen now. There had been enough television documentaries about the Pompeii eruption to inform the people of his time. The vast explosion would be accompanied by the ejection of superheated gasses and these would be forced down and out along the face of the mountain, right where the town was built. The Pyroclastic surge would generate temperatures of over a thousand degrees which would incinerate everything in its path.

He never espoused to believe in the Almighty, so he was surprised to find himself kneeling on the floor in terrified contrition, knowing what was about to hit him was compounded by his isolation both in time and space from his home. The last thing he held in his mind was a picture of Emma, the girl he was never able to obtain and that bastard Jack who had got him into this place to die. Another violent shock and the world went black.

Pain and light. Pain in his legs and back but light seeping through gummed up eyelids. Then noise, he couldn't understand it at first then he realised it was voices, human voices calling out. He tried to call back but could only manage a croak. With returning consciousness, he was able to make more sense of his surroundings. He could see a portion of sky above him where the ceiling had been and something was lying over his legs. He screamed in agony as he tried to move and realised his left arm was broken. Panting in reaction, he lay back again and almost passed out from the pain. Someone had heard his cry and there was renewed shouting somewhere in the distance. Suddenly a face appeared above him.

'Hey, there is someone here! Someone alive, come and help,' the man called to others nearby. Suddenly he was surrounded by smiling faces and he felt the weight taken of his legs. The agony of returning circulation was nevertheless a relief, at least he could feel his legs.

'Alright monsieur, we have come to rescue you,' said the stranger. 'We will get you to help. You have been very lucky. We have found no other survivors.'

He smiled up at his rescuer, 'where am I, what happened?'

'St Pierre monsieur and the volcano finally erupted but surely you remember this?'

He smiled back suddenly realising how little he knew. 'No, I don't remember, everything is a blank.'

Just before he slipped back into unconsciousness he realised he didn't even remember his name.

Chapter 2

Melissa's Diary

1786

I wonder if you will read this? I'm finding it hard enough to write with a goose feather, where are all the word processors? Hope you can decipher this scrawl. Anyway I decided to keep this journal as a rather long winded open letter to my future friends or should that be friends in the future?

Well, we arrived safely in Portsmouth, I'm not going to waste ink describing what England is like – you've seen the movies and TV shows, they're pretty good except for the smell and that's the last time I will mention that.

So Charles resigned his commission and we went to his 'house', bloody palace more like and I am now expected to rule over it as the 'mistress'. Jane Austen describes the life pretty well, we've also been to London but more of that later.

The first person I was introduced to was his mother ....

........water damage

We went to London for the first time. Charles has a large house there which is kept all year round. My God, if you thought it is bad in your time you should see it here. Total anarchy, I can't go anywhere without an escort and that's not part of polite society, it's an absolute must. Mugging is an art form, along with every other sort of vice you can think of. The 'roads' are mainly just dirt although some are cobbled and all are covered in manure and that's the nicest smell there is!!! (sorry, I said I wouldn't mention the smells any more). All the men are armed with swords and most carry pistols as well. Duelling is almost a national sport. Luckily Charles has the good sense to keep well clear. And then there are the social occasions. Charles and I have agreed that we will keep these to an absolute minimum, we don't really care if society thinks we are recluses, we have bigger fish to f........

.......mould

......*bloody doctor more like a pig ignorant butcher. The problem here is that many of the working class have their own remedies and they seem well based on centuries of experience. The so called professionals seem to just make it up. 'Vapours' and 'humours' and bleeding people, they haven't a clue, yet the Aristocracy give them credibility. Absolutely no idea about cleanliness. When I told him, all I got was condescension so I threw the bloody man out. Charles as usual understood (thank god for Charles he is my rock)but his mother went ballistic. Still with Charles's support I opened all the windows, gave her a blanket bath, started feeding her properly and in the end used up a course of my precious anti-biotics. Suddenly, she had never felt so well and suddenly I had another friend. Of course she wanted to know how I knew all these things...........*

........water damage

.....*got us thinking that if his mother could be persuaded of the truth this way, then maybe that was the tactic we could use with others. Of course, we still have to decide on what we do with our knowledge even if we are believed. We tried an idea out on the President of the Royal Society yesterday and it seems to be working. When I went through all the stuff Jack packed for us in a hurry as we left St Pierre, I came across one of those torches that works by cranking a handle, don't know how long it will last but my goodness can you use it to put the wind up these so called 'scientific gentlemen'. We allowed our tame scientist to accidentally see me using it last night. I made a quick excuse but now he is clearly desperate to know what it was. We're going to give him another day and then I'm going to let him accidentally see my watch – I've got one of those solar powered digital thingies. Soon he will desperate to believe what we have to tell him. Actually he's quite a good sort and hopefully a good conver........*

.......mice nibbled

5

1788

Well there are four of us now, Charles and me, his mum and now the President of the top scientific body of the age. We are going to have our first meeting of what we are calling the 'Jacaranda Society' – hope you like name Jack! We are working out a constitution but what we all seem to agree on is that we should not try to accelerate history (I was never good at it at school anyway). We are going to try to improve things slowly and for everyone's benefit. We all got completely tied up with the old paradox problem but we all feel we can't just let all this go to waste.

Hinchfield Hall looked magnificent. Set in rolling landscaped grounds at the end of a Beech tree lined gravel drive. The ornate, mellow, stone house basked in the early spring warmth. Hedgerows were coming to life, cow parsley, dandelions and nettle, all starting riotous growth beneath the translucent green of the newly budded beech leaves. Cattle were now in the fields having been released from their winter confinement; birds were calling in the clear blue sky, a cuckoo was making his presence felt somewhere in the woods.

Melissa, Countess Hinchfield, surveyed the scene appreciatively as she rode her horse back up the drive towards the front door. Her eyes took in the condition of her estate with approval, unlike when she first arrived; it all looked in order and well managed. She idly scratched under one armpit before consciously realising what she had done. 'Oh for fucks sake,' she swore to herself, 'I've got to get some decent bloody soap. That's the problem living amongst these bloody primitives.'

Taking the horse around the back she handed him over to Peter the groom and made her way up to the breakfast room. Charles was already there and she went up behind him and put her arms around him.

'Morning my love,' he responded. 'How was your ride? It looks like a beautiful day.'

Sitting herself down, she smiled back at him. 'Absolutely glorious, spring is such a perfect season, especially after a winter like the last one.'

Charles grimaced and nodded back. 'Yes, it was very wet and cold. We ought to try and do that 'central heating' thing you keep telling me about.'

Melissa looked sad. 'As I keep saying, some things are not possible until the technology exists and it's just too early for many of the good things we could have.'

Charles nodded, understanding perfectly. 'Are you sure you are still happy here my love? It must be so difficult for you.'

'You ask me that question almost every day and you know the answer. As long as you are with me, everything else irrelevant. I came here because of you and wouldn't have it any other way.' She reached over and squeezed his hand.

They settled into their meal but after few minutes the sound of little footsteps were heard followed by a female admonishment and a whirlwind entered the room and jumped straight onto Melissa's lap. Little Jack was almost two and despite all attempts to do otherwise was spoiled rotten by his mother and father. His nurse started to apologise but Melissa shooed her away, saying she would look after him now. It was another example of how the staff in the house were perplexed by the new mistress. Her manner and ways were so different to anything they had previously experienced. Yet they found they couldn't complain, her heart was so clearly in the right place. The mistress actually looking after her own child was the least of it.

Once little Jack was settled with a piece of toast, some of which was going in his mouth and some to the large deerhound sitting expectantly by his chair, Melissa decided it was time to broach the subject of the forthcoming days.

'Charles, I've made all the arrangements for our guests and the Society room has been prepared but we still haven't decided on the final agenda.'

Charles considered the point. 'I thought we had agreed that we would only discuss the one item this time. It's going to affect us so much and as we have discussed, if we can get them to follow our lead there is so much good we can do.'

Melissa looked relieved. 'Good, I'm glad we agree, I'll set it up that way.'

Later that day the guests started to arrive. There were several eminent scientists and professors and a few politicians but not ones in the public eye. They all came with their spouses and an entourage of servants. They were found rooms in the large house and settled in for the evening. Later on, a formal banquet was served. Melissa found these the most tiresome of all social events. The women's conversation was stilted and formal and any attempt to engage in intelligent conversation with the men was met with condescending amusement. Then just as things warmed up, the ladies withdrew to let the men carry on boozing and she was stuck with a load of vapid creatures whose conversation centred on either their children or who was being adulterous with who. As hostess, of course, she was expected to enter whole heartedly into the evening but that didn't mean she had to enjoy it. How different to parties of her youth.

The next day whilst most of the women stayed fashionably in bed until late morning, Melissa, Charles and a select number of the men made their way singly to the old folly built behind the main house in a small grove of trees. By ten o'clock, they had all entered the building. From the outside it looked like an old Greek temple, having been built by Charles's father as a garden ornament in keeping with the fashion of the times. However, in the last few years it had been carefully refurbished on the inside and contained a large table and chairs. It even had a blackboard on one wall. Strictly utilitarian, it served only one purpose; to conduct meetings of the highest secrecy. To discuss items that would be impossible to explain to anyone outside of its limited and extremely exclusive membership. That a woman was present at these meeting would also have raised eyebrows but all attendees knew why she was there and welcomed her as a founding member.

As soon as the last person was seated Charles opened the meeting. 'Gentlemen welcome to the fifteenth meeting of the Jacaranda Society. Please, as usual, do not take notes and keep all you hear today secret. Take no action unless it is agreed by us all. I am now going to hand over to my wife who will introduce you to the sole topic for discussion today.'

A few murmurs from around the table greeted this introduction. It was quite unusual to only have one topic to discuss. It was with even more than normal interest that they waited for Melissa to speak.

'Gentlemen, as you know the King of France has just about bankrupted his country supporting the revolution in the Americas and social unrest is rife. You may think that a weak France is a good thing for England but I'm afraid to tell you that within a few months a bloody revolution will sweep the country, many of the aristocrats, including the King and Queen, will be murdered and the stability of the whole of Europe will be utterly destroyed.'

Chapter 3

Jack paced up and down the small bare painted room, trying hard to keep his frustration under control. They had no right to keep him here and they knew it. He had no idea where Emma was. They had been separated as soon as they arrived and not knowing what was happening to her was adding to his misery.

He, Emma and his yacht Jacaranda had arrived back in St Lucia at the Rodney Bay marina that morning and he took her in to her usual berth and tied up alongside. He hadn't checked out with customs and immigration three weeks ago when they had left and so felt no need now to go up to the office and check in. So it was with more than some surprise that they came to him at the dock. Manny, the large man who managed the customs desk was accompanied by two policemen, who looked grim and kept their holstered pistols in clear view.

Jack invited them on board but they declined to go below for coffee or anything else.

Manny started the conversation. 'Where you been Jack? You not checked out with us and no one has seen you. This is a hard boat to miss you know.'

Jacaranda was eighty feet long and built to look like a 1930s racing boat but outfitted with every modern luxury. Jack knew she was well known and it wouldn't be hard to ask about the island and discover her whereabouts.

He looked Manny in the eye. 'Well, I suppose that's not really any of your business is it now? We didn't leave the Island and you can check with the others. They will have no record of us visiting. So what law have we broken and why are you here?' Jack knew, of course, that this was far from the truth but there was no way the St Lucian authorities could prove otherwise. Of course he also knew why they were asking the question. This was far from over but he was damned if he was going to be brow beaten by some Caribbean bureaucrat.

'Come on man, we all saw that video you posted on the web three weeks ago. The Royal Navy aren't here at the moment but

I'm pretty sure they will be heading this way as soon as they find out you've returned from wherever it is you've actually been.'

Jack was a pretty easy going character but had a stubborn streak and hated to be pushed around. Emma his girlfriend had come up from below and immediately could see what was about to happen but before she could interject Jack made his case clear.

'Manny, I have broken no laws and you have no right to be here so please leave my boat.'

Manny just looked at the two policemen and nodded. They moved to be alongside Jack and Emma. 'In that case you leave me no option. I'm afraid I am going to have to take you into custody. Come with me please.' And despite all their protestations they were taken to a large police van and driven here. Jack had been fuming in the hot confining office now for over three hours, his temper getting worse by the minute.

Eventually, Jack's feelings reached a threshold and he forced himself to start thinking rationally, rather than just reacting. The locals had made it clear that they had seen the chase on the internet, where the Royal Navy had attempted to stop them but he was pretty sure they were not able to see what had happened at end the chase. They would certainly have absolutely no idea that they had gone back to 1785 and even left two of the original crew there. As he forced himself to think it through he realised that they were probably acting on instinct and were holding him and Emma until some higher authority could make a decision.

Unfortunately, this was the Caribbean and any rights he might have for representation or to contact the consulate were subject to whim, rather than any rule of law. For that matter what would he say to a consul anyway? He had had a short chance to discuss things with Emma before they returned to the island and they had agreed in principle to be honest with the authorities but which ones? He really didn't want to try and explain things to the local low life cops. They would just laugh in his face and go down to the boat and search it for Ganja or hallucinogenic drugs. He would just have to sit tight. Maybe Robbie the Captain of the West Indies Guard Ship would appear soon, at least he would be able to talk to him about what had really happened.

Suddenly all the questions were academic. The door opened and short, slim, man in a well cut dark suit entered. When the policeman tried to come in as well, he just looked at him and the policeman beat a retreat to the other side of the door.

'Jack Vincent, we need to talk,' said the stranger in a clipped English accent. His gaze was hard and unforgiving as he sat down at the small desk opposite Jack and gazed steadily at him.

Jack could play the silent game as well and just stared back at the man. It was almost like one of those childish games one plays in the playground to see who would blink first but Jack saw no reason to respond. After all, he hadn't been asked a question.

Eventually the man sighed and broke the silence. 'We really need to know what you've been up to and what you know.'

Jack stared back. He still hadn't been asked anything.

'You will tell us you know.'

Jack didn't like threats even implied ones. He leant forward and looked into the stranger's eyes. 'You haven't asked me anything yet but I've a really good suggestion,' he said in the mildest of tones.

The stranger looked surprised and interested for a second.

'Why don't you just fuck off, go outside that door, come back in again and behave like a civilised human being?'

The man flinched and started to say something but Jack got in first. 'I've absolutely no fucking idea who you are, no fucking idea who you represent and therefore absolutely no fucking idea why I should talk to you. Oh and you sent that plod out and he's locked the door from the outside and I'm a lot bigger than you.'

The stranger's supercilious air was deserting him fast and he was at last starting to look worried, especially when he looked behind him and realised that the door was indeed locked and he was alone in a room with someone who was clearly extremely unhappy with him.

'I represent Her Majesty's government, as I am sure you can work out and we both know that you have information we need,' he blustered.

'No, I bloody don't know. Firstly you still haven't introduced yourself or shown me any ID. All you have done is make vague threats and in case you haven't noticed you are on foreign soil and have absolutely no jurisdiction in this St Lucian police cell.'

'Yes, that's as maybe,' he started to say when there was a commotion outside the door and it suddenly flew open. A large familiar figure appeared.   Commander Robbie O'Brien, Commanding Officer of HMS Suffolk and one of Jack's oldest friends grinned down at him. 'Well, me old mucker, that's you firmly in the shit. You're not going to disappear on me this time.'

Then he saw the other man and frowned. 'Lockyer you little scroat, who said you could start to interview Jack before I got here?' and then looking round, 'and where's Emma why have they been separated?'

The small man, Lockyer started to splutter. 'I don't need you permission to interview this man. May I remind you that I am the local intelligence head here. I decided to separate them to apply a bit more pressure.'

'God, you are such a twat,' responded Robbie with a grin. 'Well it's quite simple I have been contacted by London and been given full authority over this matter and if you don't believe me just give them a call. May I remind you that no laws have been broken so 'applying pressure' is a totally unacceptable tactic. Bloody hell man, we're here at the grace and favour of the St Lucian authorities, you're putting all that at risk.'

'Robbie thank you very much.   I assume Emma and I can leave now.'

Robbie turned back to Jack. 'You matey have got to be joking. After the last stunt you pulled do you really think HMG is just going to let it lie?'

Jack looked worried.

'No, you and your lovely girlfriend are coming with me to the ship, which is British soil by the way and no bloody arguing. We are going to have a nice long chat, the one we should have had a month ago.'

Chapter 4

The cool trade winds blew through and around the veranda of the large two storey grey stone building. Built on the tip a large promontory, the house dominated the estate around it. Down and to the right, the roof of the slave quarters could be seen amongst the trees. All around were similar stone buildings serving the needs of a thriving sugar plantation. The view ahead was stunning. A large, well sheltered bay, glittered in the late evening sunshine. Protected by a multitude of reefs out to seaward, it provided safe anchorage to any seaman experienced enough to run their gauntlet and gave the estate its unique advantage.

The windward coast of Martinique was different to most Caribbean Islands in that it had a number of safe havens, despite the fact that they were on a permanent lee shore. Something most sailors tried to avoid. By being able to offer shelter right next to the estate itself, it was possible to load ships with produce and steal a march on those other estates who had to haul their sugar across the island to Fort Royal for shipping. Of course they could also have used the great harbour at St Pierre but after the volcanic eruption a few years ago that had totally devastated the town and the harbour, all that was left now was a smoking ruin,

Jacques sat on a cane chair looking at the view but seeing nothing. The wind ruffled his long hair and a glass of rum lay untouched on the table to his side. The pain from the healed burns on his arm was a dull ache but otherwise he had recovered well from the physical side of his ordeal. Mentally however, even after all these years, he was still in turmoil. His dreams last night had left him troubled and once again he was having to try and reconcile two impossible worlds. He still couldn't remember any personal details, although he seemed to speak French and English with fluency. That said, his manner of speaking had seemed very strange to his benefactors when they had first pulled him out of the rubble. But how could he dream of carriages with no horses, boxes with letters and pictures on the front all hinting at a life impossible in this age?

Before he could think further, a lilting voice interrupted his reverie.

'Jacques, are you somewhere else again? I was calling your name but you didn't answer.' The speaker was a tall slim young lady. She had long dark hair held up with an ornate bone comb. Her elegant light blue dress showed her shapely bosom and hinted at her long legged figure. Her brown eyes were complemented by a smooth skinned complexion, with the hint of freckles around her pert nose. She smiled fondly down at Jacques and put her hand on his shoulder.

'You know, you called me Emma again last night. One day I would love to meet this woman, she must mean so much to you.'

Jacques flinched. 'Maybe Francine, my love but she means nothing to me now. Yet another echo of my lost past I'm afraid. You are my life now.'

Francine smiled wistfully. 'I know but I think you are still troubled by what you cannot recall.'

Four years previously, Jacques had been pulled out of the rubble of St Pierre, the only survivor from within the town of the catastrophic volcanic eruption. Briefly conscious, he had succumbed to the pain of his wounds and lain delirious for many days. He had been taken in by the La Croix family and tended by their daughter Francine who had looked after him day and night until he regained consciousness on the fifth day. During this time he had been raving and delirious. Much of what he said simply made no sense to his doctor and the young lady who attended him. However, he repeated one name many times, that of 'Jacques' and so when he finally came to and they found he could not recall anything of his previous life, the name was given to him as some form of link to his lost past.

His wounds had been surprisingly light, a broken and burned left arm plus a multitude of cuts and scrapes. However, none of it could explain his loss of memory and in the end it had been put down to the trauma of the event. However, once he had recovered, he found himself adrift in a world he only partly understood. The La Croix family were firmly of the conviction that he was, like them, an aristocrat of some sort. The quality of his clothing was one indication, but more importantly, his manner and quality of speech clearly pointed to an educated and civilised man and in 1785 that could only mean one thing. Jacques was in no position to disagree but still felt that somewhere there was another life completely unlike the one he was now living, if only he could remember what. Enquiries sent back to France came to nothing and in the end he had settled into a sort of half awake living dream, plagued by strange nightmares of things he could not understand.

Despite the trauma of his ordeal, he soon found that he had a surprisingly good head for business and the La Croix family being one of the largest landowning families on the Island had put his talents to good use. Whatever his past, he had an innate talent for commerce and soon came up with a raft of innovations that had secured his new adopted family even more wealth than before.

Monsieur Jean La Croix was the head of the family and Francine's father. Initially suspicious of the newcomer, especially with his mysterious background, he had soon realised that wherever Jacques had come from he was proving to be an asset to his family. In time he started to look on him as the son he never had and increasingly trusted Jacques with more of the day to day running of the business. Francine on the other hand, looked on him in entirely different light. Her looks and figure whilst not unbecoming did not really fit the current fashionable norms and that coupled with the dearth eligible males on the island had meant that by the age of twenty two she was still unmarried. In this age, any girl reaching such an exalted age without a suitor was destined for spinsterhood. Her mother had died in childbirth and although she loved her father dearly he clearly, he either did not or would not understand her plight. Then the volcano erupted and the whole island rushed to the scene to offer succour. She initially volunteered to nurse the survivor, purely out of a sense of duty but as he recovered, she soon realised what an extraordinary person he really was. He in turn, saw a beautiful girl, still very young by his own standards but with a bright mind and features that immediately attracted him, although he couldn't say why.

Within a year, he had approached his benefactor and been given his blessing and so became not only the husband of a beautiful young bride but also the potential heir apparent to a vast estate and fortune. All this should have made him extremely happy and content and in some ways it had. But he knew that until he unlocked the door to the room of his past he would never be truly settled.

He turned to Francine and pulled her down onto his lap, burying his head in her hair and kissing her ear. 'One day it will all come back to me, sometimes I feel that the answer is only just out of reach.'

She returned his kiss and looked him in the eye. 'As long as it doesn't affect us, then I can't wait until the day.'

'Never my love, whatever happened in my past has no bearing on the present and never will.'

Francine pulled herself away, there were other things to discuss and maybe of more immediate importance. Swinging around its anchor down in the bay was the first of the season's trading ships and Jacques had been down there this afternoon talking to its master.

'Did you find out any news from home Jacques?' she, like all the islanders called France 'home' even though she and most of the rest of them had actually never actually been there.

He frowned. 'Yes my dear and the news isn't good. There is great unrest. The Monarchy is becoming more unpopular and all sorts of rumours abound about what will happen next. You know, it's almost as if I should know what is about to happen. Something is nagging at the back of my mind but whatever it is I am sure it will be bad and will affect us greatly.'

'It seems strange that something happening so far away could be a threat to our life on this island,' she said wistfully, gazing over the peaceful bay.

'Not just this one but Guadeloupe as well my dear,' said Jacques agreeing. 'But that island has always been more belligerent. I wonder if they will react the same way. I was at the main assembly last month and several people were starting to talk openly about trying to distance ourselves from our home country, as if that were possible. Some were even saying that we should declare for England, although I really don't see why that would work. Whatever is going to happen will happen soon, of that I am sure.'

Chapter 5

Melissa's Diary

Date obscured

Last page, bottom half:

...... so you see, we're going back to the Caribbean, to Antigua !!! Charles says it will be safe even with the French problem. So I will complete this edition and leave it with my time capsule. I'll start again on return. Don't worry, I've got plans to ensure you get it. Hang on if you are reading this then I don't need to say that. Is this confusing or what....

Love Melissa

Life in France was turning to bloody chaos but at Hinchfield Hall everything was proceeding at its normal pace. It was something Melissa found extremely frustrating on occasions. But with no instant communications, it was strange how sanguine one could be about events even a few miles away, let alone in another country. The Jacaranda Society continued to meet but everyone's real focus was on events across the Channel. The latest attempts by French Royalists to form some form of government were descending into chaos. The Legislative Assembly might have worked if the King hadn't vetoed nearly every decision they made. Melissa couldn't remember much of the history but was sure that the King was signing his own death warrant.

Life went on in the peaceful English country side and Melissa and Charles were out riding and enjoying the late spring sunshine.

There was no one else about so she was riding in her normal astride fashion, not side saddle as she was forced to when amongst society.

'You know it's so frustrating Charles, I wish I had paid more attention to my history lessons at school and of course we agreed not bring any history books with us.'

'Stop fretting my love,' he responded with a smile. 'It's almost certainly better this way. You have given us enough knowledge to allow us to prepare. Let's face it, even if you could remember every detail, there is not much we could actually do. Events are happening already.'

She returned his smile. 'Yes, you're probably right and we agreed right from the start that changing history in big chunks is not really achievable. Mind you, there is a small Corsican soldier you might want to think about assassinating about now. But enough of that, you know the real problem with the men of this age?'

Puzzled he looked back. 'Er no but I'm sure you are going to tell me.'

'Absolutely right. Your problem is that you think us women are weak and feeble. You're absolutely wrong as I am going to prove to you by racing you to the summer house and beating the pants off you!' And before he had a chance to respond she let out a great whoop, tugged her horse around and set off over the meadow at a gallop.

Charles thought for a second before setting off in hot pursuit.

A few minutes later he reached the beech copse that hid their summer house just behind his wife. He grinned ruefully to himself, no doubt she would accuse him of holding back to let her win, when he actually knew she had beaten him fair and square. That she was so unlike all the other women he had ever known was one of the many things that attracted him to her.

They dismounted and led the horses through the small track between the shafts of sunlight beaming through the trees and let them loose to graze in the small meadow beyond. Melissa gave Charles a smug grin as he caught her up but otherwise they kept a companionable silence. Just further on and they came to their secret spot. Someone, possible even a Roman, as there were rumours of an old villa nearby, had diverted a loop of the river into a small man made pool. When Melissa had seen it soon after arriving at Hinchfield, she immediately had an idea. She got Charles permission to use some of the estate workers to do the work but kept her idea secret from him until everything was complete. She had the pool cleared of all its growth and lined with local stone. She then had sluice gates made on the exit of the pool so that the water level could be controlled and there it was, an Eighteenth century swimming pool. It had clear running water which would allow her to indulge in her passion for swimming admittedly only in the warmer months. She also had a small summer house made to give some shelter and shade. The place was completely private, screened by the beech wood. The main river ran only feet away and the whole little copse was alive with wildlife, from Kingfishers to Herons. The river was full of fat trout. Some even managed to get over the weir into the pool which had made Melissa jump the first time one slithered past her legs when she was swimming. As soon as Charles saw it he was entranced and they came here to be alone whenever they could.

As they reached the pool, Melissa immediately started to pull off her clothes and soon a naked golden girl, plunged in and turned to call to him. 'Come on slow coach, get your kit off and join me, it's not that cold!'

Even now Charles was finding that his wife's use of language could surprise him but he knew what she meant and needed little urging to join her. Stripping off, he also dived in emerging spluttering with the shock of the cold water. He swam up to Melissa who was floating near the middle. 'Well my little woodland nymph, what a shame the water isn't as warm as it was when we were in the Caribbean.'

She grinned impishly, her hand disappearing below the water. 'Well it may be cold but not so cold that things aren't functioning properly!'

He made a grab for her and she made no effort to resist.

Later they lay on a blanket, lying side by side looking up at the clear blue sky. Secret spot it may have been but that hadn't stopped Melissa ensuring that a hamper with bread, cheese and wine had been delivered earlier. The second wine bottle was nearing its end and all the food had long gone. She listened to the sound of the river and the call of the birds. That cuckoo was still about but she could also hear all sorts of birdsong from the trees.

The smell of spring and the warmth of the sun were slowly lulling her into a gentle doze.

'I must be the luckiest woman alive,' she murmured dreamily. 'I have no television, no car, no anything that I was bought up with,' and rolling on her elbow she looked down at Charles, 'but I have all this and I have you.'

Charles smiled gently back up at his wife. 'I only pray that it all continues, as I am also the luckiest man alive.' And he lifted his head to kiss her.

As they broke away for air, Melissa looked concerned. 'Did you mean anything by saying you pray it continues?'

'No, only with all this doubt about France. We live in troubled times my dear.'

'Charles, I've known you for long enough now to know when you are hiding something. Come on out with it.'

Charles sighed and lay back. 'As usual, you have seen right through me my dear. Yes, something has occurred that I'm fairly sure you will want to be involved in. I've been waiting for the right moment and I think that this is it.'

Melissa sat back looking at him with a raised eyebrow. 'Come on, don't keep me in suspense.'

Charles looked pained. 'My family is quite large as you know but even I wasn't aware of where some branches of the family had spread to. It seems as the Earl I have now inherited some land from a distant relative.'

Melissa frowned. 'You say that as if it was a problem. What's the catch?'

'It's in Antigua and it's a sugar plantation.' Charles stated baldly and waited for the reaction he knew was coming. He could see the emotions on his wife's face as she immediately put two and two together.

'Oh no, that means slaves, that means we now own a slave plantation, Oh my God that's dreadful.' Melissa had known that many things of the present era were going to be repugnant to her but knowing about something and being actively involved were two different matters. One thing she would never accept was slavery and Charles knew that.

'Now my dear, please don't overreact. It's thousands of miles away and there is nothing we can do from here.'

'Damn right there isn't. So that's why we are going to have to go there and do something. Even if we can't free them, we can damn well make sure their conditions are as good as we can make them.' She stared defiantly at him.

Charles knew this would be her reaction. It was quite amazing how well he had come to know this woman over the last few years.

'So my dear, that is why I've told you now. I will endeavour to find us a ship and we can take passage as soon as the Hurricane season is over.'

'How long will that be,' she asked biting her lip.

'My darling it's not like your time. We cannot just jump on one of your flying monsters but I hope we can get there safely by the end of the year.'

Chapter 6

The transatlantic trip in HMS Suffolk had been surprisingly pleasant. Robbie explained that the powers that be had decided that them staying on the ship was deemed a safer and more clandestine way to get them home rather than putting them on aircraft. The weather had been benign but even at her best speed the ship would take almost a week to get home to England. The time had allowed Jack, Emma and Robbie to sort things out as far as was possible. If nothing else, they had managed to re-establish their friendship. Jack realised that during their previous encounter, Robbie had had no choice and also that he could have been far more aggressive had he wanted to. Surprisingly, on board the crowded warship accommodation hadn't been too much of an issue. With girls serving on board nowadays, providing facilities for Emma had been easy, although due to a lack of spare cabins Jack ended up using the Sick Bay as a temporary accommodation. However, as they spent a large proportion of their time in the Captains day cabin or the Wardroom it wasn't really a problem.

For Jack it was a trip down memory lane. The motion, atmosphere and unique smells of a warship brought it all back. Despite the time away he even started feeling a little guilty about not being asked to stand a watch or two. Of course he was now just a passenger.

He and Emma had decided to come completely clean about what had happened, although they had managed to take out one small but hopefully effective insurance policy whilst they were travelling back to St Lucia. Luckily, no one knew they had returned until they arrived in Rodney bay that is except for a few friends ashore who were even now using the internet to its full advantage. However, it was one thing to thwart the navy in the heat of the moment, especially when they had a promise to a friend to keep. But now the dust had settled they both realised that trying to hide things just wasn't a workable option. Anyway, Jack wanted to know the truth of why the time anomaly was there in the first place just as much as Robbie, the navy and the British

Government wanted to know what had happened to Jack, his friends and Jacaranda.

'So, let's get this absolutely straight, you're telling me you went back to 1785, returned your visitor to his time, rescued Emma and even had dinner with Nelson? Come on Jack please tell me you're taking the piss?' asked a sceptical ship's Captain when they had first managed to get together in privacy.

'Well you saw an eighty foot yacht vanish right in front of you, explain that any other way if you can. Anyway you were the one that asked me some weeks before about anything odd going on weren't you?' responded Jack. 'So I'll do you a trade. We'll tell you everything but you've got to tell us what you know as well.'

'I'll do what I can but frankly I don't know much more than I told you last time. As I said then, it's all down to some weird wartime experiment that seems to have gone horribly wrong. Which reminds me, why weren't you honest with me then? Come on I thought we were mates.'

Jack looked pained. 'Look Robbie, your question came out of the blue. I had only just made my discovery and worked out some of the detail. In the process I made a lot of promises to a lot of people not to get them involved. I had no idea it was all going to escalate and then you went off on operations. By the time you got back, I had an unexpected visitor and more than enough problems without getting you lot involved as well. And as I eventually guessed, that shit, Paul tipped you off, so you got to find out anyway. It's just a shame we had to have our confrontation in such a public way.'

'Wasn't me with the video camera,' and then seeing the angry look appearing on Jack's face. 'Alright, we were legally in the wrong but come on, surely you can see how important this could be? The problem with you is that you always used to see things in black and white and you certainly haven't changed.'

Emma broke in before Jack had the chance. 'Now you two, we're meant to be cooperating. Jack for goodness sake just chill, I want to understand this as much as you do.'

Jack looked chastened. Emma was always able to see the full picture. 'Sorry, yes you're right as usual and when we get back to the UK, I want the powers that be to understand that as well. There's no need for the heavy handed approach that idiot tried on us in St Lucia. If they try that again, it will just guarantee me being bloody awkward.'

Robbie smiled. 'And I know just how awkward you can be. Right come on cough up. I want chapter and verse from both of you and of course you do realise it will be sent straight back home? But bugger that, before anything, what was Nelson really like?'

Jack told it all right from the very beginning when he had encountered the strange Spanish slaver, right up to when they made it back. Emma did the same, although her story was quite different in many respects as she had been separated from Jack right until he had managed to rescue her.

Robbie recorded it all and used the satellite link to forward it to London. On the third day out he received a signal and called Jack up to see it for himself.

'You're not going to like this. Sorry Jack but you can see their point of view,' Robbie said as Jack studied the piece of paper.

Jack looked grim, 'All they had to do was ask you know. I would have said yes up front. Why do they seem to want to have a confrontation all the time?'

'Yes well, with all the international attention our video got, I can see why they're a bit paranoid. They managed to cover it up by saying it was all a misunderstanding and that it was to do with drug smuggling, what else would it be out there? Don't worry we can sort this out when we get to London. Anyway we 're going to need your answer.'

Just then Emma came into the cabin and seeing the look on Jack's face realised something was wrong. 'What is it Jack?'

He handed her the signal. 'Look for yourself, it appears they tried to seize Jacaranda and for once the St Lucian authorities dug their toes in. I suspect Lewis and Martha might just have had a hand in that. Now they're telling Robbie to instruct me to tell St Lucia that the boat can be recovered back to England. Note they are instructing me not asking.'

Emma looked pained. 'Well, we did say we would cooperate. I don't suppose they mean it quite the way it reads.'

Jack snorted. 'Good on you Emma for always seeing the best side of people,' and then with a sigh, 'and of course you're right as usual. OK Robbie, I understand why they need the yacht and I will authorise her release but on one understanding and until I get that in a legally binding form I will do nothing.'

'Go on.'

'I need an undertaking from the Government that whatever they want to do with her, they will guarantee to restore her to her original condition afterwards and ship her back to St Lucia. Failing that if they have to take her apart, I want full reparation for the cost of building another yacht.'

'Well that seems reasonable to me. I'll draft a reply to that effect and we'll see what happens.'

A day later the reply arrived. Jack wasn't too happy with it as it basically stated that full details would be agreed once they were in England but he caved in knowing that in the end he had little choice. However, it didn't do anything to improve his mood as they climbed into the back of the ship's helicopter for the trip to London two days later. Robbie had passed on to them details of what he knew which seemed to be fairly sparse. They would land at the Battersea Heliport, be taken first to the MOD Main Building in Whitehall and then on for a full debriefing but where was unclear. As the helicopter approached the landing pad, Jack could see a car with blacked out windows, presumably waiting for them and two men in innocuous grey suits standing beside it. The aircraft touched down with a small thump and they waited for the engines and rotors to shut down.

The two men then approached the helicopter just as Robbie slid the large cabin door open and they all jumped onto the tarmac.

'Mr Jack Vincent?' queried the first anonymous man. 'Come with me please.' And he took hold of Jack's left arm whilst the other man did the same to Emma.

Jack angrily tried to shake off the man's rather firm grip to no avail.

'Let go of my arm. There's no need to be so aggressive.'

'Sorry Sir, we have orders to ensure you come with us.'

'Look you moron, I want to go with you, don't you get it?'

'Sorry Sir.'

'Or what? What exactly will you do?'

The man used his spare hand to pull the right side of his jacket open and expose a shoulder holster with a black pistol.

Jack saw red. Without thinking he simply reached over with his free arm and pulled out the weapon to a look of total surprised astonishment on the man's face. He then twisted his arm back and flung the pistol as hard as he could towards the edge of the landing area. There was a metallic clang as it hit the tarmac followed by a satisfying splash as it bounced over the edge and into the Thames.

There was a stunned silence. 'Now what are you going to threaten me with you wanker?'

Both men looked totally confused, this wasn't in the script. Being disarmed so simply and with the grinning witnesses of the aircrew in the nearby helicopter as well was not good. Embarrassment warred with anger on their faces.

Luckily Robbie stepped in before something unfortunate happened. 'Right, that's enough everyone.' And then turning to the man still clutching Emma's arm. 'You, let go of the girl, NOW.'

The other man let go of Emma sheepishly.

'Now these are my friends and I vouch for them. They are of considerable value to this country. They are patriots and are definitely not in the need of a threatening armed escort. Do you understand?'

One of the men looked as if he was about to argue.

'Not another word from either of you. I assume that's our transport?' he asked pointing to the parked car.

They nodded.

'Right off we go then. I believe we have a meeting arranged.'

As they walked to the car Robbie said quietly to Jack, 'bloody stupid thing to do mate but God it was worth it to see the look on that goon's face. Now look, cool it OK? These were just the monkeys, we've got the bloody organ grinders to deal with now and they won't be so easy, right?'

Jack was just coming down off the adrenalin high and wondering how on earth he had had the nerve to do what he just done. He simply nodded.

An hour later after fighting through the London traffic, they arrived in Whitehall and pulled up by the imposing white stone building of the Ministry of Defence. To their surprise they weren't taken in the through the imposing main doors but were shuffled through a little side door down a ramp to the right hand side. Jack had never been inside the building during his time in the navy so didn't really know what to expect but was not surprised when they were shown into a small room and asked to wait with the two security men. Robbie was called out but assured them he would see them soon. Jack and Emma took seats and stared moodily around them.

'More psychology I suppose, make us stew for a while,' he observed gloomily and then he added sotto voce but still loud enough so that his guards could hear. 'Still, at least I've had the satisfaction of making that security thug look a complete dick.'

The man didn't rise to the bait but Jack was sure he detected a pained expression on his face for a few seconds. He did however, receive a kick under the table from Emma. 'Stop it, we're all meant to be on the same side,' she hissed.

'Sorry, but you know me. Maybe if someone was nice just for once, I might be less grouchy.'

Emma was about to reply when the door at the end of the room opened and Robbie reappeared. 'Right you two, come with me please.' And then turning to the two guards, 'not you, your services are no longer needed.'

He led Jack and Emma down a long corridor and then down a series of staircases. At the end of the stairwell he opened a door and ushered them through. Jack stopped in surprise. Ahead of them was a large open space like a warehouse, clearly deep underground but what had surprised him was the building inside the space. It looked like an old stone chapel. What on earth was it doing here? He looked questioningly at Robbie.

'Sorry mate, you've never been to Main Building have you? This, believe it or not is Henry the Eighth's wine cellar. It was built over when the original building went up. It's usually used for social purposes but is also the most secure area in Whitehall hence we're meeting here.'

He ushered them in and closed the old fashioned wooden doors behind them. Inside Jack was surprised to see only three people, an Admiral in full uniform who he vaguely recognised and two suited civilians.

The Admiral stepped forward and held out his hand. 'Jack Vincent, you might remember me? I was Commanding Officer of Culdrose when you were doing your flying training. I'm currently Second Sea Lord and the naval lead on this subject.'

Jack immediately placed the face even though he never really knew the man.

'May I introduce Mr Alan Jenkinson who I am sure needs no introduction and his colleague John Smithers.'

'Sorry Admiral but I've no idea who Mr Jenkinson is,' said Jack as he turned and held out his hand to the man who looked rather put out.

'I, young man, am Secretary of State for Defence, surely you know that,' he said rather huffily.

'Oh terribly sorry, I haven't really looked at the UK news for years now and I certainly don't follow politics. Guess you got in last year but as I say I don't really pay much attention.'

'Yes, well, anyway my colleague Mr Smithers is the Chief Scientist on this project.'

Jack looked at the man as he shook his hand in turn and saw a thin academic looking man, with a shock of red hair, about the same age but clearly with a pallor that meant he rarely saw the sun. His firm handshake and sudden smile was in contrast to his demeanour and Jack realised that first impressions here might be misleading.

'Right everyone please take a seat,' boomed the Admiral and he indicated chairs set around a small table. The scientist poured them all some coffee from the flask on the table and a brief silence descended.

It was broken by the Minister. 'Right, Mr Vincent and Miss Jones, firstly please accept my apology for you treatment at the heliport. The Commander here told us what happened and believe me it won't happen again.' He then chuckled. 'Mind you, don't be surprised if MI5 offer you a job when the dust settles here. Oh, I also have here a legal document, guaranteeing the return of your yacht or financial remuneration as requested. I hope that's alright?'

Jack smiled looking relieved as he studied the document. At least it was one worry off his mind. It looked like at last attitudes were changing.

They talked for over an hour. They briefly summarised Jack and Emma's accounts and generally set a baseline for the way ahead. John Smithers clearly knew a lot more than he was letting on but Jack wasn't able to draw him out. By the end they had agreed a way ahead.

The Admiral summed it up. 'Thank you Jack and Emma. It's clear to me that you will be cooperating fully and that is a great weight of our collective minds. I think you appreciate now why we were so worried but from all you've said I think we can put that behind us. Now, there remains one small problem, that of getting you the security clearances you will need to get access to where we want you to go.'

Emma was surprised by the remark and said so. 'Isn't it a bit late for that? Surely in some ways we actually know more about this subject than you do.'

'You have a point there my dear said the Minister,' and turning to the other two. 'They will need access to the Farm won't they? Surely they can be given direct indoctrination and clearance? After all they will have to sign the Official Secrets Act.'

The Admiral looked at the Scientist questioningly who nodded and said, 'yes well it's pointless going on unless we take them there for full tests and a technical debrief. Maybe if I act as their chaperone for the near future then the usual background checks can be carried out at the same time.'

'Right that's settled,' said the Minister. 'I'm sorry but I'm late for my next meeting. Nice to meet you two and I will leave you in the care of Mr Smithers and look forward to his report.'

The Admiral took his leave as well and the three were left alone. Jack spoke first. 'Er what now John? And what on earth is this farm you keep talking about?'

John laughed. 'I'll keep that as a surprise but for today we have a hotel booked just up the road and I guess as long as I escort you, a bit of shopping might be in order. You don't seem to have much luggage.'

Emma was delighted, she had been wondering how she was going to replace her wardrobe which was all in St Lucia.

They left the building by more conventional means through the main exit this time. A blast of fresh air and the bustle of London met them as they walked down the steps. Suddenly, they were surprised by a middle aged woman approaching them.

'Excuse me but are you Jack and Emma Vincent?' she asked, clearly not quite sure if they were.

'Emma laughed. Well not quite yet but can we help?'

'I'm sorry but could I see some form of ID?'

Jack pulled out his passport. 'Will this do?'

She studied it for a second. 'That's fine. I have this document for you. Please, I work for a legal firm and this has been in our custody for an incredibly long time, with instructions to deliver it to you here today. We would love to know what it's all about. We were even having bets in the office whether you would really be here.'

Jack looked at it. He saw a yellow piece of what could only be parchment. It was folded over several times and sealed with a large blob of old fashioned, flaking sealing wax. He turned it over and could make out some writing. He squinted and studied the handwriting.

Emma couldn't contain herself. 'Come on Jack, what is it?'

He turned to her, a look of surprise on his face. 'It's a letter from Melissa.'

Chapter 7

The Assembly hall was hot, sweaty, crowded and noisy. Jacques didn't know whether it was that, the smell of tobacco or unwashed bodies that he disliked the most. Almost every plantation owner, merchant or politician on the island was crammed into the room and seemed to be shouting at the same time. The Island's Colonial Assembly was in chaos and the Governor and his assistant were having little success at keeping order until the frustration obviously became too much and pulled out a pistol and fired it at the ceiling.

The shattering report had the desired effect and the ensuing silence was total. All heads turned as one towards the Governor.

'That is quite enough,' he stated into the void. 'If we can't conduct this meeting properly I will dismiss all of you and make decisions on my own. Now, the situation is quite clear but I know many of you haven't heard the latest news and so I am going summarise, that is as long as you all keep quiet, understood?'

A few heads nodded and there was a murmur of acceptance from the crowd.

'As you all know, the revolution is not going to go away. It seems that the new government have decided that war is the best way to keep it going, although we also hear that the Jacobins are worried that this strengthens the hands of the military and the King. As you all also know already, they are at war with Austria and Prussia but we have now heard that The Netherlands and Great Britain have become involved. There is a serious risk that France could be defeated and where would we be then?'

A loud swell of noise greeted this announcement.

'Hold on, there's more,' shouted the Governor over the rumbling and it quickly subsided. 'As you know, I have friends back in Paris and they report to me that it is looking increasingly likely that the King himself will be arrested soon. If he goes, then all aristocrats will face incarceration or worse. Now listen,' he had to shout again over the growing noise. 'Listen, we have to decide what to do. We are a colony of France but our loyalty is to the King is it not?'

There was a loud growl of acknowledgement from the crowd at this remark. Jacques had to smile to himself. It might sound like an outpouring of Royalist passion but in reality was more an outpouring of vested self interest. Everyone who made money out of the island would be defined as an Aristocrat by these new radicals in Paris and everyone therefore felt under threat.

The Governor continued loudly. 'Gentlemen, there is one more thing. There is talk that the Convention in Paris is about to outlaw slavery.'

Order broke down completely again for several minutes. When things finally quietened down a voice was heard from the back of the room. 'We'll not have that, not for any reason, remember what happened three years ago when the slaves tried to rebel. We had to hang six of the buggers then. If they get wind that they might get freedom we will have mass insurrection on our hands.'

'Exactly,' responded the Governor. 'And I take it none of us want that to happen.'

'Except for the La Croix family,' a sarcastic voice called from somewhere.

Every eye turned on Jacques. He knew his methods hadn't been well received by the other plantation owners. Actually looking after ones slaves and treating them well was deemed to be almost revolutionary in its own right. However, the estate was now reaping the rewards of greatly increased production at far reduced cost. Since Jacques had taken over, not one slave had died through mistreatment and his work force was willing and so far more productive than any other on the island. Quite why others couldn't see this was beyond him but being so successful didn't help make friends either. He knew that there were many on the island who would just love to see him fail.

He stood and looked at the back of the room. 'I recognise your voice Bertrand.' And then looking around at the rest of the crowed hall, 'what none of you here seem to understand is that it's a simple matter of better management. If you keep beating and shagging your slaves to death you have to keep buying new ones. When will you learn? Or maybe you just can't keep it in your trousers?'

There was an almost sympathetic laugh at this remark. His jibe had hit home. His antagonist was well known for abusing his female slaves. 'And when it comes to business you all know I'm good at that. Letting these idiots in Paris ruin our lives must not happen. You can call it political ideology if you like. I call it bad business and want nothing of it. If the Governor won't come out and say it I will. We are a colony that is loyal to our King. Let us therefore declare for Great Britain until the monarchy is fully restored, that way we can retain our laws and our lives.'

Jacques sat down to more tumult satisfied that he had not only deflected the debate away from criticism of his methods but also that he had sown the seed that his friend the Governor wanted.

All afternoon the debate raged. In the end no one could see any other solution. By effectively declaring independence and siding with Britain, by bargaining with the old enemy up front, there was the best chance that the plantations and sugar industry could continue unmolested by events the other side of the world. After all most people didn't really care about who ruled them as long as they were left alone to make money. Growing sugar in the Caribbean was the way to make enormous sums of money. A consensus was finally reached when the governor dropped his last bombshell.

'Thank you all Gentlemen. I will instruct my assistant here, Monsieur Dubuc to leave for London as soon as a ship is available. However, you should know that he will not just be negotiating for us but for Guadeloupe as well. I received word yesterday that they had come to the same decision but thought it best that we debate the issue for our own reasons.'

Cheering and clapping broke out at this new announcement. It was clear the Caribbean islands wanted no part in this revolution.

As soon as he could, Jacques slipped out of the building and made his way back to the town house the La Croix family maintained here in Fort de France. As he opened the front door Francine greeted him with a hug.

'How did it go darling?' she asked, anxiously standing back to look into his eyes.

'As we expected my dear. They are going to send an envoy to London and ask for British protection. Hopefully, we can then remain independent until this mess is over. It's the only thing we can do. But we are going to have to be careful. That idiot Bertrand tried to make out I wasn't totally sympathetic to the cause. What really annoys me is that it was partly my idea in the first place. What is it with these people? Just how ignorant can they be?'

She shrugged knowing there was no answer to prejudice and stupidity. 'I think you had better go upstairs, Father wants you.'

'How is he?'

'Worse but he's still quite lucid. He 's been asking for you.'

Jacques went up the wide staircase to the first floor and into his father-in law's bedroom. Although he didn't know why he knew, the word 'cancer' kept coming to mind and he realised the old man was not long for the world. The growth in his neck was getting larger by the day. The room smelt like a sick room, stagnant and heavy. He longed to open the windows and let some air through but the doctor absolutely forbade it and who was he to argue?

'Jacques is that you?' came a frail voice from the bed.

'Yes Sir, it is I. I've just returned from the meeting and we have been successful, as we hoped.'

'Come here Jacques,' and he waved to him sit by the bed and continued in a hoarse whisper. 'You know, when you came to us I didn't know what to make of you and I certainly didn't know what to make of your ideas. Who had heard of spoiling slaves the way you do?'

'It's not spoiling Sir, its commons sense.'

'Yes, I see that now but at the time it was very strange. You said we would get double the work out of them. You were wrong you know, it was treble or even more and we don't need to pay for half as many overseers. Thanks to you, the estate is now the richest on the island. Not that I will be around much longer to see it.'

Jacque was about to utter a platitude but saw the look in the old man's eyes and stopped himself.

'Yes, we both know I have little time left. I must give you some final advice, please just attend to me.'

Jacques nodded although he suspected he knew what was coming.

'Now listen, be careful with all these new ideas. This is not a time to be making yourself too visible. This is going to be a long storm and you will need to ride it out carefully. You are responsible for Francine now and hopefully a family in due course. I only wish I could live long enough to see them. I know you still search for your past and maybe you will find it. However, I am giving you a new one. I have instructed my lawyers and have prepared papers. I will need you to change your name formally to La Croix and once you sign them you become a full member of the family with my name and my heir. Look after my legacy son, look after my daughter.'

With those final words, his eyes closed. For a second, Jacques wondered whether the old man had slipped away but ragged breathing showed that he just fallen asleep. Tip toeing out of the room he rejoined his wife in the drawing room downstairs. They talked for an hour or so and then Jacques went to the Lawyers and signed the papers. On the way back he had the strangest feeling that he ought to be overjoyed at the prospect of secure wealth and prosperity. It almost seemed as though he had done something like this before but then the memory slipped away like mist and he was left feeling confused and concerned over the future.

When he got home Francine was looking worried and pulled him to one side. 'That man is back Jacques, the one who came to see you at the estate a while ago. I thought you had told him you wanted nothing to do with him and his damned ideas.'

'I did,' hissed Jacques in anger. 'But they obviously think I have revolutionary leanings because of the way I run the estate. I'll see what he wants but don't worry my love, this time he has to go.'

Jacques found the man waiting for him in the little library. He looked like a weasel with a sharp nose and sallow skin. However, he was well dressed and clearly had a degree of substance behind him.

'Monsieur Dubert, I thought we had agreed that we would not meet again.'

The man looked hard at Jacques. 'That was before things changed. Do you really want to see this island ruled by the British?'

It was clear that the conclusions of the Assembly had been quickly disseminated amongst the population. It was hardly a surprise. 'What I want, Sir, is to be left alone to manage my estate and live my life. Anyway, we aren't intending to be ruled by the British, merely to be protected by them until the Monarchy is restored.'

The man snorted, 'You really think the British will settle for that? God, you people are naive. Anyway, that's beside the point. Look, we know that you are the only slave owner in the whole Caribbean who looks after his slaves like they were free men. I hear you even pay them a wage and allow them to better themselves.'

Jacques snorted in contempt. 'Yes I do, because it makes business sense, my productivity is over double that of any other plantation on Martinique.'

'Yet you're not worried that all this freedom will lead to unrest, to a revolution?' These last words were said in an almost fervent tone.

'You don't get it do you, you silly little man? Why do you think the home country has revolted? It's got nothing to do with your stupid ideologies. Quite simply your working class had had enough. They were repressed and exploited by the ruling Aristocracy until they finally were forced to do something about it.'

'Just like the thousands of slaves in the islands?'

Too late, Jacques saw the trap that he had walked straight in to.

Monsieur Dubert continued. 'And you emancipated your slaves for pure business reasons? That's not what I heard. I think that you, Monsieur Jacques, have a conscience and hate slavery as much as the revolution does. Deny it if you can?'

Jacques was forced to think carefully. After the volcano when he recovered enough to understand where he was, he had been shocked and disgusted. To this day, he didn't really know why and yes, his first attempts to improve the lot of the slaves were purely based on a humanitarian urge he found deep inside himself. Within a few months however, he had discovered that humanitarianism and business went hand in hand and had been able to rationalise both urges under the one umbrella. Did this odious man who there was clearly a lot more to, have a point? Unfortunately he did.

'If you are asking whether I believe in human equality, then yes I do. As far as I am concerned the colour of a man's skin is irrelevant. But and this is a big but I do not like your revolution. I don't like the stories we are hearing of what is going on in France and I have a strong intuition that it will be short lived.'

'Fair enough Monsieur La Croix but surely you have some sympathies with us? You could have me arrested after all. I am taking an enormous personal risk even talking to you.'

Jacques felt torn. On the one hand, he wanted nothing but to be left in peace with his beautiful wife. To live a life of ease on what would soon be his estate. On the other hand, he had a deep unexplainable gut hatred of what he saw everywhere on the island. He looked at his visitor and made a decision.

'Monsieur, let me make my position quite clear. Frankly, I don't care who rules my island as long as I am allowed to live my life.'

A look of disappointment started to appear on his visitors face.

'But yes, apart from that, I will do what I can to improve the lot of the slaves, to bring some degree of justice to the system. Is that enough for you?'

'It will have to be, thank you Monsieur. Please I will see myself out. I will be in touch soon.'

As the door closed Jacques sat down and looked out of the window. *'What have I just done? Dear God have I put all I love at risk?'*

Chapter 8

Antigua looked remarkably like it had the last time she had seen it. Of course to Melissa, there was still the overlay in her mind as to what it would look like in two hundred years time. Forcing herself to concentrate on the now, she hitched up her skirts and allowed Charles to hand her up into the carriage. Behind them their ship was anchored in the wide expanse of Falmouth bay. It had taken far longer to arrange passage than Charles had originally envisaged. The uncertainty in Europe which seemed intent on fighting itself to a standstill had meant that shipping was virtually impossible to charter. In the end Charles had taken the unusual step of buying his own ship. Not quite as strange an idea as some first thought. If he was going to be a sugar plantation owner then having one's own ship was actually quite a good idea. The good ship 'Polaris' was the result. Not dissimilar to Charles old command, she was also a brig sloop and even carried some long nine pounder cannons but nothing like the twenty four pound carronades of the old ship. At one point there had even been some danger that the navy would press her into service for what everyone was anticipating as the next round with the French. However, some string pulling and an early departure had put paid to that.

In some ways that had been the easiest part. The arguments they had had over who should accompany them were probably even more a stumbling block. In the end Melissa had her way by the simple expedient of refusing to go at all unless little Jack came as well. Charles pointed out the dangers of the sea passage and risk of disease at the far end of the voyage. Melissa would have none of it. She knew she could inoculate the boy once they arrived even if Charles stubbornly refused to understand the concept. And there he was, a happy little seven year old boy, sitting in the carriage, waiting for them both impatiently to get in.

'Come on Mama,' he called happily. 'Let's go.'

'Yes Jack but we are only going to the lodgings in St Johns. Mary will be looking after you there.'

'Aw mum, I want to go with you to the estate. I don't want to stay with the maid.'

Charles decided it was time to exert some fatherly discipline. 'You, young man, will do as you're told. Once we have seen what the situation is with the estate then you will be able to come.' He looked significantly at Melissa as he said it. She smiled back slightly grimly and nodded.

While the boy chatted happily as he looked out of the window at the novel surroundings and the maid did her best to keep his enthusiasm under control, Charles and Melissa talked quietly to one side.

'It's too late to go there today but I had a word with our agent quietly at the dockside. His report isn't good.' Charles said.

'What do you mean darling? The accounts show that the estate is functioning quite well. Surely things can't be that bad?'

'It's not that, it's how this man Samuel Jones is running it. I really think you should let me go alone for the first visit.' He looked at his wife and saw that look on her face again. She said nothing. 'Alright, but on your head be it my dear. I feel it could be quite unpleasant. Since my cousin died it seems the house may have not been lived in and you know how fast things deteriorate in this climate. I fear it may not be habitable at all.'

'Charles, that's not it as you well know. I want to see how the slaves are being treated. You know I would set them all free if I could.'

This had been another topic of heated debate between the two of them. And in this case Charles had won the argument through sheer logic. Setting a large number of African slaves free would probably result in them all starving to death or being captured by other estates and simply put back to work. In the end, Melissa had to accept that the social situation would not allow a compromise. However, she vowed to herself that she would do all she could to ensure they were treated properly.

The next day they set off inland. The island was quite flat unlike most Caribbean islands but the dense growth alongside the narrow tracks made visibility very limited. Their agent had joined them along with a taciturn old man who was driving the cart they had acquired for the day. Despite leaving early the day was getting very hot and Melissa was starting to sweat. In her time she would be down to bikini top and shorts in this heat. Unfortunately here and now she was forced to wear a bodice and long skirt which was totally unsuitable for the climate.

After an hour they turned up an even narrower lane that was encompassed on both sides by the tall canes of the sugar they now realised they owned. They were apparently within the confines of their new property. Suddenly the road opened out and there ahead of them in about five acres of cleared land was the house. Melissa gasped, it was beautiful, smaller than she had anticipated but beautifully proportioned with a first floor veranda running all round it to catch the breeze.

'Oh Charles, it's lovely.'

'Look closer my dear, I think more than a little work is needed.'

Indeed, as she looked closer she could see details that spoke of a long period of neglect. The paint was peeling and the roof clearly needed repair but even so the windows were intact and doors closed. It could be worse.

'Anyway, let's find the rest of the estate. I want to see the workers quarters.'

Charles and the agent looked at each other and shrugged. The cart moved past the house and suddenly Melissa could see the storage and processing sheds. They looked in good condition. Off to the right were some low buildings and she was suddenly aware of a low moaning noise coming from them. As they got closer the noise was accompanied by a smell. It was the smell of unwashed humanity with no sanitation. Suddenly there was a scream and the moaning got louder.

'Quick, hurry up,' she ordered the driver. They rounded the corner of the building to be met by a scene from hell.

A beaten earth courtyard was surrounded on three sides by the low buildings, all in a dreadful state of repair. Seated on the ground, were about two hundred black bodies all shackled together, male, female and children. Standing guard over them were six men all armed with muskets. They all carried coiled whips on their belts. However, it wasn't any of this that took the newcomers attention. Situated in the centre of the square were two wooden frames. Tied spread-eagled to both were two human beings one male one female. They were both naked. As the cart appeared a large sweating man was just raising his whip to strike the back of the woman. A savage grin split his face. He was clearly enjoying his work.

'Stop,' yelled Charles and Melissa almost in unison but the man either didn't hear or deliberately took no notice and the whip lashed the back of the woman opening up a livid red welt that immediately started oozing blood. The woman screamed and the crowd moaned again.

Charles knew he must act fast because if he didn't Melissa would get there first and God knows what might happen then. He pulled out his pistol and shot the man in the leg. It wasn't a very good shot but it had the desired effect. All eyes turned to the newcomers. The man with the whip had fallen to one knee looking at blood spurting from his calf with shocked amazement. The other guards then reacted and started to point their muskets towards the group.

The agent stepped forward. 'Put those down you men. This is the Earl of Hinchfield the new owner so be warned.'

The men looked confused for a moment and then slowly lowered their weapons. Before anyone could react further Melissa went up to the wounded man.

'Are you Jones the manager?'

He looked up at the angry young woman, not liking the look on her face one little bit.

'Yes Maam and what the hell does your husband think he is doing?' he asked angrily.

'Only what I would have done except my aim would have been better. Now, why are you acting like a bloody savage?'

The man sneered. 'Discipline, we have to maintain discipline. It's the only thing they know.'

One of the guards sniggered, 'and it makes sure he can fuck them whenever he wants.'

What did you just say?' asked Melissa striding over to the man.

'Nothing Maam,' he lied, realising that it probably wasn't the right thing to have said.

She strode back to Mr Jones but Charles intercepted her. 'Look Melissa, I told you things would be bad here. We can sort this out.'

'Too bloody right we can and the first thing to happen is that this man leaves now.' She emphasised her remark with a savage kick to his wounded leg. Jones screamed clutching his calf and fell on his back.

'Get out,' she screamed as she aimed another kick at the prone figure who scrambled clear. 'Get out, go away, you're fired, never come here again, GO.'

She turned her back on the man as he tried to stand and hobble clear and shouted at the remaining guards. 'Cut them down carefully and if they are harmed any more it will be you tied to those bloody frames, do you understand?'

They might have been hardened slave overseers but the men knew outraged authority when they saw it and hastened to obey.

Charles had to admire his wife. Most European women would have never been here in the first place let alone have the authority to command men like these. He had a quiet word with the agent to see Jones off the premises and let the man know he would get his severance but not to expect anything else. Then he went to help his wife.

Melissa worked for days and then weeks. There never seemed enough time to do the things she wanted. On more than one occasion, Charles had to physically force her to sleep. With the Hinchfield fortune behind her they were able to engage scores of workmen to restore the house which was in fundamentally good condition. In a matter of weeks, they were able to move in with local staff and at least enjoy a more relaxed style of living.

With the slaves it was a different matter. They had been abused for so long she despaired of ever gaining their trust. The original overseers didn't last long and were either fired or left in disgust at her 'soft' ways. New ones were hired but only after careful interview and an understanding and acceptance of how she wanted things to run from now on. For herself she found the whole situation overwhelming, especially when she saw the condition of the children. As non productive bodies, they had been given nothing and only survived by the sacrifices of the parents.

The worst were the half black children of which there were quite a few. The fathers obviously weren't interested and that just left the mothers to care for them.

She stopped all that and instituted an immediate regime of food for all and it was proper food. The buildings were torn down and rebuilt properly and she even consulted the men on what they wanted. Proper sanitation, clear water and privacy were her priorities. However, she got little out of them. They just didn't seem to understand the concept of a white person caring about them at all. She realised it was going to take more than a little time to change things.

She achieved her first breakthrough when the son of one of the more important men fell ill. The little child had picked up an infection and clearly they all felt he would die soon. Melissa's heart almost broke when she saw the little infant's state. Over her parent's protestations she took the child to the house to care for him. It was the closest she ever came to causing an uprising but she was damned if she would let the mite die. Using some of her carefully hoarded antibiotics she nursed him back to health. The look on the father's face ten days later when she returned a healthy son to him was worth everything. In retrospect she realised this was the tipping point. The slaves at last realised that the time of abuse was really over. The men even started working in the fields willingly. The overseers found they had little to do and production even increased.

One evening several months later, Charles and Melissa were sitting on the veranda enjoying the cool breeze and watching the sunset over the fields.

'You, my love, are a miracle.'

'What on earth do you mean by that Charles?'

'Look at what you've achieved here. What would I do without you?'

She snorted, 'seems to me you had no little hand in it yourself.'

'Yes but it's been your drive and determination that has got the results.'

'Well, I come from somewhere that would deplore what we have even now.'

'One step at a time my love. I know what will happen in the future as well but don't forget that we can only do so much. You knew that when you came here with me.'

Melissa got up, kicked his legs to one side and made herself comfortable on his lap. She kissed the tip of his nose. 'I know and your job is to remind me whenever I need it.'

He laughed looking at her clear blue eyes. 'Yes and once in a while you might even listen to me.'

'Anyway, I have some more news you might be interested in.'

'Oh, what can have happened that I haven't heard about?'

She grasped his wrist and placed it on her stomach. 'You must be one of the most unobservant people I've ever met. Surely you've noticed I've been putting on weight?'

The penny dropped and his grin grew even wider. 'How long?'

'Put it this way, little Jack should have a playmate in about five months.'

Chapter 9

Jack and Emma were travelling down the M3 in John Smither's car. Emma was sitting in the back, Jack was in the front. Jack was amazed that he hadn't dented the floor with his left foot where he was continually hitting the imaginary brake. John or 'Smithy' as he preferred to be called was the worst driver Jack had ever travelled with. He looked over his shoulder at Emma and pulled a face. She gave a sickly grin back and indicated that she was well belted in.

'So,' asked Smithy, blithely ignoring all the cars behind him as he pulled out to overtake a large articulated lorry without indicating and then also ignoring the blaring of horns and flashing lights in his mirror. 'Can I ask what was in that letter that solicitor lady handed you?' So saying, he turned and looked questioningly at Emma. Jack had to shout to get him to refocus on the road and the queue of traffic ahead.

'Oh yeah, sorry, anyway it must have been of interest and even relevance to what we're doing. Melissa was the girl who stayed in the past wasn't she?'

'I tell you what Smithy. We'll tell you everything when we arrive wherever it is we're going alright? Because we actually want to arrive alive.'

'Oops OK, don't drive too much these days and we did hit the bottle a bit last night didn't we?'

Jack reflected on that remark. The previous afternoon, they had done their shopping and got back to the hotel in good time. John Smithers agreed to meet them in the hotel bar at six and then proceeded to take them half a dozen other bars, a really good restaurant and then a few more bars. It was quite clear Smithy didn't get out much and the fact that he had effectively unlimited expenses for the night just fuelled his enthusiasm. They had specifically ignored talking about the project, whatever it was and it wasn't long before they were in no fit state to do so. Jack prided himself on being able to keep up with most drinkers, it was part of his job after all but he soon realised he was outclassed with his new best friend. By the time they all fell into bed he realised he was in the presence of a master. It was even more galling that when they met for breakfast in the late morning. The bloody man seemed to have no symptoms of alcoholic withdrawal whatsoever. That was until they experienced his driving style. Jack wondered what would happen if the Police pulled them over. He was pretty sure there was a security service escort behind them. Amazingly, the opportunity never arose.

'Not far to go now,' Smithy called cheerily as he cut up yet another car whilst exiting the dual carriageway. 'You two are just going to love this. I'll say no more. Let's see if you can work it out.'

Jack was intrigued. He though knew where all the Defence Research Establishments were. However, they were now in Hampshire in the New Forest area and he knew of nothing around here. He had assumed they would be going to Farnborough or Boscombe Down or some such place but clearly that was not so.

The car turned into a narrow side road and what was clearly a disused airfield appeared ahead. Jack caught a glimpse of some sort of War Memorial by the disused entrance which they didn't go through.

Catching his gaze, Smithy clarified, 'yes this old place was used during the war to launch most of the gliders on the Arnhem raid. That's a memorial to the poor blighters.'

Jack looked around. They were driving the old perimeter road now, broken tarmac but still passable. 'What happened to the runways? They all seem to have been dug up.'

'Oh, that was the motorways. Concrete aggregate was quite valuable when the main building programme was underway and lots of farmers sold it at quite a good profit. Anyway here we are, sort of.' And the car came to a halt on a large piece of concrete covered in farm detritus and old straw.

They all got out of the car. It was a glorious summer's day with a gentle breeze and the ripe smell of the countryside assailing their London attuned senses.

'Got it yet?' asked Smithy with a wide grin.

Jack and Emma were taken aback and looked around carefully. Suddenly a few anomalies were apparent. Jack looked around even more carefully and suddenly it all fell into place.

'Hiding in plain sight I take it?' asked Jack knowingly.

Emma was still nonplussed and said so.

'Right,' said Jack. 'The runways have been dug up but we're standing on new laid concrete and look at the edges, those are new runway edging lights. I recognise them from my flying days. Oh yes and look at all the rubbish piles around here. Only a military mind would place them so regularly. They really ought to be more random in my view. That bloody tractor over there. When did you ever see one so clean with such a smart driver? Sorry but this is all window dressing isn't it Smithy? This is what the minister called the 'Farm' isn't it?'

'Got it in one,' laughed the scientist, 'Anything else?'

Jack looked again but Emma got in first this time. 'That old black hangar there. That's all wrong.'

'Oh, how do you mean?' asked Smithy innocently.

'Well, it's obviously old, probably war time and quite battered about but it's painted a uniform black and surrounded all around by tall grass. So how does anyone actually get to it to paint it and maintain it with no access? Judging by the height of the grass, no one has been near it for months, yet the glass in all the windows is spotless.'

'Boys and girls welcome to the Farm or area 52 as we like to call it.' And seeing the puzzled looks he continued. 'Well the Yanks have area 51 so we decided to go one better. Come on, let's get out of sight.'

They got their bags out of the boot and he walked them over to the large farmhouse nearby. It was a typical British farm building with a few outhouses but once they got inside everything changed. Inside it was all antiseptic military decor. They were met by a severe looking woman in her fifties who Smithy introduced as Anne his assistant and then taken to the rear of the building where there were some bedrooms and where they left the suitcases. After that they were taken to a lobby with two lifts and ushered into one. They descended a fair way underground.

'Please don't tell me you've got an alien spaceship hidden here?' asked Jack with a wry look.

'What? No that's somewhere else,' said Smithy absently. And then realising what he had just said and seeing the look on Jacks face he laughed. 'Just kidding, no this is where we do the really clever stuff.'

Jack wasn't sure whether the man was actually joking or not but decided not to ask again. He realised that he really didn't want to know the answer.

The lift doors opened into what looked like a large open plan laboratory. They were met by several more welcoming faces and ushered sideways into a large conference room. Coffee and sandwiches were laid out and the debrief started.

It lasted weeks. They went through their experiences collectively and singly a dozen times. They were subjected to batteries of tests, medical, psychological and goodness knows what else. During that time Jacaranda arrived on the back of a chartered freighter. They all trooped down to where she was hidden in a covered dry dock in the Portsmouth Naval base. Jack dug out his special map with all their details of the weird and wonderful in the Caribbean. It was pounced upon with enthusiasm. The yacht was stripped, measured and monitored with a battery of devices that Jack couldn't even give a name to.

They also learned a lot about their hosts who they had to admit, were charm itself. Apart from Smithy and Anne, there were only six more of them and it was clear to both Jack and Emma that they were all certifiable and barking mad geniuses. But no matter how good they were, they all held their leader in awe. Professor Smithy Smithers held no less than six degrees. On more than one occasion it was pointed out that if his work ever got out into the public domain he would probably win at least two Nobel Prizes. However, it wasn't just that. The whole of area 52 was run along the lines of the American Lockheed 'Skunk Works'. Apparently it was a pre-condition laid down by Smithy. There was no quality control, no management to speak of except for guidelines laid down by Smithy himself. Everyone was expected to work as long as the current task took and was totally expected to get on with it because no one would be looking over their shoulders. It worked. The powers that be in the Defence Research Establishment hated it but didn't dare interfere because the results that Area 52 achieved were always outstanding. 'It isn't broken and no one dares try to fix it until it is.' Smithy was often quoted as saying. His workforce loved him. And it wasn't just the work. They played pretty hard too when occasion allowed. The security service personnel were often tearing their hair out when the whole lot of scientists and their two new sailing friends went out and got completely rat assed in the local pub. Jack and Emma were amazed how such dedicated people could switch off and go for it, especially on Saturday nights. Having seen their leader in London, Jack soon realised that this wasn't so surprising. Seeing how hard they worked during the week it was probably a necessary release anyway.

Almost six weeks had passed and it was getting clear to them that their presence was becoming less and less necessary. Jack collared Smithy one morning and made the point.

For a second Smithy looked nonplussed, then he collected his thoughts. 'Ah, yes, Jack you're right, er sort of. Actually, we need to discuss Phase two now. Maybe we should all get together and brainstorm it.'

'Once again you bloody mad scientist, you've left me behind. What are you talking about now? I didn't even know there was a Phase one.'

'No, I don't suppose you did and actually you two have been remarkably good at not badgering us with too many questions. Maybe it's time we did the 'coming clean' bit and all got on the same baseline. Let's meet up in the conference room after lunch, OK?'

At two o'clock the room was full with the whole team present. Smithy stood at the lectern with a slide projector set up.

'My lot have heard this before. It's the standard brief we give all the bigwigs when they come here but I'll just whip through it. Luckily, everything you two have told us only confirms what we were pretty sure we already knew. We can then get on to the fun bit and discuss what we do next.'

The lights went down and on the screen there appeared two ships, a large American destroyer and small commercial looking fishing boat.

'The Yank ship is the USS Eldridge, beloved of all conspiracy theorists everywhere. The other is the Motorised Fishing Vessel 'Poseidon' who nobody has ever heard of thank goodness. During the war both countries were experimenting with magnetic fields and other more esoteric stuff based on Einstein's Unified Field Theory. To cut a long story short there was just a little bit of disagreement over how to approach the concept. The Yanks made it work but killed half the crew in the process.' He saw the look on Jack's face and pre-empted the question that was forming.

'Believe it or not, we weren't totally sure what we were trying to achieve. Invisibility by bending light was the baseline idea. However, instantaneous transportation was also considered possible and even anti-gravity. So the Yanks went off and tried it with an all metal ship. The British scientists thought that all that metal would distort the fields and do all sorts of incalculable damage and they were right. I won't say any more, not my place really. So us clever Brits used a completely wooden ship. All conducting metal was removed with the exception of the engines which were also the generators for the power for the field system. We felt this would allow for controllable and regular field generation. We got it to work, sort of that is. The first trials were an amazing success. The ship could be made to disappear, not to radar, although we can do that now. Damn, Jack and Emma forget you heard that please. However, we decided that wasn't enough and pushed the envelope, so to say. On the last trial run the generators were tweaked to give what should have been an element of anti-gravity and the bloody thing disappeared completely this time. Never to be seen again. With your evidence Jack and Emma and all the other evidence you brought with you, we're pretty sure she didn't disappear. She simply went back in time. So in a nut shell that's where we are. Questions?'

'Jesus,' said Jack. 'Where to start? OK how come it's taken you lot so long to work this out?'

'Well it hasn't really but getting the evidence has been quite difficult and anyway for reasons I can explain, it's only the last two cycles that have been firm enough to really provide the data we need.'

'Cycles?'

'Ah yes, right. Quick bit of theory. If you go back in time let's say one week where do you end up?'

'Er, a week in the past?'

'Yup but where not when?'

'Where you started from.'

Emma broke in, 'No Jack, I've often wondered about this. Smithy, surely you'd be in space somewhere behind the planet?'

'Clever girl,' said Smithy. 'You see the planet rotates and moves through space at the same time. So if you went back a week, you'd end up where the planet was a week ago and it's moved on. Actually, it's far more complicated than that because of course the sun is moving as well. But moving relative to what? To cut a load of theory very short, we believe it is a relative effect and subject to the nearest greatest mass which in our case is the sun, inverse cube laws and all that. Any galactic movement is too small to worry about. So where did the good ship Poseidon end up? Is she floating out in orbit somewhere?'

'Hang on a second,' said Jack. 'We went back and didn't experience any spatial movement whatsoever. That theory's got to be bollocks.'

Smithy laughed, 'Good point Jack. What we think happens, is that part of the law of mass conservation has an effect here. Basically you can go back in time but only to certain points in the past that allow for a degree of mass conservation. Now this was pure theory until one of my brilliant lab rats allowed for the wobble of the earth's poles and a few variations of the earth's orbit around the sun. The consequence of a lot and believe me it was a lot of number crunching is that we believe Poseidon went back to 1722. Two Hundred and Twenty Four years to be precise, just as you did and ended up in 1785.'

'OK, why six year cycles and the last two being the most significant?'

'Same reason, polar and orbital wobble. We reckon the next cycle will be the last as the 'window' to use a general term will then no longer intercept our orbit at all and the effect will peter out.'

'But hang on, you sent a ship back in time. So presumably there is some sort of rip in time to use a science fiction term but these cycles bring people and things forward as well.'

'Yes and we would love to know why. Our theory doesn't allow for that and so our theory is clearly wrong, at least in part.'

'And how the hell did Jacaranda go back? She was far bigger than anything else we heard about. What about my little shark?'

'Ah, well we're pretty sure the shark was a complete red herring if you'll excuse the rather bad joke. We've measured your yacht rather carefully and it's quite clear that the ferric metal mass compared to the volume of ship is almost exactly the same as the Poseidon's. If anything was ever going to go through it would be your boat. I can go over the theory in more detail if you want but it doesn't help with the rather fundamental issue we have now.'

'Go on. Why do I have a bad premonition about what's coming next?'

'Because you're psychic? No listen, it's clear from our measurements that the material in your boat has not been affected by its passage though time nor has it affected your bodies, you will be glad to know. But we're absolutely sure that it will be a different matter with the metals in Poseidon because they will have been affected directly by the original fields. Not only will what we can learn from them allow us to complete our understanding of the whole process but the metal itself will have incredibly unique properties. We are talking being able to make anti-gravity a reality for a start.'

'Hang on a second,' interrupted Emma. 'Why don't you look for it now, if the ship sank, the metal would still be there surely? If she got to one of the islands, then it should be on shore somewhere.'

'Of course we've looked,' replied Smithy. 'We've done side scan sonar and magnetometer sweeps, over the whole area, as well as using a detector designed to pick up traces of the transformed metal. But there's nothing there. She didn't sink at the location she almost certainly arrived at so must have got to one of the islands and that's an enormous area to search, especially when the trail is over two hundred years old.'

'Oh bollocks, you want me to go back and hunt Poseidon don't you?'

Smithy smiled his infectious smile. 'Hey Jack its six years before we can do that and anyway, who said anything about just you.'

Chapter 10

Charles was definitely not performing the husbandly duty that he felt was expected of him. There again why should he be expect to do anything conventional where his wife was concerned? His thoughts were interrupted by another groan and then a series of grunted comments berating all bloody men the bloody world over. His hand was momentarily crushed in a vice like grip. How could someone so utterly feminine exert such strength?

He was sitting at the head of their bed. Melissa lay holding his hand whilst at the other end the midwife was doing whatever it was that midwives did. When little Jack was born Charles had managed to be away in London on business. Not this time however. On an island as small as Antigua there was nowhere to hide.

Melissa was sweating and clearly in agony. Charles really didn't know what he should be doing so reverted to the tried and trusted technique of wiping her brow and telling her how much he loved her. He was pretty sure she wasn't listening. Suddenly with a terrifying scream and encouraging imprecations from the other end of the bed there was a moments silence followed by a cry of delight from the midwife. She held something small and purple in her hands. Surely that couldn't be a baby? But it was the crying was clearly a clue. Again, after doing midwifely things it was only a matter of minutes and the mite was wrapped in a blanket and presented to the exhausted mother. She took it in her arms took a quick peak under the blanket and gave Charles an exhausted smile.

'Say hello to Emma your new daughter.' There was a slight note of challenge in her tone. He wasn't surprised by the name she had chosen and even if he wanted to argue, which he didn't, now was definitely not the time. However, she wasn't going to get it all her own way.

'That will be Emma, Victoria, my love, after my mother.' He also had a small note of challenge in his reply.

She smiled up at him. The moment was perfect for both of them. Then her eyes slowly closed and the midwife bustled him out of the room with instructions to leave them alone.

He went out to the veranda and took in a strong draft of warm Caribbean air. It was laced with the smell of the flowers Melissa had planted everywhere and the tang of molasses drifting over from the crushing sheds. Cicadas and tree frogs were fighting each other for verbal dominance. He could even faintly hear singing coming from the workers accommodation area. A bottle of brandy had been left out for him on the small table. He poured himself a generous measure and sat down in a mood of utter happiness. He looked at his watch and was amazed to see that even though it was quite dark it was only early evening. Melissa had been in labour for only four hours. He thought it was meant to take longer than that, it had certainly felt like it.

His meditation was interrupted by a polite cough from behind him.

'I hope you don't mind me barging in Charles. Your people told me what's going on but as I've come thousands miles of miles, I thought you wouldn't mind.'

Charles immediately recognised the voice and stood and spun around to see the smiling face of his old first Lieutenant and more importantly his friend from the days when he had served in the navy as Commander of the brig Andromeda.

'Thomas Deerly, you're always welcome in my house you know that,' he declared in delight. 'Oh my, that's Captain Deerly I see. Congratulations old friend. What ship?'

Tom who was wearing the blue and gold coat with epaulette of a Post Captain beamed back in pride. 'The 'Solebay', fifth rate and the best sailing frigate in the navy.'

'Of course, she would be,' Charles laughed. 'Show me a captain that doesn't love his ship above all others but how did you know I was here? Not that I mind. Here sit, have a brandy. I have a daughter to celebrate.'

'Well to answer your question,' Tom said as he took the proffered glass and seat. 'Admiral Jervis looked across the bay and saw this lovely looking brig sloop and wanted to know why it hadn't been pressed into service for his current task. I was tasked to find out. Imagine my delight when I discovered the truth.'

'So, we are going to take the French Islands then? But I thought they had declared for Britain?'

'I'm afraid we are. You haven't seen the fleet that's getting ready as most of them are at Barbados at the moment but they'll all be mustering here in a week or so. I escorted Jervis's Flagship the Boyne here early as she has some repairs to conduct in the dockyard. And yes, we don't trust the governments on the islands. France is still in bloody chaos. They've imprisoned their King for God's sake. From what we hear, the sugar islands have as many nationalists as royalists and now that the revolution is declaring an end to slavery there could be total chaos. So we are going to go and restore order. Let's face it, they should welcome us.'

'Hmm maybe but if what I've heard is true then I think you might find it a little harder than you imagine.'

'Yes and that's the second point. The Admiral would really value your appreciation of the local state of affairs. I understand you've been out here for almost a year now, so probably have a better feel for the situation on the ground than most. He has respectfully requested that you attend at your earliest convenience of course.'

'By which you mean as soon as possible. Don't worry Tom I would be delighted. The only thing is that if he wants my Polaris, he has to have her captain as well.'

'I don't suppose he expected anything else.'

'Right, that's enough for now. We have more important things to discuss. Raise your glass Sir, I offer you a toast. To Emma Victoria and her wonderful mother.'

The next morning Charles took leave of his wife and new child with the excuse of urgent business but neglected to mention what it was. She was still weak from the experience and he didn't want to tire her with explanations when he really didn't know what was going to be asked of him. They could discuss it when she was more recovered.

He and Tom made their way to the dockyard where the Admiral's and Tom's ships were anchored out. Tom's boat was waiting for them and he dropped Charles off at the towering side of the big three decker. Tom called up to explain who the visitor was, before heading off to his own ship with promises made for a more settled social engagement when Melissa was recovered.

Charles climbed the tumblehome of the big First Rate, very conscious that he was doing so as a civilian. Not for him the mustered Royal Marines and whistling of the bosun's call to welcome a serving naval Captain on board. No, as a civilian it was a simple matter of being greeted by the officer of the day as he clambered through the entry port. A polite looking Lieutenant saluted him nevertheless and welcomed him on board. It was clear he was expected.

'The Admiral is anxious to meet with you Sir and bids you join him for breakfast. This way please.'

Charles followed looking around as he did so. He was impressed with what he saw. The ship was clearly well managed. The guns were neatly stowed and the deck gleaming after its early morning holy stoning. Even more impressive was the demeanour of the men. They were all well turned out and seemed in excellent spirits. Just for a moment he felt a pang of jealousy. Where would he be if his brother hadn't been accidentally killed? Inheriting the Earldom had been unexpected and in some ways very rewarding but maybe he could have been the Captain of a ship like this by now. And then he berated himself. That was life and look at the wonderful wife and family he now had. That certainly wouldn't have happened if he had spent all his time at sea.

They reached the door to the Admiral's day cabin. The Royal Marine sentry stiffened to attention and saluted. The Lieutenant knocked. 'The Earl of Hinchfield Sir.'

Charles entered and saw a severe looking man, with a long nose and weather beaten skin. Charles had never met him but knew of his distinguished career starting with the retaking of Quebec and then action at Gibraltar and Ushant. This was a fighting Admiral who knew his business.

The Admiral stood and proffered his hand which Charles shook. 'Sir Charles so good of you to call so promptly, may I offer you refreshment,' and he indicated the table already covered with bread and platters of eggs.

Charles assented gratefully and they took their seats as the Admiral's servant poured them coffee. They chatted politely for a few minutes and Charles used the time to take the measure of the man while he was pretty sure the Admiral was doing the same thing with him. However, the conversation soon turned to the state of the French Islands.

'Now Sir, what can you tell me of the situation as you know it? They seem well inclined to us but of course nothing is ever that simple.'

Charles thought carefully. With the contacts he had made over the preceding year he had a fair idea of what was going on but wanted to make sure this feisty looking man understood the depth of the problems potentially facing him.

'Simply put Admiral, there are two opposing factions in the French islands. The vast majority of landowners and government are Royalist and want no part of the Revolution. However, they are in the overall minority. They are opposed by a smaller number of Republicans, mainly tradesmen and associated artisans. However, the slave population outnumber everyone by a factor of at least ten to one. If the Republicans get power and emancipate the slaves, in my view there will be total chaos. There are already reports of local uprisings and atrocities on both sides.'

'Ah, so the local governments will welcome our protection then?'

'No, actually I don't think they will.'

'But they've openly sided with Britain and asked to be under our jurisdiction.'

'Admiral, there is a country mile between siding with Britain and accepting military occupation. I am pretty sure they never expected or wanted that.'

The Admiral looked pained. 'So you think they will fight?'

Charles nodded.

'Well thank you for that because that is exactly what others have told me and why the British Government has provided me with the meagre forces I have. As usual they expect miracles without providing enough materiel to do the job,' he sighed. 'Our forces are spread thin you know, what with all the trouble in Europe but with some luck we should prevail. You may know that most of my ships are at Bridgetown at the moment but we will be mustering here soon. Now that brings me on to my second request. That lovely little brig of yours.'

Charles decided to play it long and simply looked interested. He knew that if it was owned by anyone else than a belted Earl it would already have been pressed into service.

'Hmmph, now look, I have a barely adequate number of ships and troops for my task. So a fleet of foot little vessel like that would be extremely useful to me, especially if she were manned and commanded by someone with good local knowledge.'

'Are you offering me naval command sir? I still hold my commission even though I am on the retired list.'

'Of course but I can't offer you Post you realise that. She would be unrated and I can only make you Master and Commander as you were in your old ship and it will only be until the situation is resolved.'

'And maybe some materiel like some extra cannon or even some carronades? I will also need extra crew. Most of mine have paid off and I won't force the remainder to sign up.'

'I'm sure that can all be arranged. If you see my Flag Captain I'm sure he can sort it all out with you. I take it you accept?'

'With alacrity Sir.' said Charles as the excitement mounted in him. Here was a chance to see some action again even if it was only on a temporary basis.

'Excellent, then maybe you and the lovely wife I hear you are hiding somewhere in the Island will be able to join me for dinner soon.'

Charles's mounting excitement ground to a sudden halt. In all the euphoria of contemplating naval command again he hadn't considered her reaction. *'Oh goodness, how on earth am I going to explain all this to Melissa?'*

Chapter 11

'Jesus, free at last,' said Jack with a groan of relief as they finally drove away from the Farm in a hire car. The last ten weeks had been amazing, frightening and even boring, often all at once. Once they had been fully debriefed and tested Smithy had agreed with them that there was little point in them staying at the Farm and convinced the Ministry that they might as well take their leave.

'I'm surprised we were let go so easily,' said Emma looking out at the country side flying past.

'Yes, well don't be too surprised if we catch the odd glimpse of strange faces and cars from time to time.'

'What, you think they'll follow us now?' She asked with surprise in her tone.

'I'm afraid so. I can't see them just letting us walk away even if we have agreed to the plan for six years hence. Maybe once things settle down a bit and they realise we're really on the level then they 'll back off.'

'Do you think the issue of Melissa's letter is sorted out now?'

'Well if a reputable and extremely long established London law firm says that the document that Melissa's letter says she left in store for us was destroyed in the Blitz, then I guess that's about it.' He turned to her and briefly held his finger to his lips, shaking his head at the same time.

Emma looked puzzled for a second and then the penny dropped. 'Oh well, that's a dead end then. So do we stick to plan A?'

'Don't see why not. We're going to be in England for at least another two months before they release Jacaranda, so let's do it all.'

As they travelled up the M3 towards Winchester and Emma's mother's house, they went over their plans again. Their own house in London was let and Jack's parents now lived in Spain so the only place they could stay was in Winchester. Emma's mother had a large old place with plenty of room and so the offer from his future mother in law was too good to turn down. It was also conveniently placed for some other things they wanted to do. They were greeted warmly on arrival and soon made to feel at home. Jack had known Emma's family ever since he was a child. Evelyn was the classic example of the adage 'if you want to know how the daughter will look when she's older look at the Mum'. Like her daughter she was still slim and attractive. It wasn't unknown for the two of them to be mistaken for sisters. It was just a shame that Emma's father wasn't there as well but he had succumbed to cancer a few years earlier.

That evening at dinner, Evelyn broached the topic she had been bursting to know about ever since they arrived.

'So you two, come on, it was quite a surprise to find you were in the country. I know Jack says it's to do with getting some specialist work being done on his boat but have you got anything else to tell me?' There was a look of predatory parental anticipation on her face.

Jack replied quickly. 'Sorry Evelyn, I've no idea what you mean. Ouch.'

The latter remark came as the result of a sharp kick on his shins under the table.

'Yes mother, we have got something to tell you. We are finally getting married as you will no doubt be glad to hear.'

'Oh at last, that's wonderful.' Evelyn was clearly delighted and they spent the rest of the evening discussing arrangements. Any thoughts that Jack might have harboured for a simple affair were quickly dispelled, as the two girls started plotting everything from the guest list to the dress. He took shelter in simple nods when required and the solace of the wine bottle, when they weren't looking, which was often. The conversation finally went on to the venue they were going to use and Jack felt that it was time he got a word in edgeways.

'Now you two I have a particular request about the venue. Somewhere north of here is an old county estate. It's called Hinchfield Hall and before we settle on anywhere else, I would like to check it out. Maybe we could be married there.'

Emma looked startled for a moment but quickly recovered. 'Oh yes, that would be great if it was possible.'

Evelyn was looking confused. 'Why there? I know where it is by the way. Its north of the town on the edge of the downs.'

Emma answered, thinking on her feet, 'Well, it's a bit odd but when we were in the Caribbean we met someone who told us a bit about the place and it sounds idyllic. I've always wanted to be married in somewhere like that.'

'Well that's the first you've said of it to me. Anyway you should be able to drive there in under an hour if you want. I'll show you where it is on the map tomorrow.'

That night Emma and Jack got out Melissa's letter once again.

'I'm glad they let us have it back,' said Emma.

Jack snorted. 'They probably knew how much fuss I would have made if they hadn't. They still managed to test it pretty painstakingly though. Shame they didn't bother reading it as carefully.'

'What? Is there something I missed? I thought I'd looked at it pretty thoroughly.'

'Ah ha, well summarise what it says then.'

'OK,' said Emma intrigued. 'It's very short. It says she's written a diary and has given it to the law firm to deliver to us. She then wishes us well. That's about it. And of course the whole of the legal firm's building was bombed to bits by the Germans in nineteen forty one, so we'll never get to read it. It's lucky we even got the letter and that was only because it was protected in a fireproof safe.'

'But that's not quite what she says. Listen, I'll read it out exactly as it's written. *'Hey you two, greetings from your past. I've been keeping diaries since I got here and the lawyers are responsible for looking after them for you. I hope you two are well and that lovely original boat of yours is too. When you get this look up my home if you get the chance.'* There're a couple of words there that are a clues I think.'

Emma looked blank. 'No I don't get it.'

'Look, she says 'diaries' not a diary. In other words there were several. Everyone is assuming there was only one or they were all in one place. Also she mentions my 'original' boat. What did she always say when I was praising Jacaranda to anyone who would listen?'

Emma thought and then her face cleared. 'She used to call her a copy, even if she was an improvement. It used to wind you up all the time which is of course why she did it. My goodness, I've got it, she left a copy of her diary somewhere at her home.'

'Well that's what I think too. There's a second diary and it's somewhere in Hinchfield Hall. I think that's the message.'

Emma looked thoughtful. 'And of course there's the other weird thing about all this.'

'Go on.'

'How on earth did she know how to tell the lawyers where and when we would be so they could deliver the letter?'

'That my dear, is a question we've all been asking. Maybe if we can find a diary, all will become clear.'

The next day they drove through the ancient cathedral town and followed the map down side roads, until they stopped in front of some imposing stone pillars and an old lodge house.

'Looks like it's seen better days,' commented Jack looking up at the state of the stonework. There was ivy growing all around the pillars and the facings were heavily frost damaged. They knocked on the door of the Lodge but there was not reply although the house was clearly occupied.

'Right then, let's see if the Lord of Manor is in, even if the flunkeys are out for the day,' said Jack as they climbed back in to the car.

They drove through the gates down a narrow tarmac road that seemed in good repair. As they cleared the entrance, they could see down the road to the house.

'Oh my God,' declared Emma. 'That is just stunning.'

The road was bordered by a solid row of beech trees at least a mile long. They were all turning a golden brown in the early autumn sunshine. Either side of the trees were fields with herds of black and white Frisian cows grazing contentedly. But it was the distant vista that took her breath away. Framed by the avenue of trees sitting regally in the parkland was Hinchfield house. It was square and made out of some sort of yellow stone that reflected the sunshine to make it look almost golden. A simple design, with a pitch roof surrounded by ornamental battlements, the proportions and setting were breathtaking.

'You are so right,' responded Jack with a catch in his voice. 'That has got to be the archetypal English Country House. Melissa must have just loved it here.'

'Well come on, lets go and find out.'

As they reached the front of the house, the road turned to gravel and encircled an ornamental stone fountain which was still in good working order. The cherub in the centre was clearly conducting his business with enormous pleasure if the manic grin on his stone face was anything to go by.

'I'll put money on a certain friend of ours commissioning that,' commented Jack with a chuckle as he got out of the car.

Emma looked over at the statue and laughed. 'I'll not take your money. That is so like her.'

Just then the door opened and a middle aged man looked out. 'Hello, can I help you? The house is closed to visitors at the moment I'm afraid.'

'Oh sorry,' said Jack. 'We were hoping to talk to the owner about possibly hiring the place for a wedding in a few weeks time.'

'Ah yes, well that's alright then,' said the man. 'You'd better come in.'

They followed him through the large ornamental doors and into a vast open hall which was surrounded on three sides by a grand ornamental carved staircase.

'You'd better come into the Library. My name is George Lonfort by the way.' And he held out his hand to Jack.

Slightly taken aback by the name, Jack looked more carefully at the man. Sandy haired and slim, his features betrayed his heritage. *'Great, great, great, great, grandchild or thereabouts,'* he thought. 'So you must be the current Earl. I'm Jack Vincent and this is my fiancée Emma.'

'Goodness, you are well informed,' laughed the man. 'Yes I am the Earl, not that that means anything these days. It's hard enough just to maintain a place like this by being a simple businessman. The aristocracy bit doesn't cut it anymore I'm afraid. Anyway, here's the library.' And he led them into a side room where all the walls were lined with leather bound books. He caught Jack's eye as he saw him look around. 'No, they're not worth anything believe me, if they were the family would have flogged them all years ago.'

They sat at a long polished table and talked about weddings. George explained that it was one of the things they specialised in and yes the dates they wanted would be fine. When they started talking prices, Jacks was glad he had decent savings because this place didn't come cheap. From what he had seen he didn't care. This was Melissa's old home and even if they couldn't tell anyone else why, this was where he wanted to get married. He looked over at Emma and was certain that she felt the same.

'Yes,' said George. 'We're still a working estate and the place has been in the family for centuries. The house is smaller than it was you know. After the war, like a lot of country houses parts of it were demolished. There used to be two big wings. They were added last century In fact it probably looks now like it did in the late eighteen hundreds. Would you like the guided tour?'

They both nodded together and their host led them outside. He first showed them the chapel where the wedding ceremony would be conducted. It was to one side of the main house in its own little copse of trees. A beautifully proportioned building, inside were rows of dark wooden pews, lit in glowing colours from the stained glass windows at the end. They went to look at the window. Suddenly Jack's eye was taken by a small detail in the lower left corner.

'What on earth is that?'

'Ah,' laughed George. 'This window was commissioned by the fifth Countess, Melissa Lonfort. Apparently she travelled a lot although not that much is really known about her. It has always been assumed that that was one of the ships she travelled on. Mind you it looks a bit odd for a vessel of those days.'

Jack looked again and pointed it out to Emma. Her eyes opened wide and she turned to him and mouthed the word 'Jacaranda' to him. Although it was a simplistic representation, it was a pretty good picture of Jack's yacht. The yacht that was currently under cover in Portsmouth Naval Base.

'Yes, that Lady had a lot to do with this place,' continued George who hadn't noticed the exchange. 'Look, here is her memorial stone,' and he pointed to the wall. 'Her grave is in the family crypt underneath us.'

Both Jack and Emma experienced the same emotion. Suddenly the reality and complete strangeness of the situation hit them. Here they were looking at the centuries old grave marker, the grave of their friend. The friend they had only said goodbye to a few months ago.

Misunderstanding their reaction for interest, George continued. 'We've a rather magnificent portrait of her in the house. Would you like to see it?'

They both nodded silently and followed him back. They mounted the sweeping staircase and there, halfway up on the wall, was an oil painting of their friends. Charles was dressed in the blue and gold uniform of a naval officer. He had a baby in his arms and was standing next to Melissa, who was surrounded by three other children, a young boy of about twelve, a girl and another boy of younger age.

Before they could say anything he informed them, 'a rather unusual pose for a family of that era. It's generated enormous debate in the family over the years. Most of us think that they were just slightly eccentric. Mind you, they weren't that daft. You know, this is the first house in the land to have what you and I would recognise as central heating and decent plumbing.'

Jack and Emma just had to smile again at that.

Suddenly, Jack's eye was taken by something strange farther up the staircase.

'George sorry but what on earth is that?' He said pointing to a large square wooden frame mounted on the wall on the next landing.

'That my friend is the blade of a guillotine, used by the French during the reign of terror. No one is quite sure how it got here, although family lore has it that the Earl down there in the picture liberated it somehow. We would love to know more but the story is lost in the mists of time I'm afraid.'

They finished the tour by looking at the bedrooms and finally the large ballroom that could be used for the reception.

George looked at his watch, 'Oh dear is that the time? Look, I'm terribly sorry but I have to go. I'm meant to be meeting my wife in town for lunch. Please, if you want to look around some more be my guest. Here is the front door key, just post it through the letter box when you're done. Honestly, you two seem to have some affinity for the place and I'm quite sure I can trust you.'

When the front door had clanked shut with an echo around the large hall, Jack turned to Emma. 'Well, I don't know about you but I think now is a really good time to go on a diary hunt. Where should we start? There's that stained glass window in the chapel or somewhere here.'

Emma thought for a moment. 'I want to go and look at that painting again. You know, there's something about it that just doesn't strike me as right.'

'I know what you mean, come on.'

They went back up the staircase and gazed in speculation at the massive oil painting.

'So, this must have been painted about Eighteen hundred because those kids ages must cover about fourteen of fifteen years since she went back to seventeen eighty five.' said Jack.

'That seems about right, maybe that's why they had the whole family included,' agreed Emma. She stepped close to the picture. 'It's nice to see her still wearing that silver cross she always wore.' She peered closer. 'Hang on a second, there's something written on it. The one I always saw her wear was plain silver.'

Jack joined her. 'I can make out four letters, 'ANAS'. I've absolutely no idea what that means. The initials of the kids names maybe?'

He stood back and looked again. 'You know there's something wrong about the overall composition.'

'What do you mean?'

'Well, look at Charles. He's in a formal posture and staring straight out of the canvas at us. But Melissa looks to be staring off to one side at something else. And look at the window behind them showing the garden, it's a weird shape.'

'It's not a window,' exclaimed Emma excitedly. 'It's a big mirror and it looks to me that it's reflecting back whatever it is that Melissa is looking at.'

'Bloody hell, you're right. So she's looking out of a window and we can see what she's looking at because of the mirror.' He peered at the painting closely again. 'That looks like some sort of folly or garden building. I didn't see anything in the garden like that, did you?'

'No but we hardly went everywhere. Hey, I reckon this was painted in the library. There are all the books behind them and the ceiling has that patterned plasterwork. Why don't we go down there and try and work out which window she was looking out of.'

As soon as they re-entered the library, it was clear that locating the window would be straightforward. There were only two and they both looked out over the large rear lawn. There was even the large mirror still in place to confirm their theory. However, there was nothing like the folly from the picture to be seen.

'Probably knocked it down, they were a bit of a fad after all,' observed Jack gloomily. 'So that's a dead end then.'

'No Jack look,' said Emma with more enthusiasm in her voice. 'There's a stand of beech trees in the right place and they're planted on some sort of mound. Maybe there's something left.'

Walking towards the trees, they both started to feel hopeful. There was clearly some sort of structure becoming visible as they got closer.

'Look,' said Emma excitedly. 'There was definitely something here. The trees are just growing around it.'

'Er yes and some are growing right through it. Here we are,' he said forcing his way through the undergrowth between two tree trunks. 'Hey this is it. Look, these are the remains of the columns we saw in the picture.' And as he pushed more growth aside he could make out a dark aperture. 'There must have been a door here in the past. Let's go inside.'

With a degree of trepidation they managed to squeeze into the ancient building. Shafts of light illuminated it from above where the roof had collapsed and several trees had grown right through it. It was dusty and full of the smell of old leaf mould. It soon became clear there was just the one room, although it was of a decent size.

'Well, if there was anything to see here it's long rotted away. A waste of time I'm afraid.'

Once again it was Emma who spotted the only thing of interest. 'Hey Jack look here, this must have been the family coat of arms,' she said pointing to a small raised crest on the rear wall. Rubbing it with her hand she revealed a shield about a foot square cut out of the stone. The shield was sectioned into four squares with heraldic symbols in each. They were quite hard to make out. One definitely looked like a bird probably a Heron but once again it looked like they had hit a dead end.

They fought their way out again and into the sunlight. Brushing themselves down, Emma summed it up. 'Well if there was anything there, it's long gone now. I'm sorry Jack but it seems time has simply defeated us.'

'I'm afraid I have to agree,' he responded wearily. 'Hey, still look on the bright side we've found a fantastic place for a wedding.'

Chapter 12

The slim, well dressed, almost effete looking man, stared thoughtfully out of the window at the bustling Paris streets. He didn't see the view. He was reflecting on how he had arrived here, how almost by accident he was now the de facto ruler of France. It only seemed such a little time ago that he was a struggling lawyer in Arras. His embrace of true revolution was the first step but the greatest step was his discovery of oratory. When he first spoke in public all those years ago he was terrified but as soon as some measure of confidence came to him, he realised he had the gift to inspire. It was the revolution that inspired him in turn. As events took their bloody course so he rose higher in the estimation of the people he worked with. Now since the riots following the death of the King, he was leading the Committee on Public Safety. Like many times before he didn't seek the post. Others had forced it upon him. However, now he could implement his philosophy of revolution and weed out its enemies. There were still plenty of those. Most of the old aristocrats had already been dealt with but now he was seeking out the rest, even moderates who had supported the original revolution. Nothing must stand in the way of the glory of what had happened. Mind you, some people were just too dangerous to deal with in the public gaze and other ways had to be found to marginalise them. His reverie was interrupted by a knock on the door. His visitor had arrived.

'Come in,' Robespierre called without turning round. Footsteps sounded behind him and then there was the sound of a chair being moved and a body settling down. He frowned in annoyance. He hadn't given the man permission to sit. Mind you it was just what he would expect from him and one of the many reasons he was here today.

'Victor, welcome,' he turned and saw a broad shouldered man with his hair fashionably long and a large aquiline nose. However, it was his eyes that always caught his attention. Whatever his face was doing they never seemed to smile. A cruel and dangerous man but a true revolutionary.

'Maximilien,' the man replied politely.

'I expect you wonder why I've asked you here today, after all we've known each other through the Jacobin club for many years. It's time we put your knowledge of the Caribbean to the test. You were born in Marseilles but grew up in Saint-Domingue I believe?'

Victor simply nodded. Clearly he wasn't going to give anything away this early in the conversation.

'So, you've seen slavery at first hand?'

'Indeed I have and it is the devil's work. If our revolution does nothing else we should look to eradicate it as soon as we can. It was a start to declare it abolished but now we need to actually do something about it.'

'So you know what's been going on in Saint-Domingue these last two years?'

'Probably better than you do Maximilien.'

'And your views?'

'Like many revolutionary principles pragmatism also has a place. There is a very complicated situation there. In a perfect world liberating the slaves immediately would be the answer but as we have seen the result tends to be chaos. When you have a population of slaves and also half black mulattos as big as there is on that island, then simplistic solutions are never going to work. Order and government must be maintained before anything else.'

'Just so. So what would you say we should do about Martinique, Guadeloupe and St Lucie?'

Victor laughed out loud. 'Well, get their governments to obey you for a start and then do something to stop the British invading because that's what they are about to do.'

A flash of anger shone across Robespierre's face. 'Don't take me for a fool Victor. Don't you think I have plans to do just that?'

'What and fight a European war at the same time? Where will the troops come from?'

'Don't you worry about that. Resources are being gathered as we speak. We need those islands for two reasons. The first is to show to the world that the revolution embraces all human beings, that our values are pure. We need to ensure that the mess in Saint-Domingue is not repeated.'

'And the second reason?'

'Quite simply, money. Those islands generate enormous wealth and at the moment we are seeing none of it. The revolution needs finance Victor. Money is the engine of change as much as anything else. As we speak, I have nine ships and eleven hundred men preparing to leave as soon as they can and I want you to go with them.' He saw the flash of greed in Victor's eyes at the mention of wealth.

'I am no soldier. What is my role in all this?'

'Take the revolution to the Caribbean Victor. Kick the British out if they are already there. There will be two Generals to do the work of the army. You are to do the work of the revolution.'

Victor nodded. 'What was it you said the other day in the assembly? Oh I remember. To punish the oppressors of humanity is clemency, to forgive them is barbarity. That I take it, is my real mission?'

Robespierre nodded looking at one of the few men he really feared and felt relief that he was agreeing to the task. Three thousand miles across the Atlantic was the best solution to sidelining him without risk and who knows he might even do a good job.

'Yes Victor that is your mission. Do it well, do it for the revolution.'

Charles drew a deep draught of pure sea air. HMS Polaris was clear of Antigua and sailing ahead of the fleet towards Martinique. He looked around his command. It was an odd feeling seeing as he actually owned the vessel as well. However, courtesy of the government there were now four, twenty four pound carronades and six extra long nine pounders to complement his original outfit of eight cannon. It wasn't as much as he had hoped for but the ship could now defend herself pretty well. He also had another sixty sailors to complement his peacetime crew of twenty five, plus another officer and a sailing master.

Admiral Jervis had explained what he wanted of Charles once the ship was ready. He was to be his forward scout. To outside eyes Polaris still looked like the armed trading ship she had been originally designed to be. Hopefully, this would allow her to get into places a warship couldn't hope to without raising suspicion. And then if it came to a fight and she had to re-join the fleet she was sufficiently well armed to be able to contribute to an action.

He had been given a week to start training the crew to behave as one ship's company and had been pleasantly surprised. The promise that the original crew would not remain pressed in service helped a great deal and all the newcomers were volunteers even though Charles suspected many of them had been volunteered by other ships to be rid of them for one reason or another.

He had even been quite surprised at Melissa's reaction to the news that he had reactivated his commission. When he first told her, he was expecting some kind of explosion but it never came. She clearly wasn't too happy but he explained that it was only temporary until the fleet was no longer needed. She did express concern that he could be dragged into something more permanent if things didn't go according to plan. He explained that the Admiral had accepted he would need to return to England in a year or two and he would not be held to anything beyond the current crisis. Melissa had already outlined that there would be further conflicts with the French in due course but she knew that those were several years hence and so accepted his assessment.

Charles's task now was to take a Martinique islander sympathetic to the British and drop him off on the island. He would assess the situation and hopefully get intelligence about how the Governor was likely to react to an armed British presence.

The next day they dropped anchor in a peaceful bay. The approach had been difficult as there were numerous offshore reefs and being on the windward side of the island it was a dead lee shore. However, it had the advantage of being out of sight of most prying eyes and the sole plantation ashore was known to be reasonably sympathetic to the British cause. Or at least that was the hope. Charles waved the man, who he only knew as Jean, over the side at first light and then made his ship ready for a quick departure. The new guns were well camouflaged and most of the crew were kept below decks. Hopefully, anyone seeing them would assume they were just a normal merchantman. He checked any desire he might have had to go ashore himself. Being at anchor in such a delicate situation could require a quick departure and he didn't want to end up stranded. Looking up to the buildings on the promontory he wondered who the owner was. It was a superb location and from what he could see, a well managed estate. However, that wasn't his business he had a ship to command.

Jacques was angry. Once again outside influences seemed to be tearing him in two. He looked out of the veranda at the little brig anchored in his bay. What right did these people have to make him a pawn in their bloody power games? The problem was that he sympathised with both parties. On the one hand, he had an irrational hatred of slavery and the Jacobins seemed to be the only people committed to stamping it out. On the other hand, they were a direct threat to his way of life if the stories coming out of France were true and the British at least offered stability. Over the last year the island had been slowly tearing itself apart. Slaves revolting, republicans agitating and the Government caught in the middle, trying to steer a course that maintained at least some form of control. Rumours were now rife that the British were preparing to invade. Governor Rochambeau who was also General of the island's forces was preparing a defence but despite some well prepared and very well armed forts, he only had a maximum of six hundred men, over half of them militia. So in Jacques opinion and that of many others, it was only a matter of time before they had to surrender. And why not surrender anyway? After all, why did they send an envoy to England last year if not to ask for British protection? All he could see coming was a lot of needless suffering. Despite his clandestine meeting with the Jacobin agent last year he had heard nothing since and now the British were asking for his help.

He turned to the man who had introduced himself simply as Jean. Francine had brought them a tray with brandy and coffee but had left them alone. Jacques had been totally honest with her after the last meeting and he would be after this one as well but she preferred to be left out of the discussions.

Jacques poured the man a coffee after he had declined a brandy and considered his words. 'Well Jean, as you say, anyone watching will think that you are just a trading captain. I am prepared to talk to you about other matters but I am no traitor, so don't push me too far.'

Jean looked thoughtful for a moment. 'I am not asking you to commit treason Sir. As I understand, it were the one who pushed for an alliance with Britain in the first place. Not only that but the idea was accepted by your government and we signed a treaty with your envoy last February.'

'Fair point but that is a world away from accepting British military occupation.'

Jean laughed. 'You would prefer to be subjected to the reign of terror? Because that is what they are calling it in Paris now.'

Jacques had heard the same and knew that this was the heart of the argument. Despite his hatred of slavery he was enough of a realist to know it would not go away overnight and he had done everything he could for his people anyway. Ever since Francine's father had died late last year he had been fighting this war in himself and now this stranger was forcing his hand. He made his decision.

'What do you want to know?'

Two day later Charles was once again in the Great Cabin of HMS Boyne. However, this time the cabin was full. Lieutenant general Sir Charles Grey the leader of the land forces and some of his staff were there, as were the captains of all the other warships; including the Captain of Boyne, George Grey, the General's son.

Charles stood beside a map of the island. 'They will fight, I'm afraid. There is no doubt of that but they only have small land forces. However, their forts are well prepared and they have over ninety cannon, especially here in Fort Royal and that is where they will take the main stand. There is only one frigate, she is in Port Royal as well and only carries thirty or so eight pounders. Rumour has it that she is not even seaworthy but I couldn't confirm that.' He went on to give all the detail that went with the general situation and then thankfully took his place to one side.

The Admiral then stood and along with the General outlined the order of battle. It would be a hard fight but hopefully not a long one. They had plenty of troops and the navy could back them up with cannon landed from the warships.

As the meeting drew to a close, the Admiral summed it up. 'Gentlemen be prepared for a fight but we must be swift. We have to move on St Lucie after this and then Guadeloupe, so be prepared for a long campaign. We land in three days.'

Chapter 13

The little chapel at Hinchfield hall was full. The fragrance of flowers was everywhere and the pews were packed with friends and relatives. Jack's parents had flown in the other day and Emma's mother was there in the front row in charge of a pack of relatives. Martha and Lewis, Jack's friends from St Lucia, had even managed to fly over. Sunlight streamed through the stained glass windows and outside it was a bright crisp autumn day.

Jack stood at the altar with his best man. Both were dressed in morning suits and had slightly sore heads. With no close friends in England, Jack had decided to ask Smithy to be his best man and not for the first time he was questioning the decision. He had forgotten how hollow the man's legs were and what had started out as a few pints in the local pub last night had got slightly out of hand. *'Why did it always seem such a good idea at the time?'* he wondered.

The little organ at the rear of the church had been wheezing out tunes for the last few minutes when suddenly Smithy gave him a nudge and the tune changed to the wedding march. Jack looked over his shoulder and his hangover melted away. He saw Emma dressed in white on the arm of her uncle walking up the aisle. She looked lovely, even if most of her face was covered in lace. When she arrived next to him she lifted the veil and smiled. Despite the fact that they had known each other since childhood and they had been living together for the last eighteen months Jack was still taken aback by her beauty. If he had had any doubts about marriage they all disappeared in a flash.

The vicar started to speak and he hardly heard a word. He supposed he must have made all the appropriate responses but he never recalled having done so afterwards. Here he was, in the chapel built by the husband of Melissa all those centuries ago and marrying the love of his life. The only thing that could have made him happier was if Charles and Melissa could have been there as well. Who knows, maybe they were in spirit.

Suddenly, it was all over. They had gone to the registry and signed the book then came back out to the congregation and started to walk down the aisle. As they looked either side and smiled at the assembled relatives and friends, Jacks eyes swept momentarily up to the rear wall. He caught sight of the Hinchfield Coat of Arms proudly mounted over the doors of the church. Just for a second something odd registered. Then it was swept away as the doors opened and they left the church to a cloud of confetti and rice.

The reception in the main hall was magnificent. Jack had originally wanted to keep it reasonably low key but Emma's mother had insisted on contributing a large amount saying it was what Emma's father would have wanted. So they all sat down to a formal late lunch. The speeches went very well. Smithy was as good an orator as he was scientist and drinker. Quite how he had managed to rake up so many dubious stories about Jack's past he wouldn't tell. What was worse was that most of them were very nearly true. Jack managed to make his speech without making a complete clot of himself and so honour was even by the time they all took a break outside afterwards for the inevitable photographs. A large marquee had been erected on the lawn and the band would be playing there in an hour so.

Jack and Emma had hardly a chance to talk to each other since leaving the church and it wasn't proving much easier now that the photographer was bossing them and all the relatives about. He managed to get a quick word in while a search was mounted for an old Aunt who seemed to have wandered off somewhere.

'Emma, I saw something odd in the church today, I'm going to sneak back there once the photographer's finished OK? I'll tell you all as soon as I can confirm it.'

'Is it about the diaries?' she asked eagerly.

'Maybe but I need to look closer, it could be nothing.' Then before they could talk further, they were herded into yet another family group and ordered to smile.

An hour later and Jack was able to make his excuses. He made his way back to the chapel. The place was eerily empty. He went into the knave and turned to look at the crest high over the entrance doors. With the light failing, it was hard to make anything out. He looked around for a light switch but if there was one, it was well hidden. Luck was with him when he went into the vestry and found a torch in an old cupboard. Going back to the rear of the church he shone it on the crest. Yes, his earlier impression was correct. Just to be sure he managed to get even closer by standing precariously on the rear of a pew. Certain now that he wasn't imagining things. He returned the torch and rejoined the party. There was nothing he could do about it now and anyway it was party time.

Later that evening, Jack was taking a break from the dance floor and flopped sweatily down into a chair. Smithy was staring into his glass at the same table.

'Hey, cheer up old chap it, may never happen,' said Jack happily.

'Oh it's all right for you. You've got the girl and the yacht. All I've got is a bloody great hole in the ground.'

Jack recognised the symptoms. Smithy always seemed to go through a maudlin phase at some stage of the evening. It was usually followed by more mayhem. He got out his telephone and stared moodily at the screen.

'Been waiting for a text reply for ages now,' he grumbled.

'From who?' asked Jack, intrigued.

'Oh no one you know, just one of my harem.'

Jack laughed knowing that Smithy had several girlfriends and none had found out about the other yet. It was one of the reasons none had been invited to the reception.

'Well, I wouldn't worry too much, that blonde over there has been eying you up for ages.'

Smithy followed his gaze and immediately perked up.

'Has she now? Well, I might just have to go an exercise my manly charm.'

Before he left, Jack suddenly had an idea. 'Hey Smithy, is that one of those modern internet thingy phones? I know what a gadget freak you are.'

'Yeah, for why you ask huh?'

'Can you Google a word for me, I need a translation.'

'Suppose so, what is it?'

'Try A, N, A, S, it may be Latin.'

'Don't need to go on line for that, I did Latin at school. That's the word for 'Duck'. Now, if you'll excuse me, my little darling over there needs some company.'

Jack sat back as the tumblers all fell into place. His earlier suspicions were confirmed, all he had to do now was go back to the folly in the grounds and prove them right.

Much later that night, Jack and Emma lay happily together in bed. They were surrounded by various artefacts that had been deposited in their bedroom by well wishers.

'You know the decor here is quite good. The balloons and toilet paper are quite tasteful really but the pair of inflatable love sheep are a bit over the top,' said Emma looking around.

'Oh I don't know, they look quite attractive to me. Maybe we should take them back to Jacaranda. They could live with the sharks.'

That got him a dig in the ribs. 'So Mr Secretive, cough up, what have you found out about the diaries?'

'Right, well I saw the coat of arms in the church and it's not the same as the one in the folly. The one in the folly has a bird of some sort in the bottom right quadrant. The one in the church has a shield of some sort.'

'They're different, so what?'

'Well, if Melissa wanted to leave us a bloody great clue, then that would be a start. Then there's that word on the silver cross in the painting 'Anas' it means 'Duck' in Latin. Smithy, the man with the brain the size of a planet and hollow legs told me.'

'No sorry, I can't see where this is going.'

'Look, what do I do every time one of our charterers asks me what sort of bird it is they've just seen?'

Comprehension was dawning on Emma's face. 'You wind them up by saying that anything with feathers and webbed feet is a duck and that's as much as you know.'

'Yes and Melissa liked the joke so much she used it as well. Now, if the Coat of Arms in the chapel is the right one and logically it should be, then the one in the folly has been altered. And that alteration is a webbed footed bird, which we would both would have said is a duck to anyone who asked. And that is the word on her cross. So my guess is that if we dig around that crest in the folly we might just find something.'

'You are such a clever bloke. I'm so glad I married you today. But that can bloody well wait. If there's anything there it's been there for hundreds of years and this is our wedding night and you have other duties to perform.

Jack needed no second bidding.

They hadn't planned a honeymoon as such as they were intending to go straight back to St Lucia after the wedding. The authorities were going to return the yacht at the same time, so it was time to go back to work. The charter season was starting soon. This meant that if they were going to investigate the folly it would have to be that morning and before anyone else was up. So first light saw them creeping through the grounds towards the tree covered mound dressed in old clothes.

'God, this better be worth it,' groaned Jack quietly. 'I've only had two hours sleep and far too much to drink.'

'How do you think I feel but I'm sure you're right, it does all seem to add up,' Emma responded looking pale in the early morning sunshine.

They squeezed into the folly again and round the tree trunks, until they were standing in front of the carved coat of arms. It was just as they remembered. There in the lower right quadrant was Melissa's duck.

'Right,' said Jack as he took a knife that he had liberated from the dining hall out of his jeans pocket. 'Let's see what we've got here.'

He scraped around the carving with flakes of old stone and moss falling to the floor. Soon the whole crest could be seen and the only alteration was definitely the first thing they had noticed.

'So, either this is just another bloody treasure hunt clue or this is where the diaries are actually hidden. If this is a lock of some sort then it's going to have to be quite simple, otherwise it wouldn't last too long.' He dug around the shape of the bird but could see no sign that the shape was just another carved part of the stone.

'I don't get it, I'm so sure I'm right but what the hell are we meant to do now?'

Emma took the knife from him and had a close look herself. 'I don't think it's the bird itself Jack. It's a very complicated shape after all but look what it's standing on.'

'That's just a line inset in the stone, presumably to represent the ground.'

'Yes but a nice straight line. Hang on a second.' And she put the point of the knife into the groove and pushed. After some little resistance it move inwards displacing soft mortar as it did so. She then started moving it from side to side, until a groove about six inches long was revealed. The movement had dislodged some more mortar at the bottom of the crest and Jack suddenly realised he was looking at a simple square shape, a rectangle about the size of a house brick. It was a brick that had been very carefully cemented in to the crest, so that only the top edge would be seen. Emma passed him the knife and he attacked the stone all around and soon he was able to prise it loose. He carefully pulled it away and looked inside.

'What do you see?' Emma asked excitedly.

'The square root of bugger all I'm afraid, it's just too dark.' So saying he put his hand inside and felt around. A few inches inside his fingers encountered something soft and damp. They quickly traced the shape of a book. With utmost care he gripped it and pulled. Slowly, after centuries of being hidden, a large leather bound book saw the light of day once again.

They both looked at it with awe. 'We were right, she did leave a copy. That's been hidden for us to find for two hundred years,' whispered Emma. 'Can you open it and see what it says?'

Jack carefully pulled at the front cover. Dust wafted away in the air and a musty smell hit them. It was clear that time had done a great deal of damage.

'No, it's definitely seen better times. We will have to look at this very carefully another time. I just pray that after all this effort there's   actually   something   left   to   read.'

Chapter 14

Charles stood on his quarterdeck, staring at the shore. Ahead were the two forts of St Lois and Bourbon. Enclosed within the arms of the bay they protected was the frigate Bienvenue and several other smaller ships. None of the enemy vessels were going anywhere. Not only were they completely bottled up by the British fleet but they had been permanently chain moored in an attempt to use their guns to augment those on the two forts. French resistance in the island had been spirited but they had inevitably been forced to fall back until all the remaining troops were in either one of the stone bastions now confronting the British.

A failed attempt to rescue some prisoners from the moored frigate few days ago had led to the current plan. Charles realised this was the first time he would actually come under enemy fire and prayed his qualms didn't show themselves to the rest of the crew who he was sure were as nervous as he was. Ahead of him, the sloop Zebra felt her way into the carenage. Polaris followed. Both ships had the shallow draft necessary to clear the sand banks in the entrance. Charles looked behind and saw the much larger sixty four gun three decker Asia follow them. Although much deeper, she carried the only pilot they could find who should be able to guide her in safely and so provide covering fire for what the two sloops intended to do. Off to one side there were assembled a number of lighters and cutters filled with marines and sailors from the Veteran and the Rose. At the same time, soldiers were to make an assault from the land. Polaris and Zebra were headed for fort St Louis, which actually had fairly low walls. Their job was to provide cover for the landing of the boats coming in swiftly behind them.

Mr Timms the sailing master looked up from the chart he had been studying as the deep thud of a cannon was heard from the top of the large mountain behind the town of Fort Royal. A plume of white smoke gave away its position near the summit. 'Three twenty four pound cannon and several mortars dragged up the side of a mountain so steep apparently even donkeys couldn't make a footing. They even had to fill in a complete river bed. That is a stunning piece of work Sir.'

Charles had heard the same astonishing story. It had given the British a commanding control of the town yet the French still resisted. 'Unfortunately, Mr Timms, despite the heroic efforts of our men, the guns cannot range as far as Fort St Louis which is why we have to do the dirty work today. I would not like to be inside the other fort however, they will be taking a pounding. As we will any minute now. Guns crews stand by,' he commanded as the fort they were heading for disappeared in a cloud of white smoke. A surge of bile rushed to his throat as the first shots struck the hull. The fort was using round shot and some grape. The mizzen sail suddenly shredded above his head. He fought the urge to throw himself to the deck and cower. Instead, he gauged the range as close enough to return the complement.

'Starboard battery fire,' he screamed over the sound of more cannon fire from the fort and Polaris shuddered from the combined effect of her own broadside and more impacts from the ashore.

'Sir, look behind,' shouted the sailing master. 'What the hell are they doing?'

Charles followed his gaze. The mighty Asia, their floating battery was turning. She had only just got in range of the shore batteries and amazingly was turning away without firing a shot.

'Dear God, well, we will just have to get on with it without her.' Charles looked at Zebra. Clearly her captain had the same idea and had altered course directly for the shore. Without the fire support from the big three decker time was going to be short and the sooner they closed with the enemy the better. Instead of paralleling the shore and pouring shot into the fort, they would have to beach the ship and take the fight to the enemy. Hopefully, once they were that close the guns on the fort walls wouldn't be able to be depressed enough to cause them any more damage. For a few more minutes they took hits from the long cannons ashore without being able to give back any in kind, as their bows pointed towards the shore battery. Several times Charles had to jump clear of falling rigging and one of the guns crews just ahead of him was cut cleanly in half buy a round shot. He was astonished how much blood could spray so far but had no time to dwell on the sight as the ship shuddered and took the ground.

'Hands over the bow, join with Zebra lads,' he shouted into the temporary silence. 'Let's show the bastards what British sailors can do.'

Leading from the bow, Charles climbed down some fallen rigging and then leaped into the shallow water with his crew streaming behind him. They joined the men from the Zebra beached just further up and started climbing the walls, just as the boats from across the harbour reached them. Suddenly, over a thousand screaming sailors and marines were climbing into the fort to a rapidly crumbling resistance. Charles had just breasted the parapet, when cheering broke out. The French soldiers were throwing their muskets down and raising their hands in surrender. Captain Nugent from the Veteran was first to the flag pole on the ramparts and personally cut down the French tricolour. Then one of his men bent on the Union flag and proudly hoisted it. Cheering was then heard from the other side of the carenage as the French themselves pulled down the flag over fort Bourbon. Martinique was theirs.

The Martinique assembly hall was in uproar once again. The Governor, flanked by several British military officers found himself in the position of trying to restore order. One of the soldiers stepped forward and called for calm in a parade ground voice and it did the trick. Slowly the noise subsided and at last the Governor found he could make himself heard.

'Gentlemen, whether you like it or not we have been defeated militarily but it is not all bad news, our new rulers are prepared to be very gracious. Any thoughts of liberating the slaves are now gone, the rule of law is re-imposed and all property will be honoured. On top of that they have promised to return us to French rule when the Monarchy is restored. This is not the situation we envisaged when we appealed to Britain for protection but at least we are to be spared the ravages of the Reign of Terror that is sweeping France as we speak. Not only that but they are intending to garrison the island in enough strength to ensure that law and order is maintained and that any attacks can be repulsed. You will not be surprised to hear that I can no longer act as Governor and the island will be run by a military board. However, this assembly will remain in place to advise the board. I will be leaving you and hand over to Colonel Stevens here who will provide the detail.'

So saying, the Governor left the room by a door at the rear as the tumult started again. He made for his office on the first floor. Wiping his brow with a large handkerchief he sat at his desk for the last time. A peaceful retirement on his estate was now all he could look forward to and suddenly the prospect seemed quite attractive.

There was a knock on the door. Jacques La Croix let himself in. 'Sorry to disturb you Martin but all that is happening downstairs is angry hysteria and nothing will be achieved until they all calm down. However, there is something I would like to talk to you about. I need someone to advise me. Can you spare me a few moments?'

The Governor nodded, indicating a chair.

Jacques sat and told him everything. How the Jacobins had approached him the previous year and how the British had done the same only recently. He kept nothing back, praying that he would be understood. When he finished, he looked expectantly at his friend.

'Well if its absolution you're after then you'd better go and find a priest.'

'Not absolution, advice. What do you think I should do now? You know I hate the whole concept of slavery but I also realise that if it were abolished overnight there would be chaos. Just look at the mess in Saint-Domingue. So the British being here will at least keep us stable and that is why I helped them. In my view, fighting them was a forlorn hope from the outset.'

The Governor sighed. 'Yes I know but we have our pride my friend and even if I had wanted to invite them in, there are just too many others who would have fought anyway. They will go on to St Lucie and Guadeloupe now you know. But why are you worried? Just settle back to managing your estates, it's what I intend to do.'

'Unfortunately, I suspect the British won't let me. They know I helped them once before and it will be only a matter of time before I am approached again. I am sure of it.'

The Governor sat back and looked shrewdly at the man he had come to know and like over so very few years. 'There's something more Jacques isn't there? I think I can say I know you as well as any man. I was there you know, when they pulled you out of the rubble, out of the remains of a beautiful city. It's something from your past isn't it?'

Jacques laughed ruefully. 'Am I so easy to read?'

'No, you're very hard to read and have some very strange notions but whatever your past, you have shown many of us how to conduct business. You would be surprised how many have copied your methods you know. So come, on tell me what is worrying you.'

Jacques stared at the man and then came to a decision. 'I know what happens next. No, don't interrupt. Please I know this sounds mad but I know that St Lucia and Guadeloupe fall to the British but I also know that the French will re-take Guadeloupe and Martinique. It will be some time this year and it will result in tragedy and enormous loss of life. I also know that the conflict between the two countries will go on for many more years yet. It's driving me insane. I am a plantation owner on Martinique, don't ask me how but I KNOW THE FUTURE.' The last was made in an almost strangled shout.

The Governor said nothing for a second and then stood and went to a sideboard and poured two large measures of rum. He handed one to Jacques and then sat down again.

'You call St Lucie, St Lucia, you hate slavery and you understand more about making money than any man I know. Six years ago, you were in the cells in the town hall in St Pierre and we have no idea of your past. Why shouldn't I believe you?'

Jacques grimaced as he took a mouthful of rum. 'And I hate the way you make bloody rum on this island. Martin, why aren't you laughing at me?'

The Governor sighed. 'My friend, it doesn't matter whether I believe you or not does it? But for the record, I probably do. There are many things in these islands that defy belief. You even being here is one of them. You are someone with an amazing past that is clear. So as I see it, you have two choices, go back to that beautiful wife of yours and make a family and even bigger fortune than you already have or go to the British and try to convince them of your beliefs. You are a man of integrity. If you think you can save lives and avert a catastrophe, then that is probably what you must do. But be careful, because if you tell them what you have just told me then they will laugh you out of the room. You must come up with a way of helping without arousing suspicion.'

Jacques nodded. 'My thoughts exactly and thank you for confirming my own conclusions. Even more for not having me arrested as a lunatic. You've no idea how it helps to be able to share this. I think I will wait a while and then offer my services at the right time. Now, I think I should leave you to tidy up. I assume that someone else will be using this office in the near future.'

Charles strode up the hill towards the Assembly rooms. The day was humid and he was hot and sweaty in his heavy full dress uniform. He should have been there an hour ago to take part in the discussions for transferring control to the new administration. As a Caribbean sugar plantation owner in his own right as well as a naval officer, albeit of the temporary variety, the Admiral had asked him to represent the navy. However, as his Polaris was the nearest ship to the Asia during the attack on the port, he had been waylaid to give evidence as to the circumstance of the action. In fact he had been unable to offer much more than an account of what he had seen and that was merely that the ship had turned when coming into range of the fort. When it was explained to him that the French pilot had suddenly refused his duty to safely steer the big three decker clear of the harbours shoals he could sympathise with her Captain. However, whether it was the right thing to do in the face of the enemy was an opinion he decided to keep to himself. He knew he would have behaved differently.

His reverie was interrupted when he saw the Assembly rooms appear at the end of the street. He instantly knew he was in the right place as it was the only three story building in sight. As he approached he could hear the sound of furious debate echoing out of the open windows.

Just as he was bracing himself to enter, a man leaving by a side door caught his eye. Unfashionably, he wore no wig rather he had long dark hair caught up in a pony tail. A dark expensive looking coat and white britches, with gleaming riding boots, clearly marked him out as gentry. He bustled past Charles without a second look. In fact from the pensive expression on his face, he was clearly far away, deep in thought.

Charles stopped dead. He may not have been recognised but he instantly knew the man. Relief that he had obviously survived the volcano, warred with deep dislike. Just as importantly, puzzlement that he hadn't been recognised in turn. He would have to enquire just what Mister Paul Smythe was actually up to here on Martinique.

Chapter 15

Jack stood back and looked with pride at the sign over the door to his new office in the complex at Rodney Bay marina. It read 'Jacaranda Caribbean Charters.' Not perhaps the most original of names but one that marked a major milestone in the development of their company.

He turned to look at Emma who grinned back at him. 'In you go then, Managing Directors first.'

Actually it was a bit on anticlimax, they had spent the last two weeks outfitting the office with furniture, filing cabinets and computers. Even so, he felt a twinge of deep satisfaction over what they had achieved in the last five years. Starting with a refurbished Jacaranda, after one season and the decision to sell their London house, they had enough money to buy a second yacht. Maintaining the policy of up-market high quality service, they had acquired a beautiful sixty footer called Jasmine. Not as big as Jacaranda, she nevertheless met his standards for luxury. With some help from the bank, two more yachts followed and he now found himself running a very successful business.

He sighed. 'You know Emma this is all very well but how often do we go out and run a charter ourselves? It seems we spend more and more time ashore and this office will be our home or even prison from now on.'

Emma laughed. 'That's rubbish and you know it. You're the boss. You can take a boat out whenever you want. Think about me, I'm forced to stay here and just get fatter every day while little Charles keeps growing.' She patted her large bump as she said it.

'Yes, remind me how that happened again will you?' he said with a grin. 'One moment it's just you and me and soon there will be three of us. My God but doesn't time fly.'

Emma frowned at the comment. 'Yes and may I remind you that in about seven months, a certain mad scientist will be taking Jacaranda out on a rather special trip.'

Jack groaned. 'I've been trying not to think about that but I guess we really need to start making plans. The conversion team will be here in the spring.'

Just then the door opened behind them and Lewis, Jack's friend and now full time employee, bounced into the room. 'Hey man, Jasmine has radioed that she's coming in early. Apparently they've had a problem with the engine. Don't worry, it's nothing your Vice President of Maintenance can't handle but I need a dock ape to help me catch her ropes. Hey Emma, see you tonight for dinner?'

Emma laughed. 'Go on Jack, make yourself useful and catch a rope for Lewis. I'll see you both tonight.'

That evening they all gathered in Martha's living room. She was Lewis's mother and as usual had prepared a communal supper. Jack had never got around to acquiring property on the island and they still lived in the apartment to the rear of the big house. It suited them all. Martha was really looking forward to being a surrogate grandmother to little Charles when he arrived and they all shared in the business one way or another.

As usual, talking shop was banned at the dinner table but once they were all at their ease in the battered comfy chairs on the veranda, then anything was allowed. Despite dire warnings to the contrary, Jack had divulged all about their experiences in England to his two friends. They already knew about the trip to the past so he saw no reason to keep them in the dark about what the British Government had been up to.

'Martha, Smithy will be out again in the spring, can we put him up here again?' asked Jack, aware that Martha had rather strong views about their friend.

'I suppose so. Just keep him away from the rum please. He may come here for holidays but he drinks like a fish and anyway he is the author of this mad idea of a return trip. You know, I'm not happy with it at all.'

'Oh come on Martha,' interjected Emma. 'We've been over this dozens of times. Look, this time we know what we're getting in to. Goodness knows, we've done enough research on 1791. It's actually quite a tranquil year for the period, unlike a few years later and Jacaranda will be modified to look far more realistic for the time.'

Martha looked unconvinced. 'I seem to remember you saying something similar last time and look how that almost turned out.'

'Yes, well, a certain Paul Smythe won't be with us on this occasion and hopefully the navy will be helping rather than chasing us,' responded Jack. 'Anyway, we know a little more about what to expect and who might be there to meet us.'

Lewis looked sceptical now. 'Just because that old diary said Charles and Melissa were going to Antigua, doesn't mean they will be there at the exact time you go. Just because we have some clues, we have no real idea on exact dates. Why would you want to go that far north anyway? The ship you're looking for was near here when it all happened.'

'Good point,' said Jack. 'However, it looks unlikely that Poseidon sank straight away. Otherwise they would have found evidence in the present time and if she survived the transition intact, then heading for Antigua would have been pretty logical. It's one of the few islands that stayed under British rule for the whole of that time period. And we do know that Melissa seems to need more shampoo so we'll have lots on board.'

Martha was still looking unhappy. 'Jack tell us again why this has to be done I still don't understand the science.'

Jack barked a sharp laugh. 'You and me both Martha but I can at least repeat what I've been told. The way Smithy has explained it, is that metals after the Second World War have been significantly irradiated by the increases in background radiation. So much so, in fact, that lead ballast in wrecks pre nineteen forty five is almost as valuable as silver. When tiny traces are used in modern computer systems the un-irradiated metals are much safer and reliable. Apparently, the same goes for the metals used in the Poseidon and they know from tests on that American destroyer in the War, that any metal that has done a full transition will be totally unique. The problem is that they can't repeat the experiment because there is not enough 'clean' metal left. Smithy knows that they only have part of the theory. Despite all his brains and all the computer power they have, they're stuck. If they can obtain a sample, even a small one, they are pretty certain they can complete their understanding of the basic principles involved. He talks about anti-gravity, limitless free energy and goodness knows what else.'

'Yeah and what about time paradoxes and all that stuff?' asked Lewis. 'We know that Melissa has done some things with that society she formed, from the little we got from the diaries. You know the old problem of going back and shooting your grandfather, what happens to you?'

Emma answered. 'We've talked to Smithy a couple of times about that but we've been very careful not to let him know about the diaries. At first, we felt it was all just personal but now we know that she did do some tweaking to history we don't want this trip to take on another aim. We already know that they want to send two Special Forces types with us for what they call protection. The last thing we need is them briefed to do something to stop Melissa. Anyway Smithy believes in the parallel world theory. Basically how he would explain the grandfather paradox is that if you did go back and shoot him, a new world would branch off. There would then be two worlds, the original one and one where the grandfather died. So with Melissa's tinkering there may be some new time streams running. The problem for us is that we can only ever perceive one at a time, so for this world, the one we are in, we simply cannot tell whether the past has been altered or not.

Jack laughed again. 'Yes, well, actually he explained it in a ridiculously more complicated way than that but Emma and I took him to the pub that night and we got a far better understanding after we got a few pints into him.'

'And we've got to take Jacaranda out of the water mid season and do the modifications,' Lewis said. 'What are we going to say to everyone and what about the loss of revenue?'

'Believe it or not, Her Majesties skinflint government are offering us full compensation and a guarantee to restore her back to original condition when we return,' said Jack deadpan. 'I actually believe them, firstly because they did so last time but far more importantly, I have a signed contract. It arrived in the post yesterday. Oh and our cover is simple. She is going to be used in an upcoming film and hence the re-profiling and other modifications to make her look contemporary to the period.'

He got up and stared out over the balcony towards the lights in Rodney Bay. It was yet another beautiful evening with a full moon producing a silver streak across the sea. Nevertheless, he shivered involuntarily. 'Guys, I've been thinking about this a lot recently. Smithy and his team are all bloody brilliant. We know that even if they do have an odd social life. But in some ways they are also bloody naïve. Being stuck in that hole in the ground doesn't exactly expose them to too much real life.'

Martha looked hard at him, she was pretty sure she knew what was coming next because she had the same misgivings. 'Jack, you don't trust him to be able to use the information responsibly if he gets it, do you?'

'Funnily enough, you're wrong there Martha, I actually do trust Smithy. But, and this is the point, I don't trust his masters. Look at the way they behaved when we went to London and I know they are still keeping an eye on us even after all these years. Give a government the keys to unlimited power and a technical revolution that is probably an order of magnitude greater than anything the human race has experienced before and what do you think they will do with it? Even if they have the right intentions to start with, others will soon get to hear about it and want a piece of the action. Dammit we know the Yanks will be in there as soon as they have a sniff. The two countries have been cooperating on this for years now. What's the betting the area will be covered in British and US warships when we come back?'

'So what are you saying?' asked Lewis. 'That they'll end up fighting over it?'

'Probably not the Yanks and us but imagine if Russia or China got wind of it. Or take it a step further. Suppose we manage to keep it under wraps? You can bet the first thing that will be done is some super bloody weapon will be developed, whether it's an antigravity fighter or whatever. What will that do to a balance of power?'

'Jack, you've got me worried now,' interjected Emma. 'What you're saying is that it could lead to all sorts of very dangerous situations.'

'Yup, just too much, too fast is exactly what I'm saying.'

'Alright, now you've got us all concerned, what are you suggesting we do about it?' Emma responded.

'That's the next problem. I just don't know. But if there is any chance we can accidentally or otherwise stop the retrieval of any of this metal, then I think we should take it, don't you?'

Chapter 16

He was walking down an impossible street. Impossible buildings, taller than could be imagined, towered over him and the streets were full of metal carriages moving at impossible speeds. In the sky above, he glimpsed an impossible shining metal monster. There were people everywhere pushing past him as though he didn't exist. All around there was noise and confusion. He found himself entering one of the buildings and walking into a small metal box. The doors closed soundlessly, yet he felt calm. Suddenly, the doors opened again and impossibly he was somewhere else. He looked out of the large window ahead of him. He appeared to be up in the sky. He looked down at the vast drop below and screamed.....

A hand was shaking him.

'Jacques, Jacques, wake up, you were dreaming again.'

He opened his eyes to see the concerned, beautiful face of his wife looking down at him.

Trying desperately to hold on to the retreating memory of the dream, whilst at the same time regaining his sanity, he found the recollection drifting away like smoke. Yet something inside him was telling him that it was true. The dream was the reality and this place, this room, this woman, was the fantasy.

He let his head fall back onto the pillow. He could see it was still dark. 'Sorry to wake you my love but these dreams, these recollections will not let me go. I feel soon the dam will break and at last I will understand who I truly am.'

'Oh Jacques I know who you are. You are starting to frighten me.'

'I'm sorry my dear but I can't stop it and today I have arranged to see the new British Governor. Somehow, I need to convince them to let me help because whatever these dreams might be, I am certain that a tragedy is about to occur.'

So that morning Jacques set off once again to Port Royal with his mind in turmoil. As soon as he arrived he was ushered upstairs into the all too familiar office. Colonel Stevens stood as he entered and the two men summed each other up. Stevens saw an unfashionably dressed but aristocratic Frenchman with a haughty manner but something in his eyes gave him a haunted look. Jacques saw a tall red haired man, who on close inspection was much younger than he expected. '*Oh God, a gingernut,*' he thought and then immediately wondered where on earth that strange phrase had come from.

The Colonel motioned to a chair and both men sat down. Jacques turned down an offer of coffee and they got down to business.

'So Monsieur La Croix,' the Colonel started in heavily accented French. 'I understand you have already provided us with some help.'

Jacques snorted and replied in fluent English. 'Not much but I did offer some advice some time ago. Oh and let's stick with English, I think it is probably better than your French,' and he smiled to take the sting out of his words.

'Yes, well thank you, I'm afraid I haven't had much chance to exercise my French lately. So, you asked for this meeting. How may I be of help?'

Jacques thought carefully. He knew he couldn't be honest with this man, as he would be laughed out of the room but he was determined to do what he could, despite the limitations this would impose.

'Firstly, you should be aware Colonel that I have also been approached by the revolutionaries. It seems they think that because I treat my slaves well, then I must sympathise with them.'

'And do you?' asked the Colonel with a raised eyebrow.

'In some ways, yes I do.' He responded with a note of defiance in his voice. 'I don't hold to the concept that men should be treated differently, just because their skin is a different colour. But I am also a pragmatist. Look what has happened elsewhere when the slaves have gone out of control. And believe me, I don't support the revolution. From what I hear they treat their own population even worse than I do my slaves.'

'You make a good point Sir but we are not here to debate philosophy.'

'No but I am here to offer my services. I assume now that St Lucie has given in without a fight that you will be moving on to Guadeloupe next.'

The Colonel looked amused. 'Well I am sure that everyone here has worked that out. Do you think they will fight like you did?'

'Not me Sir but I take your point and yes they will. We French have our pride and many feel it's worth fighting for.'

'You don't I take it?'

'Why fight for a lost cause Sir?'

'Indeed and how do you feel you can help us then?'

'Probably not with the assault. I am not a man of action. However, what really concerns me is the longer term. Tell me, do you have any intelligence that the new Revolutionary Government in France are planning to do anything in retaliation? It would seem to me that they will not take the loss of these valuable islands lying down.'

The Colonel looked shrewdly at Jacques. 'I would be very surprised. It seems the they have committed themselves to a war on many fronts in Europe. I doubt that they have the resources to send a fleet all the way here and retake them. No, we have had no intelligence of that sort. Are you telling me that you do?'

Jacques drew a mental breath. This was where he was going to have to lie. He hated doing it but it was better than trying to reveal what he felt he knew.

'I have some contacts with my trading people and yes I have heard that a force of some sort has been assembling. The rumour is they might be heading this way. No more than that I'm afraid. I presume you will want to hear if I hear anything more?'

'Indeed and what do you want for this service Monsieur?'

Jacques gave a tight lipped smile. 'Nothing, I merely want the security of the current situation to remain unchanged. I am prepared to continue with my dialogue should I be approached by the Jacobins again and be assured you will know all.'

The Colonel thought for a moment. He had already been appraised of this man's aid before the landings and he seemed sincere, almost desperately so. So be it, what had he to lose?

'Very well Sir. We would be glad of your continued help and I will look forward to hearing from you when you have more intelligence for us.'

Taking the hint Jacques stood and offered his hand before taking his leave. As he left, he mentally congratulated himself. The British seemed prepared to continue to trust him and if he played this right, maybe he could now sow enough seeds at the right time to prevent disaster.

As he walked through the town deep in thought he was suddenly woken from his reverie by shouting and commotion down by the docks. Quickening his stride, he rounded a corner to see that a ship must have arrived recently and they had set up a block to auction her wares. He realised he had never attended a slave auction before. He treated his workforce so well he had never had the need to replace any. Curious to see the proceedings he joined the throng.

'Ah, I didn't expect to see you here,' came a voice from his left.

Turning Jacques saw the smirking face of Bertrand Charliere, the most vocal critic of his business methods on the island.

'Just curious to see how you waste your money Bertrand,' and he turned away hoping the damned man would keep his mouth shut. Luckily, the bidding restarted and everyone turned to study the produce on display. Clearly the bulk of the cargo had already been sold. The last few men had gone under the hammer and now they were auctioning off the less valuable women and children. Jacques didn't really understand why but he felt a deep disgust at the proceedings. He was just about to leave when his eye was caught by the next lot to be pushed onto the block.

'Oh yes, just what I need,' muttered Bertrand who probably didn't even realise he had spoken out loud.

Two young girls were pushed onto the auction block. They were jet black, very pretty and identical to each other. They were also only about twelve years old. Suddenly, Jacques realised he couldn't let them fall into the clutches of the man next to him. He knew exactly what their fate would be. The auctioneer, sensing that the girls might raise a goodly sum had the overseer strip them of their meagre clothing and a collective sight went up around the throng. *'Jesus what a bunch of paedophile perverts,'* thought Jacques even though he wasn't sure why he thought that.

The bidding was fast and the price rocketed. When Bertrand realised that Jacques was actually bidding he gave him a smirk. 'So Mr Perfect, a little African cunt can change your mind eh?'

Jacques ignored him and kept nodding at the auctioneer. It was soon a two horse race and eventually Jacques won but not before he had committed a far greater sum than he had intended.

Bertrand was furious and rounded on Jacques. 'You bastard, they were mine, just because you have so much money doesn't mean you can behave as you like. I won't forget this.' And he stalked off towards a tavern no doubt to drown his sorrows and feed his anger. Jacques couldn't care less but wondered what on earth he was going to do with the two little girls. Maybe Francine could train them to be her maids?

Melissa gave a bark of surprised laughter although Charles could see she was not really that amused.

'Charles, are you sure it was Paul? You said you only got a glimpse.'

'Oh yes and I did some checking around afterwards. He calls himself La Croix now and it would appear he was just about the only survivor of the volcano. You know you can criticise the man all you like but apparently he is now one of the wealthiest landowners on the island and he achieved that in only a few years. It appears the daughter of an estate owner nursed him back to health and they ended up married. Paul now has the estate as the old man recently died.'

'God put that man in the shit and he comes up smelling of roses every time. So what did you do? Did you tell anyone who he really is?'

'Come on, how could I? Anyway, he is apparently very well regarded. He seems to be the only slave owner who looks after his people and is reaping the reward by all accounts.'

'He must have some ulterior motive. I'll never trust him.'

'What? Just like us? What are we doing that is so different?'

Charles saw his barb strike home.

Melissa had the grace to look sheepish. 'OK, a good point. Just don't ask me to meet him again.'

'Well I'm hardly likely to and anyway it would seem from what I can gather that he doesn't really remember much of his past. Word on the street there is that he can't recall who he was beyond the day of the eruption.'

'Probably a bloody good thing. Anyway when are you a going back? I'm far more interested in your buccaneering plans than the prospects of Mr Paul bloody Smythe or whatever he calls himself these days.

They were seated on the veranda of their estate house. Charles had been tasked to take some despatches to the island and had taken the time for a few days off with his wife. He was using the excuse of some minor repairs to the ship to delay his return to the fleet gathering off Guadeloupe.

'Tomorrow I'm afraid but at least with this last island taken we will have completed our task and then I intend to ask the Admiral to release me and the ship. Then my dear, we should return home.' He said this with a hopeful, enquiring look on his face.

To his great surprise Melissa didn't argue. 'You look as though you thought I was going to disagree Charles,' she said. 'What you don't know is that whilst you've been playing boats I've finally found an estate manager I feel I can trust to continue running things our way and I do realise we can't stay here forever. Goodness knows what that lot of idiots have been doing to the estate while we've been away and the children need to go back too.'

She stood and put her arms around him looking up into his eyes. 'Let's go home.'

He looked up at her. 'Yes my dear this will be the last voyage of HMS Polaris.'

Three days later, Charles along with all the other naval captains and senior army officers was in the great cabin of the Boyne. The Admiral started off the briefing.

'Well gentlemen hopefully this is the last time we shall meet. As you know Guadeloupe is shaped like a butterfly. Some joker named the smaller part Grande Terre and the much bigger and taller one Basse Terre. We are going to start at Grande Terre here at the port of Gosier. Once we have subdued this half of the island we will move on to the western half. My army colleagues have taken my advice that this is the best way to get troops ashore. I will hand over to my Flag Captain and you will be given your detailed orders after we break up. Oh and I would be greatly obliged if you would all dine me with me tonight.'

Charles sat and listened carefully, although it was clear that unlike the final attack on Martinique, this was likely to be much more of a land campaign. There was only one significant sea fort to be subdued and his little brig was far too small to get involved this time. So it was with some surprise that the Admiral called for him to stay behind when all the others left.

Once they were alone he indicated that Charles should sit.

'Lonfort, I've a mind to release you after this is over. I suspect you might be asking me anyway am I right?'

Charles was impressed. The Admiral was clearly no fool. 'Yes Sir, it was in my mind to return home but why do I suspect you might have one last task for me?'

The Admiral smiled. 'Touché young man, yes although it's quite simple. I have had some intelligence that the French may be contemplating a force bent on undoing all our good work. Once we are established on land then I am sanguine we are in a strong position. However, I must not be caught by surprise while we are in action. I want you to go upwind of the islands and keep a good lookout. You are to be my eyes. I must not be taken unawares.'

Charles nodded realising his ship was well suited to the task. 'Yes Sir, when do I sail?'

'Now, my secretary has your orders.'

Chapter 17

'Montserrat, what the bloody hell do we have to go to Montserrat for?' Jack was looking nonplussed and slightly annoyed as he glared at Smithy over his office table. The scientist had arrived the previous night and this was the first time they'd managed to get some peace and quiet to talk of future plans. He had the grace to look slightly sheepish.

'Not my idea old chap. The government types decided they wanted to modify Jacaranda away from prying eyes and Montserrat is the last British possession in the Caribbean. It was that or ship her home again.'

Jack looked hard at his friend. 'So tell me, have you or any of the clowns that came up with this idea actually been to the poor benighted island?'

'Er well, I certainly haven't but I'm sure that those back home know what they are doing.'

'Oh really, well, they may have forgotten but the volcano blew the hell out of the place. Most of the island is uninhabitable and there are no suitable places to refit a yacht on the bits that are left. Goddamit, they're having enough trouble building a decent dock for their new capital.'

He was interrupted by the office door opening and he looked up and all thought of Montserrat vanished as Emma, carrying a small bundle, came in.

'Hi there you two, just thought I'd introduce little Charles to his inheritance.' She smiled brightly at both of them.

Smithy jumped up and offered his seat. Emma waved him away. 'Thanks Smithy but I need to be on my feet. Exercise is what I need. Now, what was I hearing about Montserrat?'

Smithy looked pained. 'I was just explaining to Jack that that's where we've decided to refit Jacaranda for our little trip to the past.'

Emma looked at Jack and saw that he was taking it seriously. 'But Smithy that's just stupid. They've got no boat yards or anything.'

'Oh for goodness sake just let me explain. Believe it or not there is a bit more to it you know.'

He was met by two cynical stares. 'Look, I understand you two know this whole area like the back of your hand but the idea is that we will use the old town dock at Plymouth. Enough of it sticks out of the water for our purposes. We are going to increase the volcano threat level so that the whole area is sealed off and the ship we will use as our workshop will be designated a research ship. She has a crane that can lift Jacaranda and the work will be done on her deck but well screened. We really need to be alongside somewhere to keep everything steady. Even the Yanks will be unaware of what we're up to.' He looked meaningfully at Jack as he said the last part.

The penny dropped. 'Ah right, so we're going to keep our colonial cousins in the dark as well?'

'Yes, Her Majesty's Government wants to keep this one UK Eyes only. The last thing we want is a bunch of bloody Americans trampling all over us and telling us what to do.'

Emma smiled cynically. 'And of course, we get to keep the results of any discoveries?'

'Why not? It was our research in the first place,' responded Smithy.

'I just hope the bloody volcano is in on this plan.'

'Oh don't worry, we've consulted all the experts and it should be quite safe.'

'Oh yeah, that's exactly what they said just before it blew its top last time.'

A month later, Jack watched worriedly as Jacaranda was slowly lifted out of the water by the crane of the 'research' ship Argonaut. He had sailed from St Lucia the day before and rendezvoused out to sea with the big ship that morning. The sea was calm enough to get the yacht on board and screened from prying eyes before they docked at Montserrat. Her mast had been removed and she was already looking less her normal pristine self as she sat in the slings that had just been fitted around her elegant hull. He knew that over the next few weeks she would start to look completely different. Although he was worried about the lift out there were more fundamental issues that were starting to concern him.

His reverie was jolted by Smithy coming up behind him. 'What ho Jack. It's all going well isn't it?'

'Yes, she should be secure on board within the hour but frankly we need to talk.'

'Oh, what about?'

'Well let's start with the crew, the cargo we are going to be carrying and who the hell will be in charge.'

'Good questions all and I've just come down from the ship to say that Major Thomas has called a meeting in the saloon to cover just those issues.'

'Ah, he's called the meeting has he? That seems to answer one of my questions at least.' Jack's voice dripped acid.

'Come on Jack give him a chance. Someone has to manage the process.'

'Right and it can't be you? The man who knows all the issues or me for that matter, as it's my sodding boat and I'm the only one here who's actually travelled to the past. For some reason a jumped up, know it all, Special Forces type just assumes that he's in charge.'

'OK I understand and I know he rubbed you up the wrong way when you met earlier but give him a chance please. He's under an enormous amount of pressure you know.'

Not trusting himself to answer Jack merely nodded but then added. 'Tell the galloping Major I will be there once Jacky is safely on deck and not before.'

An hour later when he was finally happy that his yacht was well secure on deck he made his way down to ship's main saloon. The room was empty except for Smithy and the severe looking Major. His hair was shaved almost to his scalp and the rest of him looked just as hard. There wasn't an ounce of fat on the man, not the sort of person to pick a fight with. He purposely looked at his watch as Jack walked in. 'Right, now Mr Vincent has arrived we can start.'

Smithy looked at Jack and shook his head.

Jack took the hint but he could feel his ire rising. 'Well I'm sorry I couldn't get here earlier but we wouldn't want the star of the show damaged before we've even started now would we?'

The Major looked like he was going to respond to the remark but then clearly decided to go ahead as he had originally planned. 'Fine but now we three are here we need to address a few issues and sort out the chain of command, that sort of thing.'

Jack looked nonplussed. 'Sorry old chap, what one earth are you on about?'

The Major looked confused for a second and so Jack continued quickly before he could speak. 'As I understand it we need to replicate the circumstances of the last transition to the past as best as we can. This means no extra ferrous metal in Jacky but that's fine as all the modifications will be made of wood. Also we need a crew of five and so someone at home decided a couple of trained killers would be good to bolster security. Have I got that bit right so far?'

'That's not quite how I would have put it,' replied the Major huffily.

'Well I would and it's clear to me that you think that puts you in some sort of command.'

'That's how it was explained to me when I was given the assignment. Do you have a problem with that?'

'How can I answer that?' Replied Jack quickly as he could see that Smithy was about to interject. 'Professor Smith here is the scientific expert and knows everything about the technical side of what we need to do. I am the owner and skipper of Jacaranda, as well as the only person here who has actually been to the past. I suspect that I am also the only qualified yacht skipper here. I didn't need Special Forces people with me last time and frankly don't particularly see why I need you this time, although to be fair you could be useful pulling ropes and the like.'

'Now see here Mr Vincent, this is a task of incredible significance to our government and it was deemed necessary to put a military officer in command.'

'Ah, that's not actually true and you know it,' Smithy quickly got in. 'Don't forget that I was at all the planning meetings back at home. What was actually agreed was that it would be sensible to make up the numbers with specialist military staff to aid security. Overall responsibility for the success of this mission is actually mine. If you don't believe me then feel free to call home and confirm it. Now, I'm sure Jack and I are more than happy to defer to you on all matters to do with security in the here and now and if it comes to some form of confrontation when we get back to the past but that means we have to work as a team.'

'That's all well and good,' responded the Major. 'But someone has to be in command surely?'

'I think the Professor has already explained that,' said Jack. 'I've seen his management style and its miles away from the military approach but believe me it works. So to go back to your earlier point about the chain of command, as far as I'm concerned Smithy calls the shots. It is then up to us two to advise him when he comes up with yet another of his barking mad ideas. That said, if it becomes a maritime or military issue, I'm sure he will defer to us.' And he looked questioningly over at his friend.

Smithy nodded. 'Sounds about right and that's certainly how I envisaged it working.'

Jack continued in a more placating manner, 'come on Major, this is probably the weirdest project of all time if you'll excuse the pun. Who knows what will happen. You've been briefed on the science behind this and also on what happened to me last time I took Jacaranda through. You must realise it's far from a standard military mission.'

The Major looked as though he was about to argue and then clearly thought again. 'You both make good points and of course the professor is correct. He does have overall responsibility. Alright let's do it your way and see how it works out.'

Jack was surprised the man had given in so quickly but he was clearly no fool. Hopefully this was a good pointer to the future. Even so, he had a niggle at the back of his mind that the good Major had given in just a little too easily. He decided he would keep a careful eye on him as the project progressed.

The rest of the morning passed in a blur. They covered in detail the modifications that would be made to the yacht and also what they would be taking with them. They were just starting to discuss various scenarios when a knock on the door made them realise that lunch was about to be served and they really needed to let others use the room.

'One final quick question,' asked Jack. 'As I understand it Major, you will be bringing a Sergeant and he will meet us in Montserrat but who is to be the fifth member of the crew?'

This time both Smithy and the Major looked uncomfortable. Smithy spoke for both of them. 'Well it seems obvious to us, on the principle of keeping as much of the last trip together as possible, we rather assumed that Emma would be joining us.'

A week later, Jack was staring moodily over the stern rail of the Argonaut. The ship was berthed against the remains of the destroyed town's jetty which had stood up surprisingly well to the ravages of time and neglect. Ahead of him the town was grey, what could be seen of it that was. Half the buildings were buried in ash. The other half were starting to collapse. Above all of them the volcano brooded threateningly, although the top could not been seen. It was covered in dark grey cloud. Several large chasms had been cut through the landscape as water running off the mountain found new ways to get to the sea.

He heard a voice behind him. 'I believe you saw the last one go off in Martinique all those years ago?'

Jack recognised the voice of Derek Thomas . 'Yes Derek but that just blew up like an atomic bomb going off. The poor bastards didn't stand a chance. Thirty thousand dead in the blink of an eye. At least here nearly everyone escaped. There was plenty of warning you know.'

But didn't they have pyroclastic flows and all that?'

'Yes but it was very directional and there was no lava, just volcanic dust and ash. The real damage took several years to build up. You know if you go inland, you can find houses and even hotels that are completely intact but even now after all these years it's still just too dangerous to live there. Even further inland, whole villages are completely overgrown. This ash is very fertile. No, this part of the island will be deserted for many more years to come.'

'Still it suits our purpose perfectly. Jack are we really going to go back in time? I've had all the briefings, seen all the evidence and still can't really believe it.'

'I know how you feel and I've already done it twice. Mind you dinner with Nelson was something else. You know what the real issue is?'

'No, do go on.'

'I can't bloody well tell anyone. Apart from Emma and a few close friends who were involved I have to keep quiet. Imagine if I could tell everyone what Nelson was really like? Imagine how many parties I'd be invited to.'

Derek barked out a laugh. 'Well, if we're successful with this trip maybe that will all change. Mind you please remind me to avoid any parties that that bloody scientist is invited to.'

'Oh, I thought you SBS types were tough. What is it you say, you do all the SAS can do but with flippers on?'

'Yes but that doesn't include staying up until the small hours drinking Scotch with a loony scientist.'

'Welcome to the Smithy appreciation society. You know, you military types really aren't needed. If we meet any problems back in the past, we'll just get him to challenge them to a drinking contest.'

'There could be more truth to that than you imagine. Anyway, what are your views on your wife coming with us? You've been very quiet on the subject.'

Jack sighed again and looked back out over the bleak view. 'Yes, well, I rang her after your little revelation the other day. You haven't met but believe me she knows her own mind. Even though the last trip almost ended in disaster for her she was quite adamant. She's sorted out the baby. Martha one of my colleagues mother is going to look after him, so in the end I've agreed. Not that I'm sure I had any real choice in the matter.'

'Good I thought so. So, can you tell me why she's asked for these three things to be added to our provisions list?' He handed over a piece of paper.

Jack studied it for a second and then burst out laughing. Written on the paper were three things; Antibiotics, Shampoo and Chocolate.

Chapter 18

Victor slowly came to. His head throbbed and his mouth felt dry as though he had slept with it open all night. He desperately needed some water and the toilet. Next to him, the girl stretched and rolled over towards him. He briefly contemplated continuing their session from last night but the need for the privy was greater. He gave her a kick.

'Not this morning my dear. I've too many things to do. Go and tell that fat landlord of yours to get my breakfast ready. I will be down presently.'

When she showed a marked disinclination to move out of the bed he gave her a strong push with his foot and she slipped out of bed and onto the floor with a satisfying thump. Gathering her clothes around her naked body she pouted at him and flounced out of the room without saying a word.

Getting out of bed he went behind the screen and relieved himself noisily in the porcelain pot. As he returned to his bed and the clothes piled on the bedside chair he paused to look out of the window at the harbour. The waterway of Lorient was crowded with ships. In the jumble of masts and rigging it was hard to spot which ones were his but nine of them were. Two frigates, a sloop, a corvette and five transports. You would think that with the ships assembled and the troops already billeted in the town nothing could stop them sailing. How wrong that thought was. He sighed. He had an appointment with the General and his co-commissioner, that idiot Chretien. Still it could be worse, being stalled here with endless stupid delays meant he had an excellent suite of rooms, his pick of the town whores and a landlord who stupidly thought he would get paid for it all before he left. Yes in some ways revolutions could be a great deal of fun.

As he went down the Inn's stairs he could see into the main room. There seated by a window table was Michel Chretien. Robespierre had forgotten to mention all those months ago that he would be sending another commissioner. It was just like the man to be so two faced but Victor didn't really mind. Chretien was fat, opinionated and very, very stupid. God knows how he would cope with the climate once they arrived, maybe he wouldn't.

Victor took a seat opposite his pig eyed companion who was already sweating despite the early hour. 'Michel, good morning and where is our illustrious General?'

Michel looked up at Victor with bloodshot eyes. Clearly he had been drinking last night as well. 'Been recalled to Paris apparently, sends his apologies but should be back the day after tomorrow.'

Victor grimaced, more delays. Just then the landlord himself brought him his food. Seeing that he was with a visitor he immediately went to get another tray.

'So Michel, how much longer does that mean we are stuck in this benighted town?'

'Not as long as you might think Victor, in fact I think that when our good General returns he intends to embark the troops. So, less than a week from now, we should be on our way.'

Victor snorted in amusement as he began to devour the bread and cheese in front of him. 'How many times have we heard that my friend? I will believe it when I stand on deck and see the coast of France disappear behind me. The British will have taken Guadeloupe by now. That will be the last of our Islands and our job is going to be so much harder. If only we could have left at the start of the year.'

'You know that would not have been possible but we should be there by June which is a good time of year is it not?'

'Yes and if we leave it any longer we run the risk of large storms my friend. So you had better pray we do leave as predicted.'

'Oh Victor I'm afraid there is also some bad news.'

'Yes?'

'I received notice this morning that the Guillotine you asked for will not be arriving. Apparently Paris decided it was needed urgently elsewhere.'

Victor looked disappointed for a moment but then surprisingly he smiled. 'If that's the worst of our troubles then I can't complain and I'm sure one of our carpenters can knock one up when we arrive, now pass the butter please.'

Charles stood on the deck of Polaris and looked down the length of his ship. He still found it odd that he was here, a naval Commander but of a ship he actually personally owned. There probably weren't any other serving officers who could make that claim. Of course his crew were a mishmash as well. A number were technically his employees and mixing them with the seamen from the rest of the fleet had not been easy. However, the action at Fort de France had produced an esprit de corps amongst them. Charles was well satisfied with their performance even though they all knew now that the ship was likely to decommission in a few weeks time. However, their current duty was wearing thin. Four days at sea reaching across the wind looking for any sight of sail. Charles understood how important the duty was. Should the landing force be taken unawares even by a small French force it could easily end in disaster. However, that didn't detract from the tedium of the duty. However, there was something else beginning to worry him. He went over to Mr Timms his sailing master.

'I don't like the look of that sky Mr Timms,' and he pointed over the starboard quarter. The sky was starting to become overcast and in the far distance a much darker band of cloud was appearing.

'Aye Sir, it looks a blow is on the way. What has the barometer done in the last hour?'

'Down and going down faster. I've not been here in a tropical storm, have you?'

The sailing master grimaced. 'No Sir and I don't expect there are many that have at least and have lived to tell the tale. But surely it's too early in the year for a big one? They say the worst come in the autumn.'

'That's as maybe but I suspect no one has told the storm that.'

'Well, the wind has started to back a little Sir and hopefully that means the centre is behind us and heading north.'

'As long as it continues to back but even if we're only caught on the safer side we can still expect a mighty blow and as you know the tracks of these storms can change at a whim.'

'So what should we do Sir? Should we run back to the islands and warn the fleet.'

'No, they can see what the weather is doing as well as we can and anyway we're well out to sea. It's quite possible that the worst of this will miss them all together. I'm afraid our duty is clear. We must stay out here and watch for the French for as long as we can. At least most of their way is blocked. If they come at all they will have to skirt around this weather and so approach from the south and that is the way we need to go as well. So Mr Timms, let's strike the topmasts, break out the storm sails, rig extra stays and safety lines. We must get ready for some serious weather.'

Chapter 19

'Right you two, what aren't you telling me? I'm not daft you know. The fact that Jack hardly put up a fight about you coming with us Emma, despite you having a young baby to look after and that odd list of extra items you asked for

make believe you're up to something. You may have fobbed off the Major by saying it was things you missed last time but I'm not so easily fooled.' Smithy sat back and confronted his two friends with a stern gaze.

Jack looked at Emma and shrugged. 'Guess he's rumbled us. Shall we tell him?'

'Tell me what?'

Emma spoke first. 'Rather than tell you Smithy, I'll show you. Hang on a second.' And she went over to the large sideboard in their living room and carefully pulled out a wooden box. She placed it on the coffee table and removed the lid, carefully taking out the leather bound diary. She placed it on the table. 'Be careful, it's in very poor condition.'

Smithy looked wordlessly at both of them and studied the cover. He could see the remains of a crest embossed into the leather. 'Is that what I think it is?'

'If you mean the Lonfort family crest, then yes it is. This is Melissa's diary. Unfortunately, not much has survived but we've been able to decipher some of it.'

'But we were told it had been destroyed in the Blitz. Where did it come from?'

Jack answered. 'Remember at our wedding reception I asked you what the word Anas meant. Well, that was the last of a line of clues that Melissa left which allowed us to find this. It's a copy. She clearly decided to leave a backup. It's just a shame that most of it has been damaged beyond repair.'

'Well, you could have told me about it,' responded Smithy huffily. 'Why on earth did you decide to keep it a secret from me?'

'We would have shown it to you had we thought it relevant to this little jaunt of ours. But once we read what we could we realised it wasn't and anyway it was a personal account for us not the rest of Her Majesty's Government. You know as well as I what they would have done with it if they had got their sticky mitts on it.'

Smithy looked far from happy with the explanation, so Jack continued on. 'There are only two things we have managed to work out. The first is that they formed a thing called the Jacaranda Society to try and do some good with their knowledge of the future but it seems that was an uphill struggle most of the time and any way Melissa had very little in the way of historical or technical knowledge. As you know they didn't take any modern books with them. Those were all destroyed in the eruption in Martinique.'

'And the second thing?'

This time Emma replied. 'They inherited a sugar estate on Antigua. We haven't been able to nail the date down exactly but there is every chance they will be there at the time we're going back to. Those provisions are for her. She mentions her cravings a few times.'

'Now hang on right there. This trip is not so you can go and give your friend some chocolates. I sincerely hope you have no doubts about that because you will be severely disappointed.'

'We understand that Smithy but look, all the evidence so far indicates we will need to search the islands and Antigua is one of the logical ones to go for. If the Poseidon did survive and they worked out where and when they were it would be a logical place for them to head for.'

'Yes and yet there is no record of them arriving there or anywhere else for that matter. Alright, I sort of understand why you did this but I need to think on it and I need to study this diary myself. This Jacaranda Society thing sounds dangerous. Maybe we should look them up and ask them to stop. God knows what changes it could make to their future.'

'Not that we would ever know eh Smithy? At least that's how you described it to me last time I asked.'

'Yes, well, you've given me some things to think over and we've only a few days before we set off.' So saying he scooped up the diary and stomped out of their living room.

Jack looked at Emma. 'Well, that went well, seeing as he caught us on the hop. I was hoping to break it to him once we were back in the past. That way there would be nothing he could do about it. Let's just hope he forgives us and he doesn't let it upset all our current plans.'

Emma looked concerned. 'I don't see why it should. Give him a few hours and then I'll talk to him again. You know, the female touch. He's always a sucker for that. Now tell me about Jacaranda. What have they done to her and when do we go?'

'OK, we go as planned next Sunday. That really is the optimum date. You wouldn't recognise the boat. She has been clad with planking and looks like a contemporary cutter now. The mast and rigging have been replaced. We're now gaff rigged, the sails are made of canvas and there's not a winch in sight. She's going to be bloody hard to handle. Luckily with these two hairy arsed Special Forces types on board we'll have some muscle to hand.'

'Yes, what are they like? Will I meet them soon?'

'Well actually the Major is alright once you get to know him but the Sergeant is a bit taciturn to say the least. He insists on calling all of us Sir, which I suppose will be alright where we're going and he only answers to Sergeant Riley. I still haven't found out his Christian name. You'll have to exercise your womanly charms on him as well. As to meeting them, we leave tomorrow to go back to Argonaut. We only came ashore to collect you and the last of the stores. A helicopter will pick us up from the airport.'

'So we say goodbye to little Charles tomorrow?'

'I'm afraid so.n I hope you're not regretting wanting to come?'

Emma sighed. 'No, not really but it will be such a wrench. At least I know he'll be in good hands. Martha will be an excellent baby sitter.'

'Yes and we shouldn't be away long. A matter of a few weeks at the most.'

'So what's planned for the days before we sail?'

'We need to learn how to handle the new rig and there are some specialist navigation systems fitted that need checking out. No GPS in the past remember. So we'll spend the week on board in company with Argonaut and a naval frigate to keep prying eyes away from us before heading off on Sunday. Don't worry she's pretty much unchanged down below. We won't be uncomfortable. We've also built in some extra storage and even found room for all your little treats for Melissa. If we find her she won't be disappointed.'

Later that day they met up for a final dinner. Jack and Emma were the last to arrive in Martha's living room.

Martha looked around from the kitchen area as she saw the two of them arrive. 'Has little Charles gone down alright?'

Emma smiled wistfully. 'Yes, he's good as gold. He obviously doesn't take after his father.'

'Oh thanks for that. Who said I don't go to sleep easily.'

'Me, I'm married to you remember.'

Martha laughed. 'You two go out to the veranda the others are there and supper will be a while yet.'

They went out to join Smithy and Lewis, who both had tall glasses of rum in their hands. Seeing them Lewis went over to a cabinet and made them two more and then they all took seats overlooking the bay.

Smithy raised his glass. 'A toast. To the success of the next voyage of the good ship Jacaranda.'

'I'll drink to that,' responded Jack. 'May it have none of the unpleasant surprises of the last one.'

'Amen to that,' replied Emma with fervour.

'Now talking of our earlier conversation you two, oh and Lewis I know you are cleared to know all this but this is new so keep it under your hat as usual please. I've been studying that diary and thinking. Actually, we really ought to go and try to find you friend Melissa. We've got to talk to her about not doing anything more with this society of hers.'

'Hang on,' said Jack. 'I thought you said it didn't matter.'

'Well yes but all I have are theories and there is no reason to potentially make things worse.'

Jack was about to say something but Emma gave him a kick. 'Thanks Smithy, we appreciate your attitude over this. Please don't think we were just being obtuse over the diary. It really didn't seem to be relevant to the job.'

Martha's voice came from inside. 'Come on you lot food's ready.'

Later that night all but Smithy and Jack had gone to bed. Smithy had produced a bottle of single malt and Jack felt honour bound to ensure Smithy didn't do too much damage to it on his own.

'So, are you really ready to go into the past Smithy? It's quite a culture shock.'

'I've been dreaming of nothing else for years since we first met and I found out that it was all true. We'd only had conjecture up to that point you know. I've even learnt French and spent quite a lot of time mugging up on the local history.'

'Yeah so have I but 1791 seems to have been an odd year. No one seems to be fighting anyone, even the Brits and the French.'

'I guess everyone was a bit knackered after the American Revolution and the French one hadn't really got into its stride. Give it a few years and all that changes of course.'

'So, how hopeful are you that we'll actually get a sample of this metal? It still seems like a long shot in some ways. After all it will be quite some time after Poseidon arrived there. None of the crew should be alive even if they survived the transition.'

'One of the things I've been working on these last years is a method of detecting the metal at a reasonable range. If my theories are correct, then the metal will have certain properties that will be quite easily detected. Everyone will get one of these.' He showed Jack a small pocket fob watch. 'I wanted to use wrist watches but that would have seemed most odd in the eighteen hundreds. To be in character we'll all have these. I've even got a brooch version for Emma. If it gets even a sniff, it will vibrate and chime quite authentically until you lift up the dial when you will get an LCD screen giving a bearing to follow.'

'Wow, that's really cool. Any idea what range it will work at?'

'That depends on the size of the mass of metal. If we come across the main generators or engines, we are talking at least half a mile maybe a lot more. A small piece will only be a matter of yards.'

Jack took the watch and looked at it. 'Pretty neat, now pass the Scotch.'

The next morning they took their leave of Lewis, Martha and little Charles.

Just as he was climbing into the car to go to the airport Martha came up to Jack and pressed a small package into his hand. 'Don't look at it now Jack but remember Smithy can't explain everything that happens with science. You'll know what I mean,' she said enigmatically.

Later when they were in the helicopter flying back to the ship near Montserrat Jack opened the parcel. When he saw the contents he gave a bark of laughter. Emma looked over and smiled as well.

'What on earth is that Jack?' asked Smithy looking puzzled.

'That me old mate is Martha ensuring that all the bases are covered.'

It wasn't the original, that was somewhere deep in the Caribbean Sea but it could have been its twin. In Jacks hand was an exquisitely carved, green eyed, white, bone shark.

Chapter 20

The final week passed in a blur. Jack realised how amateurish they had been previously when he saw the preparations Smithy had arranged this time. From the moment they returned on board they were wore period clothing and acted the part. Jack had great fun explaining to the other male members of the team how the trousers worked and how all the fasteners actually did up. Emma was reasonably familiar with her wardrobe from her previous trip. However, this time she would be dressing as the wife of a trading captain and not in the finery she had been provided with in the Martinique of 1785. They even stayed in the clothing when sailing Jacaranda and becoming familiar with her new rig and sails. It didn't help that the two military crew members only had limited sailing experience. Despite the fact that they would probably only have to use the sails on limited occasions and the engines were still there and fully serviced, they needed to be reasonably proficient unless they wanted to arouse suspicion.

It took several days for Jack to be confident that they would pass muster at least from a distance. At the same time they had to inventory and then store all their provisions which were designed to give them several months of self suffiency. On top of that they had to test out the sidescan sonar and magnetometer that had been fitted during the refit. Jack was concerned that without any GPS, navigation would be far more basic and brushed up on the use of his sextant and other more traditional techniques. They had fitted an inertial navigation system taken out of an aircraft and it should be very accurate but it was of no use if they didn't actually know their starting place.

Suddenly it was the day before they were due to leave. Jacaranda was sailing under her new gaff rigged main and a foresail. Jack had been pleasantly surprised how well she still handled despite the old rig and the change of her hull shape due to the wooden cladding. The sun was setting and the crew were sitting at leisure in the cockpit.

'Right, we're as ready as we can be,' declared Jack looking at his oddly dressed crew. 'Hands up anyone who wants to back out 'cos tomorrow morning it's back to 1791.'

No one put a hand up although they all smiled. Derek looked thoughtful. 'I suppose we're really confident that this is going to happen aren't we?' he asked looking pointedly at Smithy. 'We'll look bloody stupid if nothing happens. God knows how much this has all cost the government.'

Smithy grimaced. 'Don't even go there and anyway it will be me in the shit not any of you. We know this can happen, two of us here have experienced it before and I've had my team working on this on and off for almost six years now. If we don't go back it won't be because of any lack of preparation or understanding on our part.'

Jack looked amused. 'Derek, I know exactly where you're coming from. It's how we all felt last time we tried this. But now the Royal Navy will be escorting rather than chasing us and they've got a lot of Smithy's kit on board that frigate to help us be in the right place at the right time. We can only give it our best shot. Now, we need to sail this boat out to the west and turn around at the right time, so I suggest those not on watch turn in and get some sleep. We all muster at five in the morning and soon after that we'll know whether we have been wasting our time.'

Five in the morning saw them all back in the cockpit. No one had really slept and they had all appeared well before the deadline. In an echo of their last voyage the Sergeant was busy making bacon sandwiches and mugs of coffee which were being passed up to the rest in the cockpit.

The horizon could just be seen as dawn started to make it presence felt. Off to one side by half a mile, was a naval Type 23 frigate. They could see its running lights and silhouette against the brightening sky. They were all deep in thought when the VHF radio jumped into life.

'Jacaranda this is Golf Zulu. A good morning to you all. We estimate your course is good and there are about twenty two minutes until rendezvous point. I will be launching my Merlin helicopter very soon and he will take station on the opposite side from me. Are you good to go? Over.'

Jack looked at everyone and received nods from them all. 'Golf Zulu, yes we're ready to go, all's looking good over here. We have the autopilot locked in and all the instruments are on and recording. We'll call a countdown with thirty seconds to go. Out.'

'Well this is it,' said Smithy. 'I hope you're all ready. Me, I'm going to have one last precautionary pee before we get there.' And he disappeared below.

Jack looked at Emma. 'Here we go again darling. For goodness sake keep hold of something. I don't want you knocking yourself out like you did last time.'

Emma smiled wanly back. 'Not a chance Jack, don't worry I'll be clinging on to you for dear life.'

The twenty two minutes seemed to pass in a flash. Jack and Smithy watched the chart plotter carefully as Jacaranda inexorably closed in on the position of the time rift.

'Now, you're sure there will be nothing to see before it happens and the transition will have no effect on us?' asked Smithy in a suddenly pensive voice.

'Come on old chap we've been over this hundreds of times. No, one moment you're in the present and the next everything changes. The only physical issues have been loss of the helm as the autopilot cuts out with the loss of the GPS. Right now, get ready everyone.' He got on the radio and started counting down to the attendant ship and helicopter. Emma took his arm and as promised held on tight. Smithy split his time between watching the chart plotter, the horizon and a small device he had produced from his pocket. The Major and Sergeant tensed as if expecting some form of attack.

Just before the countdown finished, Jack opened his hand and looked down at his bone shark. Emma grinned when she saw what he was up to. 'I see you don't completely trust all this scientific stuff then?'

He grinned back but kept the countdown going over the radio. He reached zero and nothing happened. He kept counting as everyone started to look concerned. He had just reached six when something did happen.

This time it felt like great internal wrench had taken his insides and just for a second turned them all inside out. The light was suddenly noon bright and indeed the sun was suddenly almost directly overhead. The frigate and helicopter had simply vanished.

'What the fuck happened? Smithy, do you know what's going on?'

The scientist was looking at his little device and frowning. 'No. Well yes, it seems the quality of the rift has deteriorated in some way. We've made the transition but not quite as smoothly as I expected and it seems the time doesn't quite align like it did before.'

Jack was looking around. 'Must be why the bloody sun is now overhead,' he stated with some asperity. 'Derek and Sergeant Riley, can you check around the boat please and see if there is any damage. Smithy, let me know anything more from all those black boxes you've got downstairs and Emma and I'll get started on the navigation.'

Meanwhile Emma had been looking all around with the binoculars. 'Jack, Smithy, stop what you're up to, we've got a real problem. Look out there.' She pointed to the horizon to the right of the bow.

Smithy looked to where she was pointing. 'Eh, I can't see anything. What are you on about Emma?'

But Jack immediately realised the problem and urgently looked all around them. 'Oh, shit, shit, don't you get it Smithy? Look over there, we should be able to see St Vincent and up to the north the bottom end of St Lucia. They're not there. So not only have we come through and the time has slipped but so has our location. We're bloody lost.'

The stunned silence was broken by the two soldiers returning. 'All looks well on deck and....' Derek stopped seeing the look on Jack's face. 'What's the matter Jack? You look really worried.'

'It's quite simple,' said Jack. 'Unless we can get some form of fix, I can't set up the inertial navigation system. We were relying on us staying in the same geographical position but we appear to have moved. I have absolutely no idea where we are and how we're going to find out for that matter.'

'Surely we can't have moved that far?' asked Emma. They all turned and looked at Smithy.

'Bloody hell, I don't know. We look to be in the same sort of area. The sea's the same colour and it's still bloody hot. Look you two, do some more navigation thinking. I'll go down and check the instrumentation and see if I can work out what's happened.'

Half an hour later they all sat down in the cockpit again. They had lowered the sails rather than sail on in possibly the wrong direction and the boat was rolling in a long deep swell.

Smithy started the debate. 'I hate to say it but from what I can see there is no real problem. My instruments showed what I would expect. I guess we just have to find the islands and get on with it.' And he looked expectantly at Jack.

'And how exactly do we do that?' asked Jack looking rather annoyed at Smithy's apparent lack of concern.

'Well, there's a good sun up there and I know you've been brushing up with your sextant. Can't you use that?'

'It's not that simple I'm afraid. I need to know the time accurately and more to the point I need to know the time of noon at Greenwich to work out our longitude even roughly. We obviously didn't arrive at the same time we left, so I've no time reference to use. It's chicken and egg. I can use the sextant to work out when local noon is but unless I know where we are, I can't use that to find our position. I tell you what, if I assume we are here on the correct day and year I can work out a very approximate latitude at noon, that'll help. My tables should be good for that. The sun appears to still be rising, so I will take continuous sights until it starts to go down. That will at least give us local noon and a start.'

Going below he retrieved his sextant and once back on deck started calling out readings to Emma who carefully wrote them down. After about half an hour the readings stared going down. As soon as they did, he shouted for noon and they all set their watches to twelve o'clock. Jack took Emma's paper down to the chart table and grabbed his nautical almanac. After five minutes he reappeared looking slightly puzzled. 'Assuming this is actually June the third seventeen ninety one, then our latitude is way off but who's to say that that's the actual date. We are in the northern hemisphere and somewhere near the latitude of the Caribbean. However, tonight if I can see the pole star I should be able to get a better assessment. But critically there is no way of working out our longitude because we have no time reference to use. I've no idea whether to turn left or right I'm afraid.'

'So what on earth do we do now?' asked Derek.

'This is how I see it,' replied Jack. 'We're about the right latitude but what we don't know is whether we are still in the Caribbean Sea in which case the islands are to the east of us or whether we are actually in the Atlantic and the islands are in the opposite direction. So we need to come up with a plan.'

'Right.' said Smithy. 'The worst case I suppose is if we turn to the east but are actually in the Atlantic. How far would it be to the nearest land?'

'Three thousand miles.'

'Sod it, we don't want that then.'

Jack looked thoughtful. 'Well I reckon we're in the Atlantic. Firstly, there is this big long swell coming from the east which you don't tend to get in the Caribbean. Also, I've spotted several birds and they are all flying west. My suggestion is that we head west for at least five hundred miles. If we haven't stumbled across land or some other clue, we think again. Also by then if I've got a better assessment of out latitude, then we might find that a north or south heading will be more productive. Any dissenters?'

Smithy nodded. 'You're the skipper. Meanwhile, I'll continue see what I can get out of my instrumentation to see if I can really find out what happened.'

'And I'll make some lunch.' said the ever practical Emma.

By that evening, they still hadn't sighted land and Jack was concerned that without a moon they ran the real risk of hitting an unlit island. So it was quite a surprise when a full moon rose just after sunset. Calling to Smithy they looked through the almanac data together. If they'd come back to the correct time there shouldn't have been any useful moon for at least another week. They were starting to realise just how much their assumptions were awry. Once it became dark Jack looked for the pole star but as he started to see the stars appear the sky started to cloud over. Within half an hour not only couldn't he see any stars but the moon was also disappearing. The wind had veered from north east to east and started to increase. Suddenly Jack had a prickling sensation down his spine. Excusing himself he went down below to look at the barometer. What he saw chilled his blood. He shot back up into the cockpit.

'Right everyone listen up, we have an even bigger problem. We know that our date and location estimates are off but that can be sorted out. What we can't sort out is what I believe is about to happen to us now. I've been looking at the weather and the barometer fell over seven millibars in the last hour. That coupled with this long swell and the changes in the wind direction could well mean we are directly in the path of an approaching tropical storm or even a hurricane. If that's the case, survival is our main issue now.'

Chapter 21

As the hours ticked by all Jack's worst fears were realised. The wind had slowly increased as fast as the barometer continued to fall. The night was black and the only thing he could see was the white spume of breaking waves as they flew at their stern. It was even difficult to breathe at times as the air was so laden with spray. He was soaked to skin and scared half to death but far too busy to worry about either. He knew their best chance was to run before the wind and waves to try and get out of the hurricane's path and onto its safer side. But that meant taking the building seas on their stern and it was soon so violent that he didn't dare allow the autopilot to keep steering. The muscles of his arms ached with the effort of continually winding the wheel from lock to lock to keep them on even a semblance of a heading. He even had both engines running in case he needed their help to maintain course. They managed to get the big mainsail down early and lash it securely on the boom leaving only a small storm sail at the front. Jack knew it was now too dangerous to even contemplate going forward to take it down and he expected it blow out at any moment. Not that it would make much difference as even under bare poles Jacaranda was soon going to be just about out of control.

He had sent everyone but himself and Derek down below. The Sergeant tried to argue but Jack wanted the minimum number of people on deck. The wind was starting to back again, which was about the only good sign so far. Hopefully they had managed to get past the centre of the storm and into its less dangerous sector. *'Unless the damn thing changes its direction of course,'* he thought grimly to himself. He prayed that this meant they would soon be able to halt their madlong dash across the front of the storm and just ride out the rest until it was all passed. Unfortunately they had no radar to help locate the storm centre. It was hardly the sort of thing to have on an eighteenth century boat after all. And that wasn't the only issue with Jacaranda's new configuration. The wooden cladding was heavy and where in the past she would have ridden the waves, now she tended to wallow, especially in the troughs between the swells. But the thing that was worrying him the most was the mast and rigging. The waves were so big now that when she was in a trough she lost most of the wind and then when the stern was lifted up like an express elevator as the next wave caught her she was suddenly exposed to the feral blast of the storm once more. With her modern rig Jack would have been fairly certain that all would hold but now she had a wooden mast and all her rigging was made of rope not wire strands. He really had no idea how strong it really was.

Suddenly the stern lifted again and started to slew around. Jack frantically wound on wheel to counteract the movement. With almost no warning he was engulfed by a wall of water crashing across their stern. Luckily they were both strapped in with their safety harness using two rather than the usual single lanyard. Without them Jack knew they would have been over the side hours ago. Coughing and choking he managed to regain control, just before the yacht broached sideways.

'Right, that's enough Derek. We're going to have to stop. Let go the foresail sheet. Don't worry about it flapping it will probably flog itself to pieces quickly enough. But for God's sake mind your fingers.'

Derek nodded and pulled out the belaying pin holding the sheet and in an instant the rope had disappeared forward. The sail started to make a dreadful sound which slowly reduced as it shredded itself to rags.

'Now listen carefully,' yelled Jack over the roar of the wind and ocean. 'I would like to turn into the wind and put out a sea anchor but turning across this sea is just too bloody dangerous. We would almost certainly be capsized and anyway it's far too risky to go forward and attempt to tie anything on. So we need to get all the ropes we can and stream them astern to slow us down. Can you get the Sergeant up to help? I daren't leave the wheel.'

Derek nodded and opened the top of the hatch to the saloon and called down. A few moments later he was handed the end of a safety harness lanyard, which he clipped to the ring by the hatch and then the sergeant followed it out safely secure before he even made it into the cockpit. He didn't look well. Jack could imagine just what sort of hell it was down below.

'How are the others holding up down there?' Jack half screamed over the howl of the wind.

The sergeant gave a sickly grin as he looked around at the storm lashed blackness. 'Fine, it's better than being up here, they're fine.'

Derek explained what they had to do and Jack pointed to the locker where all the mooring warps were stowed. One by one, they tied them to cleats and strong points and then flung them over the side. Soon there were half a dozen ropes trailing behind the yacht and Jack could feel the drag holding the stern to the waves in a more controlled manner. The steering input had reduced and with gratitude he reengaged the autopilot. It was only then did he realise how much his arms hurt from the continued strain of wrestling with the wheel. He staggered to another locker and reached under a tangle of fenders and other detritus and found what he was looking for. Derek came over without prompting and helped Jack pull out a large canvas bag.

'What's this?'

'It's a storm drogue. Now that we've slowed down using the warps we should be able to deploy this and control her even more. Here give me a hand.'

Under Jack's direction, the three of them tied the drogue onto a strongpoint which used to control the mainsail sheet in modern times. Jack also ran some extra lines to other cleats before he was happy and then they heaved the drogue over the stern. When its line reached full travel they felt an almighty jerk and for a second Jack thought it might just rip out its moorings but they held and Jacaranda slowed even more. More water was breaking over the stern now but at least she felt more under control. Satisfied that he had done all he could for the moment he sat down to gather his breath and his thoughts. He looked at his two companions blinking through sore, salt stinging eyes. 'Hopefully, we are on the safe side now.'

'Nope, you're going to have to explain that a bit more,' shouted Derek.

'Think of it like a helicopter. The rotor blade going forward has its own speed plus the speed the helicopter is going at but the blade going backwards whilst still rotating at the same speed has the speed of the aircraft working in the opposite direction. Get it?'

'OK but this is a storm not a helicopter.'

'Right but they move at up to twenty five knots or so. Suppose the wind is rotating around the storm at one hundred knots. The advancing side which is on the right, will have winds of one hundred and twenty five but the left hand side will only have seventy five. I say only because that is still enough to cause us severe trouble. The wind is over sixty knots now and I've seen much bigger gusts. We've been heading west to try and get past the centre before the wind becomes just too much but it also means we are potentially heading towards the islands without being able to see them.'

'So we're buggered either way?'

'Well, it'll be light soon and hopefully, if we do see an island, we'll see it in enough time to steer around it.' Jack wasn't at all sure that would be the case but what else could he say.

'Derek you've been up here long enough get below and at least try to dry out a bit. The Sergeant and I will manage now.'

'What about you Jack? You've been up here all night.'

Jack gave a weary grin. 'Skippers perks, I'm sure you understand.'

Before he could say another thing they were lifted up back into the wind by yet another massive swell and there was an almighty crash from up front. Jack looked up just in time to see the mast disappearing over the port side of the yacht. It all seemed to happen in seconds. He lurched to the wheel and disconnected the autopilot slamming the wheel hard over to counteract the drag of the mast and rigging in the water. It wasn't enough and the boat started to turn broadside to the waves. In desperation, Jack slammed the port engine throttle fully forwards, praying that with all the ropes over the side that the propeller wouldn't get fouled. It didn't and with the engine roaring Jacaranda stopped her turn and came to a horrible sort of equilibrium half across the breaking seas. The cockpit was a maelstrom of breaking water. Even so Jack could see the port shrouds bar taught over the side of the boat obviously still holding the mast to the hull. At the same time he could hear a hideous banging noise as the mast and boom started to batter the side of the yacht. Maybe that cladding would at last be of some use and give them some protection. Whatever happened, they couldn't stay like this for very long.

Derek had clearly worked out the danger as well. Looking at Jack he yelled, 'the Sergeant and I will have to go forward and cut it free. We daren't open the hatch to get the others to help. It will just flood the boat. Have you got an axe anywhere?'

With a sudden sickening feeling Jack realised they didn't. He had some boltcroppers designed to cut wire rigging but they would be of no use on rope. He had an idea. 'No but look in that locker there's a hacksaw, it should work on rope and take this.' And he handed over his sailing multi tool showing Derek the saw tool designed to cut rope.

Just before they left he shouted one last instruction. 'For God's sake keep your harnesses attached at all times. One hand for the boat and one for the job. Be bloody careful.'

The two men nodded and started to carefully make their way towards the splintered stump of the mast that stuck up about six foot above the deck. Several times waves washed completely over them but each time, when the water cleared he could see them clinging on like drowned rats. It seemed to take an age but they were eventually in a position to start cutting. Several lines had parted when Jack felt a particularly large wave start to lift the boat. He screamed a warning but even as he did so he knew they couldn't have heard it. Even with the port engine at full throttle the boat start to turn again across the swell. He slammed the other engine throttle into reverse but the engine groaned and shuddered to a stop. It must have picked up a rope. He had run out of ideas and hung on desperately as the boat started to roll. The whole port side went under until they were almost over at ninety degrees. Jack was flung towards the raging sea now directly below him and was only saved when his harness brought him to an abrupt stop. He actually felt when the mast and boom must have broken free because she started to slowly turn back. Suddenly, he had control again. But when he looked forward the deck was empty. Desperately looking over the side, he searched for his two companions but with a sickening feeling he knew they were gone. There was no way he could rescue them even if he could find them in that mad white maelstrom of a sea. With despair he got Jacaranda under control of sorts and wondered desperately what the hell he was going to do now.

Jack was a fighter but now he knew he was beaten. There was nothing more he could do. With the drogue deployed the boat was at least held in some form of stable condition. With no rig to react to the fury of the wind they should be safer. He was shaking with reaction and cold and knew if he stayed here in the cockpit he would either drown or pass out in which case he would probably drown anyway. He needed to get below. What was the point in keeping a lookout? They would see nothing until they hit it. With infinite care he made his way to the saloon hatch. He banged on it until it opened a crack and he saw Smithy's face looking through.

'Let me in,' he croaked through salt cracked lips.

Smithy slid the hatch open enough for Jack to clamber through followed by cascades of sea water which stopped as the hatch was slammed shut after him. He fell the last few feet and ended up on the saloon floor in a heap. Smithy and Emma rushed to him and helped him to one of the saloon benches where he jammed himself in. Somehow Emma got him a glass of water without spilling more than half and he drank it greedily. He looked around. The place was a shambles, everything was soaking wet and there was a massive jumble of cushions, books and assorted junk but at least he was out of that monstrous wind and could start to think again.

'We lost the two soldiers overboard, I'm so sorry,' he said. 'The mast went, I'm sure you heard it go and they went to cut it free but we got swamped and even those harnesses couldn't keep them safe.'

Emma jammed herself in next to him and held him tight, she could feel him shivering. 'Jack, there was nothing you could do, you must realise that. Come on, we need you now. What should we do?'

He looked blankly about. 'Sorry but there's nothing to do now but to try and wait it out. The drogue is deployed, so we shouldn't travel too far especially with no mast. It should keep us on a safe heading and stop us being capsized. We just have to pray the storm now passes us by and the weather moderates.'

Smithy was clinging to the saloon table listening to every word. 'What about the liferaft Jack? Shouldn't we think about that?'

Jack shrugged. 'We're in the best liferaft there is mate. The only time you should board one, is if you have to step up into it as the boat sinks. There are so many stories of yachts being found with no crew because they abandoned too early. But if we need it remember it's on the stern and we'll have to be bloody careful to launch it in this breeze.'

They huddled together for what seemed like a lifetime but later Jack realised could only have been a couple of hours. They listened to the scream of the storm and clung on for dear life every time Jacaranda seemed about to be tipped completely over on her side.

Jack looked at his watch and realised it should getting light and indeed when he poked his head briefly out of the hatch the sky was turning grey. However, the visibility was so poor it might just as well have been dark. However, when he looked at the steering compass he saw that they were now being blown on to a more southerly course. That could only mean one thing that the storm centre was passing them by. After the hell of the night he started to feel a glimmer of hope.

It didn't last long. Smithy, desperate for the toilet, had managed to make his way to the stairs that led down to the lower part of the boat. He suddenly reappeared. 'Jack, Emma, there's water everywhere. I think we're sinking,' he yelled in fright.

Jack clawed his way to the stairwell and looked down. His heart dropped. The floor boards were awash with sea water that flung itself everywhere as the boat moved. He suddenly realised that the boat's motion was sluggish, more so than it had been.

'Alright, don't panic everyone. It can't be that big a leak or we would have gone down ages ago. Emma, you go aft to the main cabin. Smithy, go forward and both of you start looking for the damage. I'll go and start the pumps.'

He made his way to the boats electrical control panel. Sure enough the light that said that the automatic bilge pump was working was illuminated. He quickly hit the switches that turned on the other two pumps and then made his way below to help. A cry from forward alerted him and he found Smithy in one of the port side cabins. He had pulled up the floor boards and was pointing to a bubbling fountain of water that was pulsing up from somewhere below.

Without hesitation Jack took a breath and felt down the surge of water. His fingers found splinters of wood and he quickly felt loose planks. The damage was well below the waterline and also below the level of the extra wood cladding so the damage must be to the original hull.

'It must have been caused when the mast went over. God I'm a fool. I should have checked earlier' he said to Smithy and also Emma who had joined them. 'We're going to have to try and jam something in the hole. Emma grab that mattress and pass it to me.'

They fought the water for hours. Initially the pumps made a difference, as did jamming all they could into the hole. But it soon became clear that the damage was more extensive than they initially thought and despite everything they did the water level slowly increased. Their efforts were becoming increasingly lacklustre as exhaustion slowly set in. Eventually, they were forced to abandon the lower part of the boat and Jack knew he had to make a heart wrenching decision.

'I'm sorry everyone but now it is really time to use the liferaft and by the time we get sorted we will be actually stepping up into the bloody thing. Let's do this while we still have time to think straight and do it properly. Emma, you know where the grab bag is. Smithy, go to the galley and get as many bottles of water as you can. There should still be some packaged up.'

Jack opened the saloon hatch and was surprised not to be immediately inundated with sea water. Looking around he saw that the sea was still running but the wind had definitely abated. Not only that but the sun was breaking through rifts in the clouds. With relief, he realised they were through the worst of it. Emma heaved the large yellow grab bag up the hatch and followed it up along with Smithy cradling a package of plastic water bottles.

'Jack, surely the storm has passed us now,' said Emma. 'We can't leave Jacky now.'

Jack was thinking the same thing when the yacht gave a stricken lurch and he could see water flooding in even faster down below. The saloon was almost half submerged. Something else must have given way.

'No, we've got to go. Smithy, help me here.' And he reached for the liferaft release handle 'When I pull this, the liferaft will go over the side and should inflate. Before it does, we both grab this painter and make damn sure we keep hold of it OK? We need to drag it back alongside before jumping in.'

Smithy nodded and Jack pulled the handle. The white fibreglass case fell over the side with a splash and split in half as the orange liferaft instantly inflated. Jack was relieved to see it inflate upright. They often didn't and turning it back over in these seas would have been a nightmare. Pulling desperately on the painter they dragged it back to the boat.

'Emma, you go in first. Inflate your lifejacket in case you fall out. You know the drill and then we'll pass you the grab bag and water.'

Emma jumped for the entrance and half landed on the canopy but was able to clamber inside without too much trouble. While Smithy handed down the extra water and grab bag, Jack had a final look around. If this had been his century he would have made sure they had the emergency radio beacons and satellite phone but here and now they were completely useless. He did spot his binoculars however and grabbed them before following the other two into the liferaft. His last act was to cut the painter with the knife supplied for just that task and watch the death throes of his pride and joy and their only realistic method of returning to their century slowly disappear as the wind forced them away and the waves hid her final fate.

Chapter 22

Victor Hugues stared ahead through the tangle of rigging and bodies of seamen all doing incomprehensible things with ropes. It was all accompanied by shouting from the officers behind and petty officers all around him. He decided he would never understand the ways of ships and their people. He had crossed the Atlantic several times but never in a warship before. There seemed to be far too many crew but as had been explained to him they were needed to fire the guns that seemed to fill every spare space available.

However, he was elated. At last they had left France behind. The coastline was a thin grey line on the horizon astern. Finally he could believe that he was on the way to carve out a kingdom for himself in one of the riches places on earth.

'Planning our strategy?' came the voice of his co-commissioner from somewhere behind him.

'Our strategy is simple, Michel,' he replied turning to face the man with a note of contempt in his voice. 'Our tame soldiers retake Guadeloupe if the British have taken it. We establish our position and then take the other islands. The British will be far too busy elsewhere in a few months to be able to retain sufficient forces in the islands to stop us. Especially if we recruit a local army to help us.'

'You mean to arm the slaves?'

'No, I mean to emancipate them in line with our revolutionary principles.' There was a slight sneer on his face as he said it.

'Do you not think that a large numbers of freed slaves, especially with arms, will be a danger to all?'

'Who said I would let them keep any weapons after they've served their purpose? We have to be realistic. We've seen what has happened elsewhere when too much freedom is granted.'

'And what of the rest of the population? Do we know how they feel?'

'We know the current so called government is Royalist and has aligned itself with the British but I will wager there are any number of other citizens who will embrace our cause. Most people just want to get on with their lives you know.'

'Victor, I really don't understand you. You espouse revolutionary principles yet you seem to be more of a pragmatist the more I get to know you.'

'And you Michel? Do you really believe that the revolution will improve the population's lot. Or have they just exchanged one tyranny for another?'

'Maybe, I should have said cynic.'

Victor just grunted. 'I think realist would be the best description. Don't forget I know these islands. That's one of the reasons I was chosen. There are thousands of slaves for every European. We cannot allow anarchy. Not if we want to continue to make money from the sugar estates. I will be as firm as necessary to ensure the rule of law. Whichever law we are following at the time that is.'

'And pocket a fortune in the process.'

'Do you have a problem with that Michel?'

'Not as long as you remember that there are two Commissioners and I am the other one. We share the administrative load and everything else.'

'Of course.'

'*That's if the heat or fevers of the Caribbean don't see to you first my fat friend,*' Victor thought to himself. 'Well we have at least six weeks in this wooden tub. The Captain says we will call at Madeira and then we head across the wide Atlantic. I hope you are not prone to sea sickness because it can be quite lively where we're going.'

Charles felt the fatigue making his salt stung eyes smart and on top of that a headache was coming on. It might be warm in these latitudes but a night on an open deck being constantly soaked with sea water soon made you appreciate warm, dry clothing.

Polaris had run south from the storm all night and kept clear of the worst. Even so he had never felt inclined to go below. It wasn't that he didn't trust his deck officers but just too much could happen too fast, for him to react unless he was on hand. That the ship had weathered the storm so well was a tribute to her crew.

His aim, now that the galley fire had been safely relit, was to get some hot food into all of them. However, before that happened there was one last thing to do.

After looking up at the masthead he called to the Sailing Master. 'Mr Timms, the wind has moderated enough now. Let's get some sail on her and harden up. It's going to be a long beat back to our patrol position. At least until we get a trade wind back.'

Mr Timms looked aloft as well and nodded in agreement. He shouted for the watch on deck to make sail and satisfied that all was now well, Charles finally went below for some well earned sleep. Once in his cabin he stripped off his sodden clothing and dried himself. His servant came in and enquired what he wanted for breakfast but he suddenly felt so tired he waved him away telling him to wake him at noon. He was asleep as soon as his head hit the pillow.

He was woken by a change in the noises of the ship. Cocking an ear he realised the wind had dropped completely. The great swell caused by the storm was still there and Polaris was rolling heavily. Loose gear and rigging was slamming about as she rolled. With his nose blocked and his mouth dry he swung out of his cot calling for some hot food. His watch showed almost noon. It was nice to know his internal alarm clock was still working. Lunch was a simple affair and he soon emerged back on deck holding his third cup of coffee. He blinked in the strong sunlight that poured out of a clear blue sky.

Mr Timms was off watch and it was his young Lieutenant, Peter Makepeace who had the deck.

'Well Peter, it seems the storm has killed the wind for us,' he said cheerily.

'Yes Sir but hopefully it will fill in soon. The barometer is rising again and quite fast.'

'Indeed but let's enjoy the peace while we may. And of course there is no sign of any Frenchmen eh?'

'None Sir but please excuse me, I have to take the noon sun sight and must prepare.'

'Of course, don't let me get in your way.'

Whilst his young officer squinted at the sun through his sextant, Charles looked out over the deep blue, glassy sea. '*It wasn't that long ago and I would be using my own sextant and checking every calculation,'* he mused. In some ways it was a shame that the ship would be returning to her peacetime role just as he had her worked up satisfactorily up as a warship. His eye was caught by the flash of a school of flying fish breaking out of a swell and skimming off into the distance. A pod of dolphins then broke surface which was probably why the flying fish were fleeing. Little good it would do them. It always amazed Charles how stunningly beautiful the sea could be even so soon after a violent storm. He knew he would miss this all when he was back in Hinchfield Hall.

His reverie was broken by a cry from the masthead.

'Deck there, object in the water, about two miles off the port bow.'

With little else to do and feeling the need for exercise, Charles grabbed his telescope and climbed the mainmast ratlines to join the lookout at the masthead. He arrived slightly out of breath but exhilarated at being so high above his own deck. He really should do this more often.

'Where away Williams?' he asked the seaman.

Surprised to see his Captain join him for so mundane a sighting the young man pointed out ahead. 'There Sir, it's very low in the water. At first I thought it was a whale but it's not moving.'

Charles focused his telescope using the seaman's shoulder to help keep it steady. He saw the object immediately and it definitely wasn't a whale. He realised that he could make out the stump of a mast and what looked like ropes dangling over the rear. No it was a wreck. Some poor unfortunates had been caught much closer to the centre of the storm that was good for them. He suddenly had the strangest feeling. There was something about the shape of the hull that nagged at the back of his mind. He called down to the deck. 'Mr Makepeace, launch the cutter please. It looks like we have a shipwreck to investigate.'

When he was back on deck he saw that Mr Timms was also present. 'I think I'll take the cutter if you gentlemen don't mind. I could do with the excitement.'

Mr Timms shrugged. 'More likely just an empty shell Sir. That would have been a dreadful tempest if they were caught in its full fury.'

He couldn't say why but Charles had the premonition that there would be more to this wreck but could hardly say so. He would find out for himself.

With hardly any wind the ship would take some time to catch up the cutter. They would have plenty of time to investigate. Once it was in the water under oars it didn't take long to reach the wallowing hulk. The closer they got the more puzzled he became. The lines seemed almost familiar yet the hull was simple rough planking. It looked almost like a small trading sloop but something was wrong.

He wasn't the only person to have misgivings. His Bosun also voiced concerns. 'That's one strange barky Sir. Don't think I've ever seen lines quite like that afore.'

'I know what you mean. Let's row around her first. As they crossed the wreck's stern the hairs on the back of his neck stood up. Written across her transom half awash in the swell was her name, one he never expected to see ever again and one that explained why she looked almost familiar. Picked out in gold leaf was the name 'Jacaranda'.

'Right, put the cutter alongside but no one is to accompany me. I will board alone please.'

'Are you sure Sir? That wreck doesn't look too safe.'

'She's floated this long, she must have some residual buoyancy or she'd have gone under long ago and anyway unlike most of you lot, I can actually swim.'

They held the cutter to the wreck and Charles scrambled on board. He then told them to hold off and inspect the hull from the outside to see if there was any sign of hull damage. With the water so still and clear they could probably see down to the keel.

He couldn't get below decks. She was almost completely awash. However, the cockpit was familiar although it was clear from what he could see that considerable work had been undertaken to disguise her. More importantly, there was no sign of life. He remembered where the liferaft used to be stowed and it wasn't there. A thrill of hope and even anticipation coursed through him. Whoever had come here in this boat was quite possibly still alive and probably somewhere downwind of them although there was no indication how long it was since they abandoned her.

A cry from the cutter caught his attention. He went up amidships and looked over the side where the Bosun was pointing. Looking down he could see several planks sticking out and what looked like some rags as well.

'Probably holed when they lost the mast and they tried to fill it with material from the inside,' the Bosun opined.

'I agree,' said Charles. 'Do you think we could fother it from the outside and maybe pump her out?'

The Bosun looked sceptical. 'Well yes Sir, we probably could but what would be the point? We'd be better off sinking her properly to stop her being a risk to other ships.'

'Believe me Bosun, I want this boat salvaged if at all possible. It's a vessel I am familiar with and would hate to see her sink. Let's see to it.'

Once Polaris had caught them up, Charles took charge of the salvage. They hauled an old sail around the hull and ran a pump from the ship down into Jacaranda's saloon. In a remarkably quick time she started to rise in the water to the curious gaze of the crew. Charles realised he was going to have a problem with his people once they saw what she really was. However, before he could think of a believable tale to tell he was pre-empted by the Sailing Master who was staring intently over the side at Jacaranda's stern. The wind was still very light and the water extremely clear.

'Well I'll be a Dutchman,' he said in a puzzled voice. 'Sir, what do you make of that?' And he pointed at a clearly defined propeller sticking out next to a very strange looking rudder.

Charles knew he had to come up with something at least half believable very fast.

'Mr Timms, gentlemen,' he said to the assembled throng. 'This may be an amazing coincidence but I have actually been on this vessel before. I even know her owner or rather knew him as the storm will probably have taken him. What you see is an experimental ship he was developing for the Admiralty. Those strange devices are called propellers and are driven by a small steam engine in the hull. It's not a new idea as you may know. We already have a several vessels like this in England. The difference here is that they use paddle wheels whereas this vessel uses these devices. She must have been on some sort of proving voyage and been caught out in the storm.'

He waited to see how his words would be taken. To his surprise there was little debate, although quite a lot of muttering broke out. It seemed his explanation was being accepted for the moment at least.

With that sorted out they managed to get the hull almost watertight and Charles went below to inspect the wreck. In the saloon it was very much as he remembered, although there seemed to be more electrical devices than he remembered. He wondered what they were for but knew he would never find out not the least because they were clearly wrecked, having been totally submerged. He quickly found why she had remained afloat. The engine room had been shut tight and when he opened the door found it surprisingly dry. The buoyancy of this one compartment coupled with that wood planking over the hull was probably enough. He also found the hole from the inside and could see what they had done with an old mattress and other bits and pieces. He could also see that due to the external water pressure, the sail on the outside had not only covered the hole well but had also forced much of the sprung planking back into position. There was surprisingly little leakage. Satisfied that she would now stay afloat he returned on board Polaris.

'Right gentlemen, I think we need to tow the wreck back to Guadeloupe. We are at the end of our patrol time anyway, so we might as well head back. The wind is starting to set back into the east and we can set course easily enough. Oh and on the way we must keep a good eye out for any survivors. If they did manage to take to a boat then they are most probably downwind of the wreck and so between us and the Island.'

Chapter 23

Jack retched over the side of the liferaft again. This time virtually nothing came up. He sat back feeling slightly less nauseous and grimaced at Emma and Smithy who looked no better than him.

'I've been sailing for years and never thrown up. They say a liferaft's motion is the worst there is. They weren't bloody joking.'

Emma smiled back wanly. 'Take another pill Jack. I don't think the last one stayed down long enough to even reach your stomach.' She handed him the packet.

Smithy sat forward and looked out. There was nothing in sight except sea and sky. 'At least the weather is moderating. It's quite nice out there now. Any idea how long we can last in this rubber bag Jack?'

'Good question. We have enough available water for at least five days and food for at least a week. But actually it's far better than that as we've got a solar still and fishing gear so we could probably last almost indefinitely. There is enough moisture in raw fish to keep the body alive. It's been done before you know.' Suddenly the thought of raw fish sent him back to the side to throw up again. 'Oh bugger, Emma hand me yet another pill please.'

Emma did so. 'But we still don't know where we are. If we're still in the Atlantic then presumably we might sight an island but suppose we're not, what then?'

'Well the current and wind is from the east, so we will gradually be set westwards. At the worst, we will end up somewhere in central America.' He did a quick mental calculation. 'Assuming a drift of say three knots, that's 70 miles a day so it could take a minimum of twenty days or so.'

Smithy lay back against the rubber bulkhead. 'God that means I have to look at your beautiful visage for that long and no booze on board. How will I survive?'

'Hey, we have to look at you as well you know,' responded Emma giving him a gentle kick.

'Yes well, we'd better pray that we land somewhere where there are actual people. That part of the world is pretty sparsely populated in this era. And most of those that are there are bloody pirates. Lucky we packed a gun in the grab bag. Why do I keep getting this feeling of déjà vu?' Jack asked despondently.

Emma managed a wan smile. 'Because last time you came back to the past you ended up losing Jacaranda and ended up adrift with only a pistol and two friends for company.'

'Tell me about it.'

They were interrupted by a whoop of joy from Smithy. 'Hey guys, look over there. A sail.'

Jack grabbed his binoculars and focused on where Smithy was pointing. 'A local fishing boat by the looks of it. Shit, I wonder what they'll make of a bright orange blob in the water?'

They didn't have long to find out. The boat had obviously seen them and altered course towards the liferaft. However, as soon as they started waving and shouting, the boat sheared off and headed away. Excitement turned to disappointment as it disappeared.

'What the hell was that all about?' asked a disgruntled Smithy. 'Surely they could see we needed help.'

Jack was not so sure. 'Look at it from the perspective of someone from this century. They see something in the water that's a colour they've probably never seen before and definitely a shape they've not seen before either and then people appear and start shouting at them. I'm not sure I would hang about either.'

'You don't seem that upset though.'

'Actually I'm not, because I recognised the type of boat and if that wasn't a Caribbean design, I'm a banana. In fact we sailed something very similar last time I was here. So we must be fairly close to an island. They don't venture far offshore. And thinking about it that means we must still be upwind of the islands as we travelled quite a distance in Jacaranda. We'd have never seen that boat if we had started out in the middle of the Caribbean Sea.

Jack's optimism was soon rewarded when a few hours later through his binoculars he spotted the hills of an island to the south west. It took surprisingly little time for another two islands to appear. One almost dead ahead and one to the north west.

'Right, everyone, I know where we are at bloody last,' he announced with a savage grin. The big island to the south is Dominica, the big one to the north is Guadeloupe and the one it looks like we might hit is Marie Galante, which belongs to Guadeloupe. So we better make sure our French is up to scratch as in 1791 they belong to France.'

Emma felt relief wash over her. She knew the area as well as Jack. 'Do you think we'll be washed ashore Jack?'

'Can't really tell this far out I'm afraid and at this rate it'll be dark before we get anywhere. But if we don't get close to Marie Galante then the Saintes are just behind them and whatever happens we should be able to swim to one of them.'

'The Saintes?' asked Smithy.

'Yes, another group of small islands just further on. It was off there that Admiral Rodney kicked the French fleet's ass at the end of the American War of Independence. Now look, I think we need to consider how we get ashore. Emma and I are strong swimmers. How about you Smithy?'

'Well I can swim but it's not something I do regularly I'm afraid. But why are you assuming we'll have to swim for it. Didn't you say we might very well be washed up ashore anyway?'

'Yes but I'm now thinking of our cover story. What do you think anyone of this time will make of the liferaft and some of the stuff in it if they find us with it? My suggestion is that at the appropriate time we bundle up our clothing and supplies in the grab bag and that other dry bag we have and use them for flotation. We then de-inflate the liferaft, even sink it if we can and then swim ashore. Our clothing is of the correct period and I put some identification material in the grab bag before we sailed. We can then just claim to be shipwrecked mariners.'

The idea met with general agreement and they went on to discuss their cover identities. They had all kept their current names, although Jack was now an 'Honourable' and Smithy had become Smythe. They even had had the forethought to put some papers in the gab bag to support their identities. Hopefully, those and their clothing would be enough to allow them to pass as authentic occupants of the eighteenth century. All they had to do now was wait and hope they would get close enough to land to swim for it.

As darkness set in they could see in the moonlight that Marie Galante was going to pass too far away. Clearly the current was sweeping in a curve between the two larger islands. However Jack wasn't worried, as this should set them directly towards the Saintes. A few hours later, they were startled by several large flashes that lit the horizon over Guadeloupe. A few seconds later there was the roll of what sounded like thunder.

'What the hell is that?' asked Smithy. 'I can't see any clouds over there.'

Suddenly, there was a crackling noise and then more flashes and deep booms. It went on for at least half an hour and then as suddenly as it started, silence descended again. They debated the cause but all they could think of was some sort of firework display.

'After all this is one of the few quiet periods in Caribbean history,' observed Jack. 'Not like it will be a few years from now.'

Sometime later in the middle of the night Jack, judged they were as close as they were going to get.

'Emma, Smithy, time for a swim. It looks less than half a mile. Let's get our clothes and everything we're taking into the bags.'

They stripped down to their underwear and were soon in the water holding onto the liferaft. The two dry bags gave plenty of buoyancy so Jack took the knife and started to puncture the liferaft which hissing slowly, subsided into an inert bag. It soon became clear that it wasn't going to sink as there was just too much trapped air and Jack didn't want to waste too much time in case they were swept past their target island. Leaving the deflated raft to its fate they struck out for shore.

It hadn't seemed far from the comfort of the liferaft but as soon as they started swimming Jack prayed he hadn't misjudged it. Progress seemed painfully slow even though the current was clearly still helping them. Luckily, with the water so warm, they shouldn't get cold. Smithy was the first to tire. Jack wasn't surprised he hardly led a physical lifestyle. He and Emma put him between them, with the two bags to aid buoyancy and half pushed him along. After what seemed like hours, they could hear the sound of surf. Soon it started to sound quite loud and Jack started to get worried that they might get dashed onto some rocks. He knew the coast they were approaching was mainly beach but there were steep cliffs at either end. It didn't help that the moon was beginning to set. Then before any of them could react the swell started to build up as the shore started shoaling fast and they were on a roller coaster that couldn't be stopped. The waves started to break over them and it was only a matter of seconds before they could see the beach through the breaking surf.

'Just think of it as a surfing holiday and keep swimming even if you get sucked back by the undertow. Smithy you keep the bags. Emma and I will swim for it together.' And then there was no more time as the surf took them. Jack soon lost hold of Emma but knew she was a strong swimmer and anyway they used to play in waves like these. Not at night and exhausted by lack of sleep and seasickness mind you but he was sure she would be fine. Suddenly he was picked up by a large wave and was hurtling forward. He couldn't see the shore but suddenly he could feel it. Rough sand and stones grazed his knees and before he could stand he was being sucked back. Digging in for all he was worth he managed to keep his position and then with the next wave he was pushed even further up the beach. Suddenly he was standing, with the water receding behind him. Making his way ashore he could make out pale sand and some vegetation further inland. However, his concentration was on the waves.

A shout alerted him and he could see a body struggling in the surf. He waded out and grabbed something. It turned out to be the two bags with a half drowned Smithy attached. Jack half dragged him above the surf line where he slumped gratefully as he caught his breath. Where was Emma?

A shout to his right caught his attention and there she was walking towards them.

'Well we made it Jack,' she gasped as she sat down by the recovering scientist and shaking the water from her hair.

They all sat for a while getting their breath back. Smithy opened one of the bags and passed around a bottle of water which they all used to take the taste of salt from their mouths.

Jack hadn't realised just how thirsty he was until he was offered the bottle. 'It may be the Caribbean but I'm getting bloody cold. Let's get dressed and ditch anything that's not contemporary. The water bottle for a start and then I guess we'd better start looking for some form of life.'

Once they were all ready he led them off down the beach. The main town should be over the rise ahead of them, although he wasn't sure how much of a town there would be in this era. Suddenly, as they reached the end of the beach, he saw the shape of two people just before they stumbled into them.

He called out in French. 'Hello, can you help us? We've been shipwrecked.'

Before he could say anymore, to his surprise one of the figures responded in English. 'Oh, not some more bloody crapauds.'

And then something swung towards his head and with a terrible thud his world turned black.

Chapter 24

It took Polaris longer than expected to make it back to Guadeloupe. Towing Jacaranda hadn't been easy. Charles had had to put several men on board to steer her but with strict instructions to stay on the upper deck. Even so, she had a habit of sheering about which made the tow long and frustrating.

However, they eventually made it back and anchored off the town of Point a Pitre where the rest of the British ships were sheltering. Apparently the storm had affected the landings badly and driven some of the ships clear for a few days but now Grand Terre was theirs and Basse Terre was about to fall. Charles had been summoned on board the largest warship present, the frigate Winchelsea. Her Captain had been wounded, so he met briefly with her First Lieutenant on the quarterdeck. The man looked harassed and clearly wanted Charles away as soon as possible. He handed him a sealed packet of orders.

'From the Admiral Sir. He has gone to St Kitts now that things are settled here but as I understand it you are to be decommissioned and are a private ship once more.' There was a note of asperity in the man's voice.

'*Maybe I should volunteer to stay on.*' He thought. But no, the Admiral had given him his orders and far more importantly Melissa had given him her orders and he really needed to clear up the mystery of the yacht he had in tow.

'One last thing,' the man continued. 'You are to head back to Antigua to decommission and hand over any naval stores and your cannon. The detail is in the orders. Before that however, we would be obliged if you went over to the Saintes and transferred some of your naval seamen into HMS Rose who is sore need of prime hands.' And then clearly with curiosity overcoming his reticence he asked. 'And may I enquire Sir, why you have that strange vessel in tow? I assume she is salvage from the storm?'

'Indeed she is,' responded Charles who had no intention of providing any detail. 'She may be worth something to me if I can repair her. As my recovery of her was not the result of enemy action then she is mine to dispose of as I am sure you know. On that matter have there been any reports of shipwrecked mariners? It looks likely she was abandoned so her crew may have survived.'

'No I'm sorry we've heard nothing and from what we saw of the tempest I would be surprised if anyone caught in it could have survived.'

Unsurprised but disappointed by the reply, Charles could only agree with the assessment. He simply nodded and took his leave. On the short run over to the Saintes he read his orders, which simply confirmed the conversation on the deck of the frigate but included a letter from the Admiral thanking him for his services and wishing him good fortune. Charles was impressed and not a little surprised that an Admiral would write to a lowly Master and Commander. But there again he was also an Earl and no doubt the Admiral was thinking of his return to England some time soon.

Late that afternoon they arrived in the lovely little bay of the Saintes. HMS Rose was there and as soon as he dropped anchor, Charles headed over to the frigate. He noted the Union Flag flying over the fort at the entrance to the bay. This time he was ushered into the great cabin and introduced to Captain Scott who was all affability. Hardly surprising as he was getting an influx of trained seamen when he least expected it. Once again the subject of his strange salvage became a point of discussion. Charles explained how he had discovered her and intended to take her back to Antigua with him.

Scott looked strangely at him. 'Is there any indication of her nationality?'

Charles was surprised by the question but as he knew the answer he saw no reason to prevaricate.

'Actually, although it's quite a coincidence, I know the boat and knew the owner assuming he has now perished. She's British why do you ask?'

'Well last night, two of my seamen discovered three people on the beach near here. Two men and a woman and they claimed to be shipwrecked mariners but as they spoke to our men in French we're holding them in the fort up there. I wonder if they're your missing crew?'

Jack came to with a splitting headache. Waves of pain pulsed across his eyes. He suddenly heard Emma's voice. 'Smithy, he's awake at last, get some water.'

He felt his head lifted up and cold clear water dribbled into his mouth. Some went down the wrong way and he started to choke and cough. It didn't help his headache but forced him to sit up. He managed to focus on his surroundings and saw that he was in a small. grey. stone room with straw on the floor and one tiny barred window on one side. On the other was a large substantial looking wooden door.

'Where are we? What happened?' he croaked.

Smithy answered first. 'Seems they think we're French spies. You shouldn't have spoken to that man in French last night. They seem convinced and won't take no for an answer.'

'Who? Who thinks we're French?'

'They're British Jack,' answered Emma. 'They've taken us to that fort. You know, the one that's a museum in our time. They took all our belongings and just chucked us in here.'

Jacks mind was clearing fast. 'Hang on that can't be right. These islands are French in 1791.'

'Sorry mate but it looks like we've arrived even further off target than we imagined.'

'Hang on a second, Guadeloupe was briefly in British hands in 1794 if I remember my history correctly. Jesus, have we arrived three years late?'

'Seems so but don't ask me why. But it does explain why all your sextant calculations were so far off.'

Jack realised there were more pressing matters and looked at Emma. 'How are you darling? It seems I was the only one to get clobbered.'

Smithy answered first. 'You should have seen her Jack. That poor seaman didn't have a chance. She really laid into him. I guess as we were all talking English at that point they calmed down a bit.'

'Yes well,' said Emma. 'I wasn't going to let them get away with just clubbing us to the ground and anyway I got really angry. But the bastards took all our stuff Jack. Then some poncy officer came in this morning and wanted to know who we really were. I explained our cover story to him and said if he bothered to look at the letters with our possessions he would find out we were telling the truth.'

'He asked why we were speaking French Jack,' added Smithy. 'I explained that we thought the islands were French. It seems like the British only took them over this week but he didn't say anything to that, he just left. They brought us some food and water if you call stale bread and cheese food.'

Jack sat back still feeling very rough. 'Can I have some more of that water? How does my head look Emma, it feels like I've got a balloon stuck to my forehead.'

'It probably feels worse than it looks Jack. I've checked as much as I can but I know what a thick skull you've got,' she said with a grin. 'I'm pretty sure there's no fracture, just a bit of a gash and a bloody great bruise.'

With nothing else to do, they spent the day speculating what might have gone wrong.

'All I can think of is that there was some form of magnetic field anomaly as we went through,' said Smithy. 'But it would have had to have been on board and we were so careful to keep Jacaranda's metallic and magnetic configuration as close as possible to her original one.'

'So what does that mean for us returning to our time Smithy?' asked a recovering Jack. 'If we can get a boat, can we find the rift in the original place? We will be three years late.'

'Well unless I can find out what happened in the first place that's going be very doubtful I'm afraid.'

'Well, I guess we'll never know what with Jacaranda sitting at the bottom of the eighteenth century Atlantic. So let's face it, we're in survival mode now. All I can think of doing is to try and convince these idiots we aren't enemies and then get to England. At least we should be able to look up a certain Earl and his wife.'

Emma was starting to feel forlorn. Having recovered from the trauma of the hurricane and losing Jacaranda and now that Jack seemed to be better she suddenly realised how far from home she was. What was worse this was the second time this had happened to her but this time she had lost her little baby and there seemed there would be no way of returning home. She cuddled up to her husband and held on to him for comfort just as the door opened.

At first they didn't recognise the fair haired naval officer as he strode in but then he spoke.

'Jack, Emma, I thought it might be you two. You've no idea how glad I am to see you and I see you have a companion. I bet you'll be surprised to know that I discovered and salvaged a waterlogged yacht out at sea the other day and prayed you might still be around. How would you like to be reunited with Jacaranda and my wife?'

Chapter 25

At last they had arrived. The French fleet stood cautiously in towards the Guadeloupe coast at Gosier. Victor stood with the other officers on the quarterdeck waiting from the call from the top of the mast.

'Deck there, the anchorage is deserted, no vessels in sight.'

A surprised babble broke out but Victor stayed silent savouring the moment. The voyage had been despicable but crossing the Atlantic was always a lottery especially at this time of years. Squalls, electrical storm, calms and tempest, they had experienced them all. But now they were here and he was on his own. As he had predicted the stresses and heat of a long crossing had taken its toll on his companion. Michel had been committed to the deep two days ago. 'Heart failure,' said the surgeon. *'A life time of gluttony and indolence,'* thought Victor. Now it meant there was no one to gainsay him. Once the soldiers had occupied the island it was his, every bit of it. There were more to follow.

Several hours later the boat they had sent ashore returned with news. It wasn't as good as they had all hoped. The British had taken the island some weeks ago and there were several small garrisons of troops scattered about but luckily the Royal Navy was nowhere to be seen. They had all left some weeks ago and were supposed to have either returned home or withdrawn to Antigua or St Christopher. The strength of the nearest garrison at the strong point of Fleur d'Epee was estimated at no more than 300 men and some Royalists sympathisers. It was clearly their first target but first the men had to be put ashore. All that afternoon that's what happened. Boats plied tirelessly between ship and beach. Victor elected to stay on board. He had no desire to leave the comforts of a ship until there were comparable comforts for him ashore. That night he heard the sounds of righteous retribution as the first estates were liberated by his men.

The next morning he went to the beach where his men had several captives to show him. He set up a small court on the sand and had them brought in front of him. There were two men and three women. They weren't in a good condition. Both men had been severely beaten and had to be supported by soldiers either side of them. The three women were little better. Two were quite young only in their teens and would have been quite pretty once. One was much older but still striking. Looking carefully he could see a family resemblance. Whatever their relationship they had been ill used, practically naked, the signs of rape and other abuses were clear on their weeping faces. Only the older one showed any spirit, staring straight into his eyes as he took his seat.

'Who are they?' he asked in clipped tones.

A soldier stepped forward. 'The owners of the plantation next to the British Fort Sir. We found them trying to escape. They had a cart full of valuables and were heading towards the fort but we got to them first. The two men are the husband and the overseer and the women are his wife and daughters.'

'Who gave you permission to beat them like this? The women look like they've been raped and sodomised by the whole army,' he asked with a note of anger in his voice.

At his question the captives looked up at him with a glimmer of hope appearing in their eyes.

'Why you Sir,' replied the soldier. 'You said that no mercy should be shown to enemies of the revolution and that we could treat them as we saw fit.'

Victor smiled. 'Oh yes so I did. Are you sure they are actually Royalists though? Mind you it's a bit late if they aren't,' he chuckled

'Oh yes Sir and we freed all their slaves but they just ran off.'

Now Victor really got angry. 'You idiot, what did I also say? Slaves would be freed but only once they were recruited into the Army. In future you keep them under confinement until myself or one of my staff talk to them understand?'

The soldier looked sheepish. 'As you say Sir but what about the captives?'

'Hmm, we need to dispense justice in the revolutionary way.' Turning to one of his men he told him to find the frigate's carpenter. He knew he was around somewhere.

The man was soon brought to him. 'How are you progressing on that little task I set you citizen?'

The man glanced at the dishevelled captives and then back to the unsmiling Victor. 'All the woodwork is complete but until this morning I had no blade. However, I've now found some materials. I will have the forge set up on the beach and the complete guillotine should be ready by tomorrow.'

He turned back to the captives who had heard every word just as he intended. 'Excellent, then I pronounce all five of you enemies of the revolution and condemn you all to death.'

One of the men struggled and tried to say something but was immediately clubbed senseless to the ground with a rifle butt.

'Oh and in the meantime,' he turned to the carpenter. 'Can you quickly make me three sets of stocks? To confine someone standing but bent over?'

'Of course Sir one of my assistants should be able to do that within the hour.'

Excellent, when they are ready, completely strip the women and put them in the stocks. They might as well entertain my troops while they await my justice.'

The next day the executions took place on the beach. Victor was impressed with the carpenters work and the guillotine soon demonstrated its efficiency. He had the two young girls beheaded first. Neither put up any form of struggle although one had clearly lost her mind. She simply drooled and sang nursery rhymes right up to the end. However, the mother was made of sterner stuff and called out 'Vive le Roi' as the blade descended. It didn't help her much he laughed to himself as the blood fountained for feet into the already red sand. The husband was next and to prevent any further Royalist outpourings he had the man gagged. Just as the last man was being led to his fate he put up his hand and had him bought to him.

'You were only the overseer at the estate Monsieur?'

The man nodded. Victor suspected he was past being able to talk. 'Very well and are you a true Royalist or were you only obeying your master's orders?'

'Orders.' The man croaked.

'Very well, I believe you have suffered enough, I am prepared to merciful. You are free to go.'

The look of confusion and then hope that appeared on the man's face was almost comical. He looked around, expecting some form of trick but there was none. Victor waved in the direction of Point a Pitre and the man took the hint and started running. No one followed.

Victor smiled and turned to one of his aids. 'That man will tell everyone he meets of the quality of my justice and also of my mercy. Citizen Robespierre believes in the power of terror and so do I.'

Jacques found himself closeted with Colonel Stevens once again. The day was burning hot without a breath of wind. The office was like an oven. Not unusual for this time of year but it made him wonder why they all insisted on wearing such heavy clothing.

As he looked over at the red faced, sweating man he realised he probably looked just the same. 'So the rumours are true then, the Jacobins have returned?'

The Colonel looked even more uncomfortable. 'It appears so. Jervis is mustering his fleet but we don't have many troops. They are either garrisoning the islands or have been sent home.'

'I'm hardly surprised. You may recall I warned you of the possibility some time ago.'

'Yes, well that's as may be. We have to deal with the situation as we find it now.'

Jacques smiled tightly. 'Now you want my help I take it?'

'Well. you did say you would try to continue your dialogue with them. Have you had any contact?'

'The only man I've spoken to is a certain Monsieur Dubert. After he contacted me I did a little digging. He lives on Guadeloupe and is merchant running a warehouse on Grande Terre. But I've seen neither hide nor hair of him since our last meeting.'

The Colonel sat back in his chair looking at Jacques. He seemed to make a decision because he steepled his fingers and then sat forward again. 'Would you go there and make contact? On our behalf of course.'

The question threw Jacques. He had expected something but nothing this involved.

'To what purpose? Surely we have people there already.'

'No one like you though Monsieur. It would appear that they will trust you so much more because of your previous contact. If you go to them and offer to supply information about Martinique for instance I'm sure you would get into their confidence, would you not?'

'I say again, to what purpose?'

'We need to know their intentions. We're already hearing stories of atrocities being visited on the local Royalists. The revolutionary leader is someone called Hugues and apparently he has been very harsh on anyone not supporting the revolution. Beatings, rapes and even the use of a Guillotine are being reported to us. Between you and me we may lose Guadeloupe. Our troops are suffering badly from Yellow Fever and there is a rumour going around that Hugues is about to liberate and then arm the slaves. I don't have to tell you what that will do to the size of his army. They may not be trained but they will fight hard if freedom is within their grasp.'

Jacques snorted. 'Are you surprised at that?'

'No Sir I'm not. But I am a soldier and I deal in tactics not politics. However, if he does take the island what will he do next? We need to know and you can find out for us.'

Jacques thought hard about the idea. He still had the premonition that something bad could happen and maybe by going directly to the source he could do something about it.

'But what about the risks?' he thought. *'If the situation was that bad in Guadeloupe, did he really want to get involved in it? What would they do to him if they found out who he was actually working for? What was he going to tell Francine?'*

And then he realised he was already thinking in terms of doing the task rather than considering the options.

'Alright, I will take my small sloop and try to contact the man and see what I can find out. However, I have one condition.'

'Name it.'

'If something should happen to me and the French try to retake Martinique, you will ensure that my wife is evacuated to safety.'

'That is hardly likely Monsieur.'

'Nevertheless I insist.'

'Very well, you have my word.'

The next day Jacques was back at his estate trying to explain his reasoning to his distraught wife.

'Jacques, what were you thinking? You can't do this, it is madness.' She cried with tears streaming down her face. 'We know what these pigs are like. There are already dreadful stories being told. Why do you have to risk your life, why?'

Jacque's problem was that he didn't really know himself. He put his arms round Francine and held her tight. Her hair smelled fresh and he nuzzled her neck. 'I don't know and before you say anything, I know that's not an answer but it's all I've got. Somehow, I know I need to go there. Maybe it will help me regain my memory. Maybe I will be able to do some good. I just don't know.'

His answer hardly consoled Francine but she could also hear a strange determination in his voice. Maybe he was right, maybe it would help slay the demons that had been tormenting him more and more over the last few months. Would he ever be whole until his memory returned or would that change the man she knew and loved beyond measure? She knew she had no choice.

Pushing him back so she could see his face she sniffed back more tears and looked into his eyes. 'Alright my love but promise me you will return. We have a long life ahead of us.'

Jacques could only nod.

Chapter 26

The house rang with laughter. The wine was flowing and the level of conversation was slowly getting louder as it flowed. The room was full of the cream of Antiguan Society invited by The Earl of Hinchfield, to celebrate the preservation of his friends, the Honourable Jack Vincent and Emma his wife along with Doctor Smythe the eminent scientist.

Charles looked around. Emma and Melissa were talking to the Governor and General Shirley. Jack was in deep conversation with several estate owners and Smithy had managed to corner three of the prettiest girls on the island and seemed to be regaling them with stories of tempest and shipwreck. They were laughing and simpering as he waved his hands, clearly in the depths of his story. Charles moved to join his wife.

The General was holding forth. 'Antigua has been lucky you know and it cannot last. In the last confrontation with the French, they simply sailed past us. We may not be so lucky next time. We need more fortifications.'

Charles clapped him on the shoulder. 'Well as you know General, the government only pays for the troops. You will have to get us skinflint landowners to cough up for any building work and that's like getting blood out of a stone as you well know.'

'The General loves his hobby horse,' quipped the Governor and turning to Charles. 'Come on Sir, pray tell us of your gallant rescue and that new acquisition of yours. The one that you have hidden from our eyes down in the harbour.'

As Charles wondered how to answer that he thought back to the trip and the subsequent reunions.

He immediately had the three survivors released into his custody. Explaining to the Major in charge of the fort that he would vouch for them and no they really weren't French spies. They were soon on Polaris although Jack insisted on an inspection of Jacaranda as they rowed past. Once in his great cabin he arranged for food and poured them all some wine.

'You have no idea how wonderful it is to see you,' he said looking at his old friends. 'When I found Jacaranda almost sinking and no sign of any crew I feared the worst.'

'We thought we were gonners as well, you know,' replied Jack. 'That was one hell of a storm. So what are your intentions now?'

Charles briefly explained what he had been doing and that he was now free to return to Antigua and Melissa. He also gave then a brief overview of the situation. With the French Islands secure, he had intended returning to England in the near future. He noticed Jack and Smithy exchanging glances.

'Does that mean you know something I don't and maybe something I should?'

Smithy spoke for them. 'Look Charles, of course we know a lot about the period. We prepared very carefully for this trip and studied the local history. You must understand that we want to minimise our footprint here. I'm sure you realise why. We must do as little as possible to change the past.'

Charles nodded. 'Then maybe you could explain why you're actually here? I never expected to see you again after we left Martinique the last time.'

Between them they gave Charles a simplified version. Smithy saw no reason not to let him know that they were looking for a form of technical treasure. Despite all that had happened, he still had a mission to perform and Charles was clearly in the best position to help with that now. Emma finished by saying that hopefully the stores in Jacaranda were safe as they were stored in watertight compartments behind the wood planking. She would have some surprises for Melissa.

So they sailed for Antigua with Jacaranda still in tow. Before they left they took some time to make further repairs. Jack astounded the crew of Polaris when he jumped into the sea and started to dive under the water to look at her hull. Despite their fears that he was in the process of drowning he was able to nail some of the sprung planks back in place as well as some battens over the fothered sail, making her much more watertight. He knew there was nothing more he could do until he could get her out of the water but even then he wondered if she would ever sail again.

It took three days to get to Falmouth harbour on Antigua's south coast. Charles wanted to stay clear of the neighbouring naval dockyard and get Jacaranda away from prying eyes as soon as he could. Without a modern crane the only way to repair the hull would be to careen her onto her side. Grateful to have arrived they all agreed this could wait for a day or two. However, they did go over to the yacht and retrieve Melissa's stores which had thankfully survived intact. Charles loaded them all into a carriage and they drove out to his estate.

Without any foreknowledge of their arrival the look of astonishment on Melissa's face was something to behold. For several seconds she stood stock still and then with a little scream as recognition fully dawned, she tried to hug Jack and Emma at the same time. She started laughing and crying and then Emma joined in. Jack managed a more manly demeanour but was still quite overwhelmed. When the first surprise was over and Smithy had also been introduced they showed Melissa the contents of the boxes taken out of Jacaranda.

'Oh, you've brought loads of antibiotics. Thank you, I had just about run out,' she said delightedly. Then she almost screamed in delight when she saw the shampoo. But when she saw the chocolate she simply stopped talking, tore a packet open and stuffed some in her mouth. She turned grinning to her friends with her mouth full.

'You've no idea how much you miss something until you try it again,' she managed between ecstatic chews.

The others all laughed at her obvious delight. As soon as things settled slightly the two children were sent for and introduced to the newcomers and they all retired to the veranda to talk. Between them it didn't take long to explain the bones of how they had all arrived. Charles had already explained his and Melissa's side of things so they concentrated on Jacaranda's hair raising voyage and how Charles had rescued them. While all the talking was going on Jack studied Melissa. She may have been nine years older but she didn't look it. Clearly living in the past had been good for her.

Melissa caught Jack studying her. 'So Jack, you're a father now and a successful business man as well? I have to say you look good on it.'

'I guess so but dammit Melissa it looks like the eighteenth century agrees with you pretty well too.'

'Yes, well I'm sure we'll all talk more but it's been hard at times you know.' A shadow crossed her face for a second. 'But never mind that. let's get you settled in there'll be plenty of time to talk in the future.'

The next few days were a bit of a blur as they caught up on each other's news. Smithy attempted to explain the science behind the reasons for the trip and probably managed to make some of his meaning clear. One thing that he did ask for was for there to be no more meddling in the future. Jack and Emma promised to explain about the diaries but then Smithy broke in and suggested they drop the subject before the paradox issue became even more confusing even to him.

As with all small islands, local society soon found out about the miraculous rescue of the newcomers and their strange boat. Well-tuned to her surrounds Melissa decided to arrange a party two days after the reunion. Ending ill-informed speculation was the first reason but introducing her three guests to the strange ways of this century was a secondary aim.

Charles thought about the Governor's question. It wasn't the first and surely wouldn't be the last time he was asked to recount their adventures but getting the story straight with this man would be a good start. And he could counter some of the stranger rumours already circulating.

He launched into a factual account of his encounter with the waterlogged yacht and finding the crew incarcerated in the fort in the Saintes. He managed to attract Jack's attention and then got him to recount the story they had all agreed on. Having made some claims to already know the origins of the yacht when she was salvaged they had decided to use that as the basis of Jack's story.

'Yes Sir, she is an experimental vessel,' said Jack. 'We have been using a small steam engine to propel her but of course our prime means of propulsion will still be sail. I don't suppose that will ever change. We were on a simple proving trip to see how it would behave at sea for a prolonged time and then the hurricane hit us. The rest you know.' And then in a lowered tone, 'of course Sir you discretion in this matter is most essential. As I am sure you understand our government will be very keen to keep her secrets intact.' As he said it he prayed the man would swallow such a silly tale. However, it was immediately clear that the Governor was impressed and also quite taken with the idea of being in on the secret.

'Rest assured young man,' he said pompously. 'The government of Antigua is at your disposal.'

The discussion then ranged onto wider matters not the least the on-going French War. Jack was surprised that everyone saw war with France as an almost natural state of affairs. The last few years of peace were merely a breathing space before they went at it again. However, the big difference this time was that they were fighting French peasants who had overthrown their monarchy and there was an almost palpable aura of paranoia whenever the topic came up. The British had clearly been given a wakeup call and were terrified that it might happen to them.

Later that night Jack and Emma finally made it to their bedroom.

Jack struggled with his eighteenth century clothes swearing at the various items as they refused to come undone. 'Stupid bloody clothes. I've been sweating my bollocks off all evening. Why the hell do they have to dress as if they're in England in winter?'

'You should complain,' said Emma, similarly struggling with various petticoats. 'You know Melissa did offer me the services of a maid to help me get undressed.'

Jack's eyebrows shot up. 'Wow and would she be able to help me too?'

'Don't go there big boy, we're twenty first century people remember.'

'Drat, foiled again.'

Finally they made it to bed and lay panting in the heat even though they had discarded all the bedclothes.

'Jack, what happens now? We've been so focused on being rescued and getting here that we haven't really given it much consideration.'

He thought for a moment. 'Well, the priority has to be to see if we can get Jacaranda seaworthy again. Smithy needs to find out why we ended up at the wrong time in the wrong place. Then we'll have to decide whether we can go home or not.'

Emma didn't answer she just rolled over and held him tight.

Charles watched his wife undress from the comfort of his bed. It was something he never tired of doing. Melissa, well aware of his gaze gave her usual excellent performance. As soon as she had put her clothes neatly to one side and removed her last shift she sidled up to her man.

'Enjoying the view sailor?'

'Oh yes. Now come here,' and he made a lunge which only got him fresh air as she neatly sidestepped his arms. A few seconds later he made contact and she squealed in mock terror as he pulled her down.

Sometime later they lay in each other's arms. Melissa rolled over and looked at Charles. 'You know the last few days have been amazing. I never expected to see Jack and Emma again but I really wonder how they're going to get home. From what that scientist said they should have arrived three years ago. How are they going to return?'

'You know I can't answer that. We're going down to Jacaranda tomorrow to start looking at her. Maybe there will be a clue on board.'

Melissa lay back with a sigh. 'And if they can't go back?'

'Then they come to England and live with us or make their own way whatever they wish. They will have my full support.'

'Thank you.'

Smithy was also having trouble with his clothing. But in his case it was because he was also trying to remove the clothing of the delightful young lady he had sneaked into his room as the house guests retired to bed. In the case of the Lady Clare Stevens, her father thought she was tucked up in her bed and indeed by morning she probably would be. However, for the next few hours she seemed determined to test the mettle of this new addition to Antiguan society.

'There are so few single men here,' she had complained when they first met and then went on to make it quite clear why she saw that as a bad thing.

Now she was rectifying the situation. 'Oh let me do it you clumsy oaf,' she said with frustration as she found the fastenings of his trousers. 'Anyone would think you didn't know what to do.'

'Oh, believe me I do,' he responded with a laugh as he managed to loosen her bodice at the same time. 'Although maybe I should have paid more attention to Pride and Prejudice when I was forced to read it at school.'

'What are you talking about?'

'Never mind,' and the talking stopped for quite a while.

Chapter 27

The town of Point a Pitre had turned out en masse to welcome its new liberator. Cheering crowds waved and threw flowers at Victor in his carriage as he made his way down the main street followed by the ranks of his soldiers. The town had fallen without a shot being fired. Looking at the sweaty faces of the populace he wondered if they had cheered the British with the same enthusiasm only a few months ago. He suspected that his little demonstration of revolutionary justice on the beach may have been one of the reasons for such a sudden change of heart.

He turned to Jean his aid, a thin, sallow, studious lawyer from Nantes but nevertheless a rabid revolutionary and just the sort of man to support Victor in his activities. 'It seems they are glad to see us Jean unlike those at the fort.'

Jean snorted cynically. 'The British seemed brave enough but the Royalists were pure cowards. The day they tried to attack us they dropped their arms and ran at the first shot.'

'Yes, I agree about the British but they clearly underestimated our numbers. However, I want any that we capture to be treated with dignity. If necessary we can use them for prisoner exchanges and I don't want our revolution to be seen as barbaric to our enemies.'

'But not for our own people?'

'That's not the same. We need to inspire terror in order to rule. Once the benefits of our system become manifest to everyone there will be no resistance anyway and so no need for extremes. Who knows, maybe even the British people will rise against their aristocracy?' Victor said all this with a straight face knowing that Jean believed it implicitly. 'So now we must prepare our defences. They will be back soon you can count on it.'

'What will we do with the landowner royalists we capture?'

'That's simple, we keep them until we have a good number and then Madame Guillotine can have her day.'

Jacques was tired. The trip from Martinique hadn't been easy. With a permanent east trade wind and strong westerly current it meant being hard on the wind until he cleared the island of Dominica and only then could he free off a little and head directly for Grande Terre whilst skirting around the low flat island of Marie Galante. He knew the French had landed at Gosier and were now almost certainly in Point a Pitre so that was where he was heading. He had two of his local crew with him but even so sailing the sixty foot trading cutter was hard work. As the carenage at Point a Pitre came in sight he saw that it was crowded with ships. Once they had approached a bit closer he could see the French flag flying on all of them. So far so good.

He was surprised that no one challenged him as he made his way to anchor near the loading quay in the main port area. But such a small vessel hardly represented a threat to anyone. However, that all changed once he got ashore. As soon as he stepped out of his dinghy a soldier armed with a musket approached and demanded that he state his business. He said he was looking for Monsieur Dubert the merchant to discuss trade but the soldier wasn't prepared to take his word and marched him up the quay to see his officer. Jacques repeated his story to the hard looking man. He decided it would not be good to admit he was from Martinique, merely stating that he had come around from Basse Terre when he heard that the French had arrived. The officer seemed sceptical and Jacques stated to get worried that he was talking himself into some sort of trouble, especially as that part of the island was still in British hands. Eventually he suggested that Monsieur Dubert be sent for and he prayed silently that the man would vouch for him. It seemed that Dubert was well known and Jacques didn't have to wait long before he bustled into the little room asking querulously why he had had his morning interrupted.

However, as soon as he saw Jacques he smiled and told the officer that he would take responsibility for him. Shepherding him outside he said briefly, 'don't say anything Monsieur until we are alone.'

They walked along the quay which was eerily quiet without the normal bustle of trade and went into the large warehouse at one end. Entering a small office, Dubert motioned for Jacques to sit and then seated himself behind a cluttered desk.

'So Monsieur La Croix, I hear you are now head of your family and continuing in you good fortune. What brings you to Guadeloupe in these interesting times?'

'Monsieur Dubert, I have been reflecting on our last conversation.'

'Oh no. please call me Pascal.'

'Very well and I am Jacques. Anyway, we have all heard how the revolution has now come to the island and I have decided that maybe it is time for me to choose a side. It has been too easy to let things run their course. The British are firmly in charge on Martinique and frankly until I heard the news of the French arrival here I felt there was little I could do, even had I wanted to.'

'I seem to remember that you were quite disparaging about the revolution last time we talked. Has something occurred to change your mind?'

'In a way, yes. The British are firmly decided upon maintaining the status quo and all the other landowners are of the same mind. I find myself in a minority of one when it comes to a more liberal approach. I have come to the conclusion that if things are to change then I cannot sit idly by when such wrongs continue to perpetrated. Don't get me wrong, I don't think very much of your revolution either but it at least offers some hope.'

Dubert sat back and thought for a second. He wasn't totally convinced by what appeared to be a serious change of heart but this man could be just what they needed. He would need to test him further.

'Excuse my scepticism Jacques but surely now that you have inherited the whole estate there is even more reason for you to keep you head down in these troubled times? Has something else happened to generate this new enlightened point of view?'

Jacques had expected the question and had prepared his answer. 'Pascal, some time ago I attended an auction in Fort de France, a slave auction. At the auction I bought two little twin girls of about twelve years old. And before you make any remark, I did this to stop another of the estate owners buying them. They are now working as maids for my wife and are turning into beautiful intelligent human beings, full of life. If I hadn't bought them by now they would have been abused, raped and then quite possibly murdered. What is worse is that no one would have cared and no one would have even broken any law. At that point I made a decision to do all I could to end this appalling system. Your revolution is the only light on the horizon.' As he said all this, Jacques realised he really meant it. However, he also felt that familiar tug of conflict within himself over his other overriding conviction that he was also doing the right thing by helping the British.

Pascal could not miss the fervent tone of conviction in Jacques voice. *'Yes this man really does believe in what he says and an idealist is always the best. I wonder what he will think when he finds out just how Victor has been conducting the revolution since he arrived. He may not be such a convert when he finds out,'* he thought grimly to himself.

'Very well Jacques,' he responded. 'I think we can work together. I think I had better introduce you to our new commissioner and see where we can go from here.

A few hours later and Jacques and Pascal were ushered into the presence of the new ruler of Grande Terre. Pascal had already seen Victor in private earlier and explained who Jacques was and they both agreed the man could prove invaluable when the time came to reclaim Martinique.

Victor stood up when they entered and warmly shook Jacques hand, offering him a seat and telling his servant to get some brandy.

Jacques studied the man before him and didn't like what he saw. He spoke and acted like any other arrogant aristocrat he had ever met and nothing like a dedicated revolutionary Jacobin. Jacques quickly decided that this was a man who was primarily interested in furthering his own interests and damn anyone or anything that got in his way. Not that it mattered, Jacques was here for his own reasons as well and so he did his best to hide any reactions.

'So Jacques, to sum up, once this island is fully in our hands you are willing to help us in the capture of Martinique, is that so?'

Jacques nodded. 'Yes Victor I am. As we've discussed I am pretty sure that I can get you ashore unopposed and that should guarantee you victory.'

'Excellent. then I look forward to working with you in the future but maybe it would be best for you to return home now until the time is right. I will leave it to you and Pascal to arrange a method of communication.'

Jacques was about to nod agreement when there was an urgent knocking on the door and it flew open before anyone could answer. The troubled face of a soldier appeared.

'Sir, forgive my interruption but the British fleet have been seen; several ships of the line and other smaller warships. We have been told they are in the process of anchoring in Gosier bay.'

Victor didn't appear too troubled by the news and waved the soldier away. 'Well gentlemen, it would appear that we are now about to have the fight we were expecting. I think the British will be in for a shock when we see how many troops we now have even if most of them were slaves until only a few days ago.' And then turning to Jacques, 'sorry Monsieur but it looks like you will have to remain my guest for a little while longer.'

Chapter 28

'Come on,' roared Jack. 'One last effort. Heave!'

With a final desperate pull on the ropes by the assembled men Jacaranda tipped up to the vertical and her keel slipped into the hole that had been dug by the shoreline.

'OK now,' shouted Jack. 'Get the support props in place and we're done.' He stood back and admired his handiwork with satisfaction. Jacaranda was ashore just above the high water line of the beach with her keel and lower part of her hull sitting in a purpose made hole. Her rudder and propellers were clear of the ground. Wooden posts were being placed around the hull to give final stability. It had taken all morning to pull her close to the waterline and then over on to her side. Her keel weighed in the order of almost twenty tons. If it hadn't been for Charles volunteering his field hands to provide the muscle power they would never have done the job. After that, they dragged her sideways on wooden rollers until clear of the water and then dug the pit. The final trick had been to allow the keel to fall into the man-made hole under careful control and then haul her back upright. It was something Jack had seen done when securing yachts against hurricanes although having the use of a crane made it a great deal easier.

Charles came over to him. Like everyone else he was stripped to the waist and sweating in the tropical heat. He was wiping his face with a large cloth. 'Well done Jack, your idea worked. Of course, what you haven't explained is how we get her back in to the water.'

Jack laughed. 'Actually that's the easy bit. We dig a channel to the sea and dig the pit out a bit more. Then we breach the final wall to the sea and give her a sideways push. She should settle onto her hull and just float out. That is if you don't mind lending me these fine fellows again,' he said looking at the now resting field hands. He refused to call them slaves and it was clear that they were far from unhappy in their work.

'No, not at all. Let's just hope it will be worth re-launching her.'

'Oh it will be Charles, now I can see the hull damage I'm certain it can be safely patched, especially with the quality of the carpenters around here and an application of twenty first century fibre glass on the inside.'

'I'm glad you're so confident, even if I've no idea what fibre glass is. What about the rest of her?'

'I've had a preliminary look and of course most of the modern equipment is beyond repair but I'm pretty sure we can make her seaworthy and possibly get one or even both engines working again.'

He was interrupted by a call from behind and turned to see a cart with the girls and Smithy approaching. The cart was laden with food and drinks for the men and soon they were all standing around happily eating a late lunch.

Afterwards, they all went on board Jacaranda and surveyed the devastation. The upper deck didn't look too bad with the exception of the ragged stump of a mast. However, down below was a turgid mess of wet cushions, paper and the contents of various drawers.

'Right, first things first, let's empty out all this crap and get a clear picture of what might be salvageable. Then we can audit the machinery and other fixed equipment and see what might be made to work again,' said Jack in a firm tone. 'It's probably not as bad as it looks but let's quantify what needs to be done.'

'I tell you what,' said Melissa. 'Let me take all these loose fittings, bedding and the like up to the estate and we can wash them all in fresh water and see what can be recovered. Some of my girls are quite good seamstresses and we can probably repair much of it.'

'Good idea Melissa. Oh and Smithy you need to look at all your stuff. I'm afraid that anything with electronics is going to be trash but you ought to look at the heavy machinery we installed in the stern compartment. That may be salvageable.'

Smithy just nodded and made his way back on deck to open the hatch to the large area of the stern where the sidescan sonar and special magnetometer had been installed.

They worked all afternoon and soon had at least a semblance of order appearing out of the chaos. Jack had just finished inspecting the engines and batteries when Smithy joined him.

'As you said Jack, all the electronics are buggered but I might just be able to get the magnetometer functional with a jury rig to display its output. Of course we'll need electricity for that'

'Well that's good news and you'll be pleased to know that I think I might be able to get power back on board. Out batteries are sealed units and seem to have survived their bath. Mind you, the wiring is going to have to be checked out very carefully. I don't suppose you've found anything yet that might explain our mysterious three year error?'

'Nope, how about you? Anything you didn't expect?'

'No sorry,' and then he had an odd thought. 'Smithy, did you vet all the stuff the soldiers brought on board?'

'Of course, it's quite an arsenal but I went through the list very carefully.'

'Yes but did you physically check it out?'

'Well no, it didn't seem necessary.'

'On the basis that it's the only place we haven't looked yet, why don't we check it out now?'

Jack unclipped a large panel on the port side of the boat. When the extra exterior cladding had been added, two large voids had resulted on either side of the boat. These had been sealed to make them watertight and provided useful extra storage space. The starboard side had been largely filled with Melissa's supplies and emergency stores. However, the port side had been allocated to the SF soldiers to store weaponry and all the rest of their military supplies.

Shining torch into the space Jack gave out a low whistle of surprise. 'Jesus Smithy, did you really know how much crap they put in here? There's enough weaponry to start a small bloody war.'

'I saw the items on paper but I'm not that way inclined as you know and anyway it was their judgement call.'

'Guess you're right, let's get this stuff out and make sure it's safe. It looks like it's stayed dry in here which is always good when explosives are around.'

So saying Jack started passing out various items, starting with five SA80 rifles, one for each of them he presumed. These were followed by several containers of ammunition, some handguns, two boxes of hand grenades, one box ominously marked as high explosive and another as containing detonators.

Surveying the pile on the cabin sole he was not impressed. 'For goodness sake Smithy, what were they thinking? What sort of situation did they think we could get ourselves into that would need all this firepower?'

'That's the military mind for you I guess but there's something missing. Jack are you sure the compartment is empty?'

'Why, what am I looking for?' asked Jack as he peered in again with his torch.

'It should be quite big, in a long container of some sort.'

Jack shone the torch all around and then realised that the bottom of the compartment was much too high and in fact what he was looking at was a long thin wooden crate that spanned the whole length of the space. Two rope handles protruded up either side. Tugging at one he felt the crate move but it was inordinately heavy.

'Smithy, there's a crate on the floor but I'm buggered if I can work out how they got it in here, it weighs a ton.'

Smithy peered past Jack. 'Maybe they put the empty case in first then the gun in afterwards.'

'Hang on, you know what's in here?'

'Er yes, they wanted to bring a bigger piece of weaponry as well as that lot. If I remember the list it was called a one inch calibre, recoilless, multipurpose rifle.'

'One inch calibre? That's a fucking cannon Smithy. You could take out a modern tank with something that powerful. Bloody hell, these soldiers were really paranoid. Oh well, let's check it out.'

He looked back in and saw clips along the lid which he was able to undo and then remove the whole top, which he handed out to Smithy behind him.

'It's largely made of carbon fibre Jack which is why I approved them bringing it.'

Jack looked at the vicious device nestled in black foam protection. He had never seen anything quite like it. Painted in matt green, it had a bulbous main section with what was clearly the barrel sticking out of the front. Where most guns he had ever seen were covered in levers and sights and whatever, this was smooth without any signs of controls. He pulled it up and could see what was clearly a trigger but that was about it. He heaved the barrel out to Smithy and together they half dragged the extraordinarily heavy gun out of its hiding place.

'If that's just made out of carbon fibre I'm a banana,' said Jack panting with exertion. He looked back into the crate and could now see a tripod which was presumably there to allow a human being to actually operate the thing and towards the front several compartments clearly labelled as containing ammunition of various types. He also spotted what looked like a small book which he pulled out. He studied the title, flicked through a few pages and then handed it to Smithy without a word.

Smithy took it and started reading and then turned white. 'Fuck, well that explains it. Dammit, this is all my fault. I should have checked their stuff out personally. On the list they gave me they missed out one bloody word and it's made all the difference.'

That evening back at the estate Smithy explained to them all the consequences of having the rifle on board.

'The gun is recoilless. A human couldn't fire a weapon of that calibre. The recoil would just be too much. It would smash him to a pulp. However, the bloody thing uses a series of very powerful magnets to absorb the energy of the round being fired. It's all here in the manual,' he said waving the little book at them all. 'Unfortunately, the military forgot that one key word when describing it to me in their inventory and I didn't think it worthwhile to check. I can only apologise.'

'Why is it so critical Smithy?' asked Melissa.

'Sorry Melissa, basically the whole time travel thing hinges on the manipulation of electromagnetic fields and the one thing we were careful to do was minimise any of those within Jacaranda. The fact that such a powerful one was present completely screwed up our transition.'

'OK Smithy,' interjected Jack. 'Isn't this actually a good thing in some ways? Now we know what caused the problem can't you do your Mad Scientist thing and work out the numbers. Surely you have enough data now to work out how we can get home.'

Smithy's brow furrowed. 'Yes, although it's going to take me quite a while and there will be a large margin of error. Jack, didn't you say we would have power on Jacaranda?'

'Yes hopefully, why what do you need?'

'The only calculating power I've got is my telephone and that will need twelve volts to keep it charged and I will need to use it quite a lot.'

'Well tomorrow you start on your numbers and I'll make it a priority to get the generator back on line.'

They then went on to a general discussion on the state of Jacaranda. Jack summarised it for all of them.

'The rig can be replaced. Charles you say you can get the dockyard to do that for us?'

Charles nodded. 'Yes, the master shipwright owes me a few favours and will be over tomorrow to survey the task and will also look at the hull repair.'

'Good. now as to the equipment. All the electronics including the autopilot are written off. But the good news is that generator is probably alright and the fuel seems to have survived without sea water contamination. The biggest task is that I am going to have to survey all the wiring before I dare connect anything. However, the engines are a different matter. Both have got contaminated oil. The water must have come in through the exhausts because the engine room stayed mostly dry. I have enough spare oil on board to refill one, so we should be able to restore some motive power. That's the good news. The bad news is that I'm afraid the fridge, freezer and water maker are all completely buggered but the stove can probably be made to work again.'

Charles laughed. 'So poor old Jacaranda is going to have to operate as a real eighteenth century vessel now Jack? Don't worry, I'm sure I can find some oil lamps for the saloon and some hammocks for the crew.'

'Thank you so much Charles but at least we will still have an engine and some electricity and now we have some hope that we can eventually return home.'

'Please don't forget we came here for a reason, all of you,' interjected Smithy. 'I still have some instrumentation on board and we all have our personal detectors. So not only will we have

Jacaranda back and hopefully a way home but there is now a chance that we can still do the job we came to do in the first place.'

Chapter 29

The headaches were back and this time with a vengeance. What was worse was that every time Jacques tried to sleep the dreams returned. He would wake up in a sweat, trying desperately to hang onto the fleeing echo and always fail. Pascal had offered him accommodation in his house by the waterfront and Jacques had gladly agreed even though he knew it was so they could keep an eye on him. Whether it was the forced idleness or homesickness or something else the last few weeks were turning into a nightmare.

The British had landed in exactly the same place that the French had only weeks previously but it was clear they were short on troops. The ships might have made an impressive display offshore but were of no use when fighting on land was the requirement. Some seamen had been seen ashore to supplement the meagre troop numbers but there would never be enough if the British Admiral wanted to man his ships with any safety. Even though the result was stalemate of a sort, it didn't help Jacques who was stuck in the town until something changed.

This morning he at least had something to look forward to although Victor had been keeping the actual activity he was planning a close secret.

He made his way downstairs for breakfast and joined Pascal and his wife Marie in the dining room.

'Good morning Jacques,' said Marie as he entered. 'Goodness, you look like you haven't slept at all.'

He gave a wan smile. 'You're probably right Marie but don't worry I'll be fine.'

'You really should let the doctor bleed you. He has many other remedies as well.'

Jacques grimaced at the thought. 'Not a chance Marie. I know you mean well but I wouldn't let that charlatan near me.'

'Goodness, you do have some strange ideas. Anyway, help yourself. I'm sure even you would agree that a good breakfast is beneficial.'

'So are you up to coming to Victor's demonstration this morning Jacques?' queried Pascal. 'He promises something quite spectacular.'

'Of course, although I pray it is not a repetition of what I heard he did on the beach when he landed.'

'Ah you've heard about that.'

'I could hardly fail to do so. The whole town is talking about it. If his aim was to scare everyone into submission then he succeeded spectacularly. Personally, I am revolted and it only confirms my feelings about your so called revolution.'

Jacques had thought long and hard about how to react when he had heard about the atrocities on the beach. Sanguine acceptance would have been very suspicious bearing in mind his previous views. He decided he would be as honest as he could whilst still maintaining his basic posture of accepting the revolution as the lesser of two evils.

Pascal looked hard at Jacques. 'You don't overthrow centuries of arrogance and prejudice without spilling little blood on the way. Imagine how many people would have lost their lives if the town had put up a fight. Anyway, one must be pragmatic in these troubled times. We all have our own lives to lead.'

'Yes, well don't expect me to become involved.'

'Of course not, we need your help in other ways my friend.'

Later that morning, Jacques and Pascal forced their way through the gathering crowd to the town square. They were given seats not far from where Victor and his entourage were gathered. Victor saw them arrive and nodded a quick acknowledgement before turning back to face the square. At the stroke of noon he called for silence.

'Citizens, when revolution comes, justice always follows. As you know the British have failed to subdue us. Indeed they rot on the beach only a few miles from here victims of their own repressive system and not a little Yellow Fever.'

A small ripple of laughter ran through the crowd. It was well known that the unseasoned enemy troops were suffering badly.

'Now is the time to cleanse this island of the Royalist scum who have repressed you for too long.' He clapped his hands and from round the corner of the building behind him came the guillotine mounted on a wheeled trolley and pulled by two horses. A collective sigh went up from the crowd. It was towed into the centre of the square where it was dismounted from the trolley and the horses led away.

'For the last two weeks we have been collecting those who would oppose us. Now is the time for justice.' He clapped his hands again.

From the other side of the square, guarded by soldiers, a file of chained people was herded into the square. They all bore marks of their recent harsh treatment and most seemed apathetic even when they saw what was waiting for them. The crowd booed and hissed and several stones were thrown.

Jacques was appalled. 'So, yet another demonstration of revolutionary viciousness,' he whispered to Pascal.

'Be thankful it's just the men, at least he has spared their wives and children this time,' Pascal hissed back.

Jacques felt the tug of another headache coming on but realised he couldn't leave, not if he wanted to maintain some form of credibility with these barbaric people.

The first man was unshackled and dragged by two soldiers to the guillotine. Despite desperate struggles his head and hands were forced onto the block and secured with the wooden stocks. A wicker basket was placed in front of him.

'*Oh god this can't really be happening,*' thought Jacques desperately. His vision felt odd as the headache took over and he realised he could no longer hear the baying anticipation of the crowd. His sole focus was on the poor wretch pinioned in the barbaric death machine. He didn't hear Victor give the order but he saw the executioner pull the release lever and the sun glint on the metal blade as it made an almost slow motion descent. He was suddenly assailed by the stench as the man's bowels and bladder let loose, just before the dreadful thunk of the blade hitting home. His head simply dropped into the waiting basket. But the last thing Jacques remembered was the fountain of blood, blasting spectacularly across the sand of the square. One part of his mind was clinically surprised by how much there was and how far it actually sprayed. The other part rejected the whole scene and everything went black.

Paul, Jacques, Smythe, La Croix woke up to darkness. He quickly realised that he was in his bed back in the room at Pascal's house. He felt hot and feverish but conversely for the first time in ages he felt at peace. This time he could recall his dreams.

He knew who he was.

He could remember everything; his parents, his first day at school, entering the Army and leaving it. There was the slippery climb up the corporate pole that had ended up with the ultimate promotion and the ultimate disaster. Jack and Emma and that ridiculous trip into the past where he had made a complete ass of himself. With hindsight, he now realised it was more a nervous breakdown than anything else. But that didn't excuse that bastard Jack incarcerating him in the jail in St Pierre just as the volcano was about to erupt. No hang on, that couldn't be right. The others would never have let him do that. He must have known that people survived in the jail. Oh God, maybe he had actually saved his life, after all it was his own idea to insist on staying behind. Then being rescued and starting his new life. No wonder he had railed against the attitudes of the time. No wonder his business acumen had generated such success. Then he suddenly realised why he was here in Guadeloupe and what had been worrying him. He knew a little of the history of the Caribbean of this time. Now he remembered what it was that concerned him so much and why he was working for the British. With a rush of final understanding he realised that his reasons remained sound.

He found himself idly scratching his arm. He could feel scabs there. Bloody hell that quack doctor had been bleeding him. He would see about that when morning came. Lying back on the pillows, his frantic thoughts slowly settled a little. The situation reminded him of when he was nursed back to health all those years ago. Then he recalled the savage day in the town square where that maniac Hugues had used the guillotine and the dangers of the age asserted themselves. He realised what a perilous situation he had got himself into but found that he didn't care. Although his thoughts still churned in turmoil, he now had a fixed anchor to hold on to. His universe had a centre to it. Despite everything he now remembered and some of the shameful things he had done in the past, he had purpose and love. A face appeared and it was the only thing that mattered.

Francine.

Chapter 30

'Hi, you two, have you seen anything of our Mad Scientist?' asked Jack.

Emma and Melissa both looked up from a gurgling baby Emma as Jack posed the question.

'Sorry Jack,' replied Emma. 'Ever since he got the bit between his teeth working out all his numbers, he's been hiding in his room. He's presumably working out how to get us home.'

'As long as he hasn't got another of the island's ladies up there helping him. I still don't know how Lady Clare's father found out. I was very impressed with how Charles managed to calm him down. Talking of him, where is Charles? I've been down on the boat all day and thought you'd all like to hear how we're progressing.'

'He's been down at Falmouth on some mysterious business he won't talk about,' said Melissa. 'He should be home any minute now.'

'Someone talking about me?' called a cheerful Charles as the door to the nursery opened. 'For some reason, I thought I'd find you girls in here. Bit surprised about you though Jack.'

'Listen Charles, in our century, the blokes have to muck in with all the tasks.'

Emma chuckled. 'Yeah right, Mister 'I'm always busy when it's nappy time.''

Jack didn't know whether to look smug or embarrassed but was saved from having to dig himself in even deeper by Smithy himself putting his head around the door.

'Ah there you all are. I've spent four solid days reinventing mainframe software to run on my telephone and recreating dimensional algorithms from scratch. I've inputted the extra fields based on a number of assumptions of Tessla strengths and iterated a number of four dimensional solutions and I now need a rum. A large one please.'

'I and probably everyone in here haven't clue what you just said Smithy,' said Emma. 'Although, I suspect we all understood the rum word. Are you saying you've solved the problem of us getting back?'

'Hey, isn't that what I just said? Anyway, if you can tear yourselves away from that little monster in the cot and join me on the veranda, you might get even more sense out of me. Don't wait too long I know where Charles keeps his stash.'

A short while later they all joined Smithy to hear his explanation.

Standing in front of them with a very serious rum to hand, he launched into a detailed scientific explanation.

Jack very quickly butted in before he got into full flow. 'Smithy, stop it, you know damn well we haven't a clue what you're talking about. I also know you're bloody well doing it deliberately to try and impress us with your superior brain. Just remember, we've all seen the other Smithy, you know the one that gets titled ladies into trouble and lets Charles dig you out of the mire afterwards.'

'Oops, got me there. Right in simpleton's words then. Based on the strength of the magnetic field in that damned gun, Jacks best navigational estimates of where we arrived and of course when we arrived, I'm pretty sure we can head back to a similar position offset by two miles to the south and the window should be there.'

'That's fantastic but how long have we got?' asked Jack. 'The original window only lasted six months.'

'Same with this one. Basically our coming through dragged the original gate with us. By my calculations we have at least another four months before we're stranded completely. I assume you can get the yacht fixed in that time Jack?'

'Oh yes and that's what I wanted to tell you all. As you know the generator was fixed a few days ago and I charged a battery for Smithy to keep his phone topped up. Well, I've now got one engine working properly, fixed up some wiring for lighting inside and checked the steering gear. The hole has been really well patched inside and out and I've inspected the rest of the hull and it's all sound. If we put her back in the water now we have a working vessel, albeit a mast and a few sails might come in handy.'

'Well done Jack and Professor Smith,' said Charles. 'On top of all that, I think you might be interested to hear my news. I may have tracked down your mystery ship.'

All eyes turned to Charles in surprise.

'I've been putting the word out amongst the locals. Down in Falmouth is a very old man who has been fishing these waters for years. When I explained to him that I was in on the secret of the anomaly out to the west, I managed to get him to open up. That and a few bottles of rum of course. Apparently, when he was a teenager there was a strange story circulating about a ship that had been spotted moving very fast without any sails. It had initially been spotted down by St Lucia. It made no effort to hide itself and scared the hell out of many people at the time. They all called it a devil ship. No one would go near it. However, it then disappeared. That year was apparently very bad for hurricanes and everyone assumed that the weather had done for it. But this is where it gets interesting. His father claimed to have seen it and described it in detail to him. Some years later the chap was also caught out in bad weather and almost died when his boat was swept onto a lee shore. They just managed to claw their way clear but he swears he saw a strange boat answering the description of the mystery ship wrecked on a reef.'

'Where, which island?' asked Smithy with mounting excitement.

'He says he doesn't know exactly. They had been fighting the storm for several days and the visibility was very poor. I suspect you know exactly what he means after you own experience in Jacaranda. However, he says he knows where it wasn't if that makes sense. He says it can't have been south of Martinique because of the time it took them to return to Antigua when the weather abated. The shapes of the islands are all pretty unique and he is pretty certain that it wasn't Dominica, as the island he saw had low lying land as well as mountain peaks. So that leaves Martinique or Guadeloupe somewhere on the windward side.'

'I wonder why Poseidon, if that is who it was, didn't try to make landfall at one of the islands right at the start?' mused Jack.

'They probably decided to head for England if their reception here was so confusing for them. They had the fuel for it,' said Smithy. 'I guess we'll never know for sure. Charles, can I talk to this old guy, try and get a description of what he saw and any more detail?'

'Of course, we can go down tomorrow.'

Just then there was a discreet cough at the door and Charles's agent from the dock stepped in. 'Sorry to interrupt Sir,' he said. 'But I think you should know that a ship has just come in to Falmouth and it's loaded with refugees.'

'My goodness, where are they from?' asked Melissa with concern.

The man looked at Charles questioningly.

'It's alright, there's no need to talk to me in private. These are my friends.'

'Indeed Sir but the news is pretty desperate.'

'Go on.'

'Well Sir, they're from Guadeloupe. Apparently a short time ago a French fleet arrived and landed on Basse Terre. They have taken that part of the island and the British fleet seems powerless to kick them out. Apparently the French have armed the slaves and seriously outnumber our soldiers.'

'Yes but what about the refugees?' Melissa asked.

'They're mainly women and children plus a few old men. Their husbands were the leading Royalists on that part of the island. The story is that they were all guillotined only a few days ago. I'm sorry.'

After the man had left there was silence. The euphoria of the last half an hour had completely evaporated. Charles was immediately thinking whether a recall was likely. It was the last thing he needed at the moment. Melissa was worried for the same reason. But for the other three it was a serious reality jolt.

Jack voiced their thoughts first. 'Jesus Christ, I'd almost forgotten where and more importantly, when we are now. This really is a savage benighted age isn't it?'

Melissa was stung by Jack's unthinking remark. 'No it isn't, there is as much good here as bad. The difference now is that much of it is visible to the naked eye. What the hell do you think goes on in countries around the world in your time Jack? Public executions in China are even televised for God's sake,

Guantanamo Bay, genocide in Africa, how long would you like me to go on?'

Taken aback by the vehemence in her tone Jack immediately apologised. 'Sorry Melissa, I guess that living with you has protected us from the reality of what's going on around us.'

'Yes, when I went back to England with Charles, I got the same culture shock,' responded Melissa in a conciliatory tone. 'Raw and bloody it may be Jack, medicine may be primitive and the average life expectancy may be lower but it is also invigorating and surprisingly liberating.' Seeing the look on her friend's faces she continued. 'In this age, you have to be prepared to accept the consequences of your own actions. If a man decides to marry and have children then he expects to be able to provide for them. If he fails in that then the whole family suffer. There is absolutely no system, no safety net to help. But he wouldn't expect help anyway. It's not how anyone thinks. In your time unmarried mothers receive handouts for every new unwanted mouth that they bring into the world. Try that in our age and all that will happen is that they will starve. So guess what? It doesn't happen.'

'Melissa that's dreadful,' said Emma.

'No Emma you don't get it. Very few people starve because they have deliberately had children to get some form of handout, because there are no hand outs in the first place. Do you see? Look, let me give you another example. Jack you've been to Hinchfield hall. Suppose you lived there in the twenty first century. One day you decide to go to your house in London. What would you do?'

'Er, I would get in my car and drive there or drive to Winchester train station and catch a train.'

'Right and be there in an hour or so. In my time, we would plan the journey for several days in advance. We would take our coach as it's too far to ride with any baggage. Our coach doesn't carry our coat of arms as it might do in London, as it would be too good an advertisement to be robbed. We would take a coachman and probably another footman and they would all carry weapons. Assuming that the coach doesn't lose a wheel or be damaged in any other way, then it would be unlikely that we could make it in one day. Not because of the distance but because the roads are almost non-existent. So we would have had to arrange overnight accommodation at an Inn or a friend's house. Should anything go wrong, we would have to fix it ourselves because there are no such things as insurance, breakdown cover, police, fire, ambulances, nothing.'

'That sounds dreadful. I hadn't thought of it that way.'

'Yes but by the same token there's no nanny state. There are no hordes of bureaucrats breathing down your neck continually making rules every time something happens to stop it happening again. You take responsibility for your own actions. Health and safety exists but it's down to you, no one else. If something goes wrong, there are no teams of lawyers ready to help you sue all and sundry. I'm not sure if I'm explaining this at all well but I actually love it. It just takes some getting used to that's all.'

'But what about child mortality and all the Dickensian stories we were bought up on?' asked Emma.

Melissa laughed. 'Well Dickens is well into our future now and yes the lack of decent medicine can be tragic but as no one knows any better then they don't worry about it. And the family unit is very strong. I guess it's the equivalent of the modern welfare state. You know, I've had to revise my opinions enormously over recent years. Take the slavery system for example.'

'Oh come on you can't say you support that?' scoffed Jack. 'I know you too well Melissa

'No of course not, I abhor it but the way it's portrayed in your time is so skewed. Look, slaves are only available because they are sold to European countries by their own people. If they weren't sold to us, they would either be killed outright, enslaved in their own country or sold to Arab slavers. Don't think that the Caribbean trade has increased demand significantly because it hasn't. The Arabs have been dealing in African slaves for centuries. And transporting them here is a lucrative business because they are extremely valuable. What ship's captain would deliberately allow his precious cargo to perish en route? I'm sure you've seen those dreadful pictures of the inside of a slave ship and yes they are horrible but believe it or not most slaves arrive here well fed and healthy,.'

'I'm betting that most slaves aren't treated as well as those on your estate though,' said Emma. 'How do you defend what goes on in the islands?'

'I don't, I can't but I've done all I can for our people, as I'm sure you've seen already and made damn sure they will continue to be looked after when we leave to go home. Look I've learnt that you can't mend all the world's ills no matter how much you might want to.'

'Yes, I can see that,' said Emma. 'Oh Melissa, it must have been so hard for you.'

'Yes well, I had more than a little support,' she said looking at Charles, who grinned conspiratorially back.

'More rum anyone?' asked Smithy innocently.

Chapter 31

He became aware of light filtering through his eyelids and then he was startled into full wakefulness by a gentle snore. Opening his eyes he saw he was still in his bed. He felt washed out but clear headed and he still had all his memories. '*It hadn't been another dream then,*' he thought. Another snort drew his eyes to one side. Sitting in an armchair fast asleep was his wife.

'Francine,' he tried to call but it just came out a croak.

Her eyes flew open and she was instantly by his side. 'Oh Jacques, you're back, thank God. Here, drink some of this.' She lifted his head and offered him a glass of water which he drank gratefully before falling back on the pillow suddenly realising how weak he felt.

He cleared his throat and found he could at least talk better now. 'My dear what are you doing here? How did you get here? What about the British?'

'Shh, you've been unwell for quite some time. The doctor said it was a brain fever. It looked more like Yellow fever to me but whatever it was you're over it now. I got here when you friend Pascal sent one of his boats to tell me what had happened. I could hardly stay away could I?'

'Yes but how did you get past the British fleet?'

'They've gone. Some days ago they withdrew all their troops and have apparently sailed around to Basse Terre and are making a stand there.'

Suddenly the fact of Francine's presence sank in, in all its horror. 'My dear, did they force you to come? You realise this will make my task here impossible. What have you told them?'

'Hush, I've told them nothing. They still think you are the idealist who is fighting against slavery nothing more.'

'But they will be able to use you as a hostage. What are we going to do?'

'Please let's not worry about that now. You almost died and now we need to get you better.' She smiled conspiratorially at him, 'I threw that doctor out you know. He was bleeding you and doing all the things you say are so stupid.'

He smiled back looking at his wonderful wife and wondering what to say next. He knew he couldn't hide the truth about his past but wasn't sure how much of it she could take. He was still having trouble assimilating it himself.

'Francine, you should know one thing. I've have my memory back. Maybe it was the fever or the shock of witnessing those executions but I now remember everything.'

He studied her face for her reaction. Before she could say anything he continued. 'It doesn't change a thing. I remember who I was and what I did before the volcano erupted. I also remember our time together and how happy we are now. Nothing can change that.'

It was like the sun coming out when she smiled down at him.

'I am so glad to hear that Jacques because I have some news as well.' She reached for his hand and placed it on her stomach. 'We're going to have a family soon.'

It took another week before Jacques felt strong enough to get up. The fever had really weakened him. Thinking back, Jacques, or was it Paul, had realised that he had forgotten to get his jabs before coming out on holiday to St Lucia. He smiled ruefully to himself when he remembered how hectic his life had been all those lifetimes ago. He and Francine had been able to talk for hours and he had explained much of his past, although he had deliberately not explained that his previous life had been in the future. He made up the fiction that he had been a successful merchant trading from France and England and had lost his fortune in the revolution before coming out to the West Indies to try again. It was close enough to the truth that he could dissemble confidently. He vowed to himself that some time in the future, when they had regained their normal life, he would tell her the full story.

The story which also gained him some credibility with his hosts who were more than a little concerned that when he was delirious he often shouted out in English. By the time he was able to sit out in the sun with Francine everything seemed to be settling back into place.

It was a beautiful morning. They were sitting in the little garden to the rear of Pascal's house having coffee in the shade of a large coconut palm. Marie was as usual fussing around them both when the door behind them opened and Pascal came in ushering a smiling Victor.

'Victor, may I introduce Francine La Croix, wife of our esteemed colleague from Martinique.' Francine rose and Victor gallantly kissed her hand while appraising her form. He liked what he saw even if she was clearly pregnant.

'Please take a seat everyone,' he said magnanimously. Even though it wasn't his house, no one seemed to mind.

Jacques who hadn't risen on Victor's entrance stared back, his gaze challenging. 'A triumphant return Victor? Your enemies banished across the water so we hear.'

'Indeed, we kicked the last of the British out of Basse Terre last week. The island is ours and hopefully Martinique will be next. With your help of course.'

'Not if you are going to use that bloody machine of yours to murder more people.'

'Murder? Jacques, that was justice and I'm sorry but you had better get used to that.' He said with steel in his voice. Then his tone changed back to hearty affability. 'Anyway there is no need to use her any more. As I said the island is now ours.'

'What about the slaves you released and armed? What are you going to do about them?'

Victor looked at Jacques thoughtfully. 'You tell me Jacques. Are you aware of the situation on Saint-Domingue?'

Jacques wondered what he meant for a moment and then realised Victor was talking about the island of Haiti in his time. One of the poorest and most desperate islands in the Caribbean. He knew the history; that it was the first island to have a successful slave revolt and one that led to anarchy almost up to the present day. He also saw what Victor was driving at. He immediately realised his quandary. '*How would Jacques the idealist react,*' he thought desperately.

'You can't be suggesting that you re-enslave them. That would be barbaric.'

'What choice do I have? Do you wish to see this island descend into anarchy and barbarity? You complain about a few executions, yet you would see all the whites on the island murdered by rampaging mobs of free Negros, including your beautiful wife. Imagine what they would do to her. No, it must not be allowed to happen. In time, we can be more liberal but for now we have already recovered their weapons and they are being taken back to the estates.'

Before Jacques could react Victor spoke again. 'Now ladies, I wonder if you would excuse us. I need to talk to Jacques and Pascal alone. We have our future strategy to discuss.'

With no recourse but to obey gracefully, the ladies left. Francine caught Jacque's eye as she walked past but there was nothing he could do or say.

When they were alone Victor turned to Jacques. 'Jacques I must congratulate you. Such a pretty wife and soon to be a mother as well. You are very fortunate and I hear you have recovered from your fever. I hope you are in a good frame of mind to aid us in our task now.'

Jacques ground his teeth. The threat was quite clear and he knew he couldn't react. *'Why on earth did Francine have to come here,'* he thought. But of course he knew the answer even as the thought was forming. Well, all he could do now was cooperate and pray that something came up.

'Yes Victor, what do you have in mind?'

'It will take several weeks if not longer to regroup all my soldiers or at least that is what my General says and we will need to ensure that this island is fully secure. So I was thinking of making a move in about six weeks time. I understand that your estate is on the eastern coast of the island and has a secure anchorage? It would seem ideal for us and would take the British by surprise if we were able to march on them from an unexpected direction.'

'Yes but the approach to the anchorage is very dangerous even in daylight and good visibility, unless you have good local knowledge that is.'

'Ah, yes but you have that knowledge do you not?'

'Not really, I tend to rely on my skippers for that.'

'I understand. Here is what I am suggesting. You go back to your estate and look at ways of guiding my ships in, preferably at night. Surely you could arrange to set up some leading lights or something could you not?'

Jacques thought about it. It would be quite feasible but he would have to talk to several of his men before he would admit to it being really practical.

'Yes, I think something could be done.'

Victor beamed. 'Excellent, then Pascal will arrange to get you home and set up methods of communication.'

'And my wife, she will come with me?'

'Oh no my friend, in her condition she shouldn't travel. I'm sure you agree. She will be well looked after here. I insist on it.'

Chapter 32

Jack was happy and content. He was back in his element. Jacaranda was at sea and flying across the blue Caribbean swell on a broad reach just to the south of Antigua. The low brown and green coastline was in clear sight to the north. The rig that the dockyard had supplied was similar in many respects to the one they had travelled here with and so it hadn't taken long to get to grips with it. She was working superbly. Down below was a different matter. It was still a bit of a mess and most things didn't work anymore but there was enough functional equipment, not the least the galley stove, the toilets and refurbished bedding to make her habitable. The last time Jack had sailed his yacht in these waters was for the annual New Year, Nelson's Pursuit race. From this far out nothing much had seemed to have changed. He smiled as yet another sheet of spray flew up from the bow and splattered him with warm drops of Caribbean Sea. Emma ducked the spray and then looked up at Jack and laughed. He just shrugged. 'Tastes and feels just the same as in our time and the sun is just as warm.'

'Yes but there seem to be so many more fish about,' replied Emma as the school of dolphins that had been playing in Jacaranda's bow wave continued to leap and play.

Seeing her gaze, he replied. 'Dolphins aren't fish.'

'Are you two bickering again?' asked a smiling Smithy who was lounging in the cockpit with them.

'Nah, just making sure my wife's fish recognition remains up to scratch.'

'Bit like you bird recognition then,' responded Emma.

'Hey you lot,' interrupted Melissa from the cockpit hatch. 'Coffee and bacon sandwiches a la eighteenth century for anyone?'

'Yes please,' was the chorused reply. And then curious, Smithy asked. 'What's the difference between those and modern ones?'

'Ah, well the bread is homemade and manually sliced and so is the pig and believe me they taste so much better for it.'

Some minutes later there was broad agreement in the cockpit that this was yet another aspect of the current time that beat the modern day equivalent hands down.

'Nice to see you've even got eighteenth century man trained to do the cooking,' Jack observed as Charles finally made it into the cockpit.

Charles gave him a disparaging look. 'So future man, I haven't seen you slaving over a hot galley recently.'

'Ah but I'm the skipper here and so have to remain aloof and in command.'

That remark got him a kick from Emma and bread crust in the forehead from Melissa.

'Right you mutinous lot, let's just go over our plan such as it is. Now that Jacky appears to be fully functional, we need to go off on our treasure hunt. Smithy says he's got the big metal detector thingy in the stern working and we have at least some data to refine our search after talking to that old guy.'

'Yes,' said Smithy. 'The 'detector thingy' or magnetometer to the less ignorant, survived quite well. Unfortunately its electronics didn't. I've rigged up a simple analogue gauge to it. If we get a reading the needle will move. As we don't want to spend all our time staring at it, if the needle moves any distance it hits a metal post and makes a simple circuit to ring a buzzer I managed to salvage of one of the printed circuit boards. So we have a basic search capability. Of course we will need to go and look carefully at several likely coastlines using the world famous Mark One eyeball.'

'OK,' said Jack who then turned to Charles and Melissa. 'What about you two? I've no right to ask it as I know you have your own plans but you're welcome to come along.'

Melissa looked at Charles. No words were said but clearly some form of communication occurred because she turned back to Jack. 'You just try keeping us away sunshine. The children will be fine back on the estate and I wouldn't miss this for the world.'

Jack turned to Charles and raised an eyebrow.

'I think the modern phrase is 'what she said,'' he responded. 'Oh and you should know that I received a letter from the Admiral thanking for my offer but declining my services. It seems that the government have decided that retaking Guadeloupe is not so much of a priority anymore and as no more troops are being sent out, he tacitly admitted that the island is lost or will be soon. They are going to withdraw to Martinique and concentrate on holding on there. You must understand the dangers this represents and that means all of you,' he said meaningfully. 'Jacaranda is fast and hopefully has the use of at least one engine but if we should fall in with an enemy ship and they are going to be out there, then even a small cannon could blast her to bits. You could of course just head over to your calculated position and simply return home.'

Smithy was first to respond. 'Charles, we have the opportunity to gain knowledge that could have the most profound effect on humanity since the invention of the wheel. I think I speak for everyone when I say that it would be criminal if we didn't give it our best shot. Dammit we survived a hurricane and God knows what else and despite all that we are still in good shape. ' He looked at his two companions.

'What he said,' replied Jack and Emma nodded.

'Alright,' said Charles. 'What I propose is that we head back now. I'll get Polaris ready and send her down to Martinique so that she can support us if needed. We can then store up Jacaranda and work out a detailed search plan.'

A week later and Jacaranda was back at sea with her five crew. They had sailed in company with Polaris but soon left the lumbering brig behind. Jack had decided to initially head out into the Atlantic and keep well to windward of the islands and use the ever present trade winds to send them south. The last thing he needed was to get becalmed in the lee of an island and have to use an engine to avoid interception. Martinique would be their first island to search as it was much safer. They would only move up to Guadeloupe if they didn't find anything there.

Jack and Charles were on deck. The sun had just risen in a fantastic display of colour. 'It's nice to see that the sunrises don't change,' said Jack. 'Charles, are you listening?'

Charles was standing and scanning the horizon intently through Jack's binoculars. 'Sorry Jack but it's standard procedure to be alert at sunrise. If anyone is around with bad intent, then this is the most dangerous time. Don't forget that warships will have a permanent masthead lookout, which means they will see us long before we see them.'

'Good point. I guess I don't have the same automatic mind-set that says any sail I see is possibly an enemy and could be trying to kill me. The worst I normally have to face is incompetent charter boats who don't have a clue about the collision regulations.'

'Yes, well I'm glad I did look because there is a sail out there to windward and it looks like they have already seen us.'

'Let me see,' said Jack. Charles handed over the binoculars and Jack looked where he was pointing. There on the far horizon, was a tiny triangle of grey. Not much to look at but Jack immediately realised the problem. 'I suppose this is what you mean by having the weather gauge?'

'Yes, I'm afraid so. He can run down on us with the wind behind him. Our normal course of action would be to turn downwind and try to outrun him but with our speed we should be able to bear away a little, speed up and simply sail away.'

'I'll take your advice Charles. You're the naval expert here.'

Jack woke the others and they all spent an anxious morning as the strange sail got closer. First the rest of her masts became visible, all three of them and then her hull. Charles identified her as a thirty six gun frigate. Because she was heading towards them it was hard to make out her ensign and hence her nationality. She apparently had the lines of a French built ship but that meant nothing as many British frigates had started out life as French only to be captured and pressed into their enemy's service.

Jack had been maintaining a check on her bearing and it soon became clear that it was moving slowly aft. The frigate also quickly seemed to realise this and turned to port in an effort to maintain an intercept heading. It also then became clear that she was not going to do it as her bearing continued to change and draw aft. However, it did allow them to see the massive French ensign at her stern.

'What do you think her intentions are Charles?' asked an anxious Jack. 'Surely we're small fry. Why are they bothering?'

'Well, there are several answers to that Jack. We're not flying an Ensign and it's a bit late to put one up now. We could show a French one but then they'd want to come and talk to us as a minimum and would expect us to heave to and wait. If we didn't then clearly we must be an enemy. If we fly a British one we're the enemy anyway. We might be small fry as you put it but would be a legitimate capture. Who knows what intelligence we might be carrying?'

'Right, so run away is the order of the day?'

'Absolutely, there's nothing wrong with that.'

So that's what they did. Later in the afternoon the Frigate clearly decided it wasn't worth the effort as Jacaranda obviously had the speed to outrun her. Also the hills of Martinique were at last appearing over the horizon to leeward and the Frenchman probably didn't want to get too close to the British held island. A collective sigh of relief went up when they saw the aspect of her sails change as she wore away and headed off over the horizon.

Jack called a council of war. 'I guess that was a bit of a wakeup call. Anyway, we'd better sort out a detailed plan now. As we agreed simply sailing up and down the coast is almost certainly a waste of time. If Poseidon was wrecked on the shore somewhere then she will almost certainly have been smashed to pieces by now. I suspect the locals would have been fairly keen to salvage what they could as well. So probably the best thing is to go ashore and start talking to people. The real question is where? This coast is quite dangerous in the wrong conditions and we will have to be careful.'

'Why not go round to Fort de France Jack?' asked Charles. 'It should be quite safe.'

'Two reasons, firstly, it's on the other side of the island and we would have to come over to this coast, find accommodation and do all the work on foot. Secondly, Jacaranda still attracts rather too much attention and I would like to keep her away from prying eyes. Anyway, I have an idea where we could go that would be safe and convenient.'

He produced the chart he had been studying earlier and pointed to a narrow peninsular that jutted out from the coast. 'In my time this is a bit of a tourist attraction. It's a restored sugar plantation. The buildings are just shells but in this time it should be a thriving estate. More to the point, the bay it shelters is very safe once you get in. I've been in many times over the years and even without any marker buoys I'm confident we can get in.'

Charles looked at the chart and immediately recognised the bay he had brought the British agent too what seemed like and age ago but was in fact only a few months past. 'I know this place Jack, I was here recently but I had a local expert with me. Your memory of here is two hundred years out of date. If that's the right way of looking at it and reefs move, it may not be the same,' replied Charles. 'Your charts may not be that accurate and your memory might be a wrong as well.'

'True but we have another modern aid.'

'Oh, what's that?'

'You. You're pretty used to going up masts I believe, so we'll send you up with the binoculars and some Polaroid sunglasses and you can look out for shallow water for us.'

They had to wait until the next morning to ensure the light was good enough, so the night was spent sailing close to the coast and listening to the detector that Smithy had rigged up. It stayed stubbornly silent all night.

The next morning with Charles standing on the crosstrees, wearing the sunglasses which worked surprisingly well at seeing below the sea's surface and Jack carefully conning Jacaranda, they crept into the bay. Once inside, they could see a small trading cutter anchored close to the shore but no other signs of life. However, once they had dropped the anchor it was clear they had been seen. A small boat rowed out from the shore below the imposing house on the top of the bluff.

The man in the boat introduced himself as one of the estate staff and politely asked their business. At the same time he was clearly casting a professional eye over Jacaranda and her crew.

Thinking on his feet, Jack said they had come in to talk to the estate owner about possible trade issues and so the man invited him ashore. Jack insisted that all his crew come with him and the man demurred without complaint but was clearly surprised by there being two women on board. He kept his counsel as he rowed them ashore and then led them up a winding track to the house. They were deposited in a side room off the imposing hall while the man went to fetch his master. They were admiring the view and the books lining the walls when the sound of the door opening drew everyone's attention.

Standing in the doorway was a dark haired man dressed in a casual shirt and breeches. He looked questioningly at his guests for a few seconds before dawning recognition suffused his face.

Almost comically the same expression was appearing one everyone else's countenance as well.

Jack and the man spoke at the same time.

'Bloody hell, Jack Vincent.'

'Bloody hell, Paul Smythe.'

Chapter 33

Paul spoke first. 'I haven't the slightest idea how or why you are here. But I don't know whether to punch you in the face or thank you Jack.'

'Well. I knew the town goal was the one place you had a chance of surviving. What else was I supposed to do? You were the one who insisted on staying in Martinique.'

Paul grinned wryly. 'You know, for the last nine years I didn't know who I was. I only got my memory back a few weeks ago. But I kind of worked out what you'd done. I also remember what an asshole I'd been. I guess it's me who should be asking for your forgiveness. I seem to remember we were all great friends once.'

As he spoke the words Melissa broke ranks and walked over to Paul and put her arms around him. 'I think more than enough time has passed for us to be able to forgive each other don't you?'

The ice melted and everyone started talking at once.

'Stop, everyone stop,' Paul called over the babble. 'We obviously have a lot of catching up to do and I really need to know how you found me and what you are doing here but one at a time. Look, it's almost lunch time. Let me get something arranged and we can talk over a drink and something to eat.'

It didn't take long and they were all seated in the dining room enjoying an impromptu lunch. Smithy was introduced and he gave a very brief synopsis of why they were here. Jack and Charles followed it up with an oversight of their travails since arriving back in the past again.

'So that's Jacaranda down in the bay? I thought there was something familiar about her. Mind you she looks a great deal more contemporary than last time she was here. You've disguised her well this time.'

Charles answered. 'Yes, she looks quite the part. Now tell me Paul or should that be Jacques? I actually heard you were here some time ago. I saw you briefly in Fort de France but there wasn't time to meet.'

'You're right Charles. All of you, as far as I'm concerned I'm Jacques La Croix now.' He gave a similarly brief overview of his past but then realised there was a lot more to tell about recent events. 'Before I go on I need to ask a question. Are you involved in this tragic little war between the French and British in any way? Or is your trip here only involved in the chase for this mysterious metal?'

Smithy answered for them. 'Our mission is to recover a sample of the untainted metal from Poseidon, no more.'

Jack interrupted, he realised there was more to the question. 'Yes but I think there's something more you are asking Paul. How about you tell us what it is that's worrying you?'

Paul thought for a second and then launched into brief history of the recent activities of Jacques La Croix the sugar plantation owner.

'You should understand that I volunteered to work under cover for the British authorities recently to try and head off the massacre. Even before I got my memory back I knew something dreadful was due to happen. Unfortunately, that has been totally compromised by my wife now being effectively held hostage on Guadeloupe. Understand this all of you, despite everything that happened in our time earlier, there has never been a woman for me like Francine. She owns my heart and my soul. You may wonder at the old Paul Smythe making a remark like that. But Paul La Croix is a different man and believe me when I say that I will do anything to ensure her safety, I will. That includes letting the massacre happen.' He looked expectantly at his audience with an air of defiance.

Jack was the first to respond. 'Paul I think I speak for all of us. We haven't a clue what you're talking about. We studied local history very carefully this time before coming here and even though we arrived just a tad late, we still have a pretty good knowledge of events. What on earth is this massacre you're on about?'

Paul looked confused. 'Oh come on guys, if you know the history you'll know that Hugues takes the British by surprise. He captures Martinique and rounds up all the Royalists. He murders them, their wives and children in a public display in Fort de France. Bloody hell, there are hundreds of them. It takes days and becomes one of the most notorious events of the French revolution.'

His words fell into silence. 'Come on? Please tell me you know what I'm talking about?'

Smithy spoke. 'Paul, what happened in nineteen thirty nine?'

Looking nonplussed Paul replied. 'The second World War started.'

'Led by?'

'Adolph Hitler. Look, what the hell are you on about?'

'Bear with me. So who won?'

'We did, although the Yanks came in late as usual and helped out. Is that what you want to know?'

'OK and just one more. Who is Saddam Hussein and what happened to him?'

'You mean who was he? He was the leader of Iraq and got kicked out by the Yanks and us in a dodgy war. They found him in a hole and he ended up being hung. How's that, did I pass?'

Smithy smiled although he still looked tight lipped. 'Yes you did but I can only think we've got a lot to blame the bloody butterflies for.'

'Right Smithy,' said Emma. 'As usual you've got us all mystified. Paul, sorry about our scientist friend but he has a habit of talking bollocks and then explaining why in fact it all makes perfect sense.'

'OK,' said Smithy. 'It's quite clear that Paul recalls an incident in Caribbean history that none of us do. I'm sure we all think that Martinique stays in British hands throughout the French revolution. Am I right?'

A chorus of nods greeted the question.

'Yet Paul recalls a different version of local history but two key events far in the future seem to be common for all of us. Surely if he was right, his and our history would be different? Well I've had a theory about this and now it seems I've been proved right again. Hey Jack, pass that bottle of red over to the clever scientist.'

Jack reached for the wine bottle but then paused. 'Not a chance matey, not until we get to understand about the butterflies.'

'Look pass the bloody wine anyway and I'll explain.'

Reluctantly Jack let him have the bottle. Smithy topped up his glass and then looked around smugly. 'Right who's heard the story about butterflies causing hurricanes?'

Melissa caught on first. 'Oh I know that one. It's the idea that the gust of air from a butterfly wing can be the eventual cause of a hurricane forming. A sort of cause and effect thingy, chaos theory. Isn't that it?'

'Yup, got it in one. That's why most people are scared silly that if you go into the past then you will inevitably change the future and set off parallel universes. Until this conversation I was sort of that mind as well as you all know. But I've always had reservations. Here we have some great evidence that the theory is actually bollocks. Oops sorry, that's a technical term by the way.'

He saw Jack reach over to retrieve his bottle and swatted his hand away. 'Look, Paul remembers the same key events from our shared future, so history can't have been changed significantly, if at all. I'm betting that in fact it's exactly the same bar the one incident. Now going back to the butterfly theory. It's such a pretty idea that no one ever queries how likely it is that the bloody insects wings actually cause anything other than a local disturbance in the atmosphere. Any idea what the actual odds are that a butterfly's fart actually does anything at all?'

He received nothing but silence to his question. 'The answer is that although possible, it's more than highly unlikely by several orders of magnitude. Taking the analogy further, so what if Martinique stays British or changes hands a few years earlier? We all know the revolution was led by a bunch of psychopathic, bloodthirsty morons. It is quite clear to me therefore, that either event can occur and it won't make a jot of difference to the future. I guess none of our grandfathers gets killed if you want to look at it that way.'

'So, what you're saying,' said Paul. 'Is that relatively small events are unlikely to change history overall. Is that right?'

'Sort of, they may or more likely they probably won't,' said Smithy taking a large gulp of his wine. 'It's clear to me that in this case the latter is true.'

Paul was starting to look stricken. 'Then if I thwart Hugue's plans I can save hundreds of innocent lives and not actually screw up the future.'

'Got it in one.'

'Shit. Look everyone, this is going to be hard to admit to but as I said I will do anything to keep Francine safe. I thought that as the massacre had happened in my future, then there was nothing I could do to stop it. That meant I could cooperate and keep Francine safe. From what you've just said that's not the case. Jesus, what am I going to do now? If I alert the British or do something to screw up the attack that bastard will kill my pregnant wife.'

His announcement was met with silence as everyone assimilated the problem. Emma was the first person to break it.

'In that case, we'll just have to rescue her won't we?'

'What? No I can't ask you to do that and anyway it would be just about impossible. Point a Pitre is an armed camp It's absolutely swarming with soldiers. The slightest sniff that I wasn't totally cooperating would sign her death warrant.'

Jack looked thoughtful. 'Alright but if they all head over here to invade, then the town will be empty right?'

Charles was the first to object. No Jack, for two reasons. Firstly, there will still be some military there and who's to say that Hugues will be part of the actual operation. More importantly, I am not prepared to let a crime like the one Paul just described actually take place. No, we've got to do both things, preserve Paul's wife and stop the invasion.'

Paul was managing to look hopeful and worried at the same time. 'Guys, this isn't your fight. I've no right to get you involved.'

Melissa spoke for them all. 'Bollocks Paul, we go back too far. Despite a certain incident in the recent past, I remember what good friends we've been over the years. Don't argue. We're going to help any way we can.' Emma and Jack nodded agreement.

Paul noticed that Smithy was about to speak and got in first. 'What can I say? I'm overwhelmed. But maybe I can help pay you back. You see, I think I know where your mystery ship might be.'

Chapter 34

'Bloody hell, this really is a day for revelations,' said Jack. 'Come on then spill it Paul.'

'Alright, this is more than second hand but it sort of fits with what Smithy said earlier. Now you say the wreck was seen on a lee shore, which looked flat but had mountains in the distance. Is that right?'

'Yes,' Charles replied. 'It sounded to us like either part of the coast here or somewhere on Guadeloupe.'

'Now, a hurricane can cause the wind to come from just about any direction right? So it doesn't mean the coast was facing east.'

'OK but the fisherman said they had been fishing upwind of the Islands.'

'Fine but they could easily have been picked up by a southerly wind if they were in that part of the circulation and if they did, then the southern coast of Grande Terre would answer your description pretty well. Hang on, I'll get some charts.' He went to a side board and fished around in a drawer and dug out a large parchment chart. He cleared room on the dining table and spread it out.'

'Bet this would be worth a fortune in your day Jack but for navigation they are adequate even nowadays. Now look here, this is the bay of Gosier, which currently seems to be everyone's favourite destination when invading. Of course it's well sheltered and has a flat beach which is great for getting troops ashore. Now, look at the eastern end, see the reef sticking out?' He pointed to a clearly marked underwater reef pushing out into the bay with several rocks identified as remaining above the waterline.

'I know that reef from my day and its not the place to hit in any weather, let alone a hurricane,' mused Jack. 'What's it called? There's nothing on the chart.'

'Very good question,' replied Paul. 'On the charts it has no name but all the locals call it Devil Ship reef. I wonder why that might be?'

'That ties in I guess,' responded Charles, 'Is there any sign of a wreck on it?'

'It's not the sort of place I would venture too close to even in good weather. Even with a modest Atlantic swell, the waves pile up on it quite enormously. Any wooden ship stuck on it wouldn't last for long. However, if she had some heavy metal machinery on board that could easily have survived, even now. Mind you, getting there is going to be interesting. It's only a few miles from Point a Pitre and is overlooked by the fort just here.'

'So,' said Jack. 'We have three things to achieve now. We need to rescue Paul's wife, stop this invasion and somehow get close enough to this reef to try and see if there is anything worth salvaging. Any ideas anyone?'

'Why don't we just tell the British here about it and then they can stop the French? Why do we need to get involved at all?' asked Emma.

'Because,' said Paul. 'As I said before, I'm damned sure that I'm not the only person reporting back to Victor. If he heard that his plans had been compromised there would be no doubt who had done it and then what would happen to Francine?'

'You're right Paul,' said Charles. 'The first thing we need to do is somehow thwart the invasion which will give us time to get over to Point a Pitre and rescue the lady.' Then seeing the look on Smithy's face. 'That should also allow us time to come back via this reef and check it out.'

'Hang on a second,' said Paul and he went and laid out another chart. 'Hugues will need to get here without being detected. The last part of the trip and the initial landing will have to be at night or at least at dawn. I've already thought about this as you can imagine. Now the best beach to land here,is just below the house but to get into the bay you have to sail past two reefs.'

'Tell us about it Paul,' said Jack. 'We had to pick our way in this morning. I'd forgotten how difficult things are without GPS. So, how were you thinking of guiding in ships in the darkness?'

'Simple, I set up some temporary leading lights. We put twin sets of lights here, here and here,' he said pointing to the chart. 'You just follow each set until the next line up and then turn.'

'So, if we accidentally moved the lights we could get the whole fleet to pile up on the rocks?'

'Hmm,' said Charles thoughtfully. 'You might get the first ship to run aground but the ones following would either see or hear something. Of course, they might then all collide with each other as they tried to turn around and if all the leading lights went out, they would all be in serious trouble, so yes it could work but what about warships? I presume they have some as well as transports. We saw a thirty six gun frigate on the way here. I don't think they will be tempted into shallow water. My guess is that they will stay offshore to fend off any attack by British warships.'

'Yes and we would need to ensure that the ships ended up where they aren't able to get their troops ashore, at least not until the British can be summoned. Even a small force will be enough to start to take over local estates to liberate and then arm the slaves. It's how they took Guadeloupe,' said Paul. 'Of course, once they are here then warning the British is no longer a problem for me. All we would have to do is ensure that the landings are such a mess that they don't get organised in time. We could even send a message to Fort de France the day before because all of Victor's fleet will be at sea by then.'

'Hmm, there may be the making of a plan there Paul,' said Jack. 'But how about rescuing your wife?'

'Well, if most of the military and especially Victor are mired down here we should be able to get to Guadeloupe pretty fast in Jacaranda and well before the news of any problems arrives. It should be quite easy to just walk in and collect her and then we can return via the reef at Gosier. It's probably about the only chance you'll get.'

'That still leaves the warships,' said Jack. 'What on earth do we do about them?'

'Nothing,' replied Charles. 'We use Jacaranda as Paul has suggested and simply outrun them.'

Ah, you've still got engines I take it then?' asked Paul.

'Only one I'm afraid due to a lack of oil but one should be enough.'

The rest of the afternoon was spent talking over detail and then before supper Jack invited Paul down to Jacaranda for a visit. Paul was keen to see what had been done to her and Jack wanted a private conversation away from the others.

'So Paul,' said Jack after they had looked around. 'The others know about this but I suspect they haven't realised the significance. I would value you expert opinion, after all you were in the Army for quite a while and had a thing for guns.'

He pulled open the Port side storage locker and motioned for Paul to look in. 'What do you think?'

'Ah,' responded Paul with a feral grin. 'That dear chap is what they call a force multiplier. I heard about these things but never actually saw one. It could make the whole thing so much easier.'

Chapter 35

Just over two weeks later and they were all once again sitting in Jacaranda's cockpit. Dawn wasn't far off and so far nothing had been seen. There were no bacon sandwiches this time. Everyone was tense and silent. The yacht was at a mooring well clear of the entrance to the bay but with a grandstand seat of the forthcoming activities. As soon as they dared they would be off to Guadeloupe, while hopefully the French would remain occupied here.

After their initial meeting Paul had reluctantly gone back to Guadeloupe to confer with Victor. When he returned he was at least able to report that Francine was well and being looked after in comfort by Marie Dubert. However, Paul's plan had been accepted and a date set. They needed a moonless night and tonight was it. Victor was going to put four transports into the bay and as expected the two frigates, Thetis and Pique, would stay out at sea to guard the landings. Victor would be on board the Thetis.

Emma whispered to Jack. 'Jack look over there, is that a light?' and she pointed towards the horizon to the north.

Jack followed her finger and saw it too. It was hard to see, the night was overcast so there wasn't even any starlight but it was flashing the agreed signal. Suddenly, two lights appeared on the shore one higher than the other.

'About bloody time too,' said Jack. 'Typical Frogs, they're almost two hours late. Let's hope it stays dark long enough.'

'Right,' said Paul. 'My people ashore are doing their job. We probably won't be able to see the other transits as the lights are shielded from the side. However, give it half an hour and all hell should break loose.'

'Especially if you end up using that bloody thing,' said Emma pointing to the deck forward of the cockpit where Paul had mounted the Special Forces rifle on its tripod.

'Contingency my dear, you know a plan never survives the first shot of the enemy. That little monster could just save the day.'

'And you're just dying to play with it aren't you?' However, Melissa's words were accompanied by an encouraging smile. She knew how good Paul was with guns and for once was really glad he was here.

'Believe it or not,' he replied with a catch in his voice. 'I pray we don't have to use it. I want the plan to work. I've only one aim and that's to rescue Francine. Nothing else matters to me.'

Melissa put her arm round him and gave him an encouraging hug. This was a different Paul and one she decided she now really liked. She just prayed that they were successful. There had almost been a dreadful row with Jack when she and Emma had insisted on coming along. But in the end it was agreed that it was probably safer at sea in Jacaranda than on shore with potentially hundreds of angry French soldiers rampaging around. It didn't stop a shiver of fear running through her. This could get very serious, very soon.

'There look,' said Jack interrupting her thoughts. 'It must be the stern light of the first transport.'

They watched as the first three ships, seen only by a blue lantern at their stern slid slowly past. The fourth ship needed no lights but Jack suddenly realised he could make out its bulk which could only mean that the sky was starting brighten.

Nothing happened for what seemed like hours but was probably only minutes. Suddenly, there was a groaning creaking noise followed by a large crash and distant shouting. At the same time all the shore lights went out.

'So, if Victor wasn't sure if he would be betrayed, he bloody well does now.' said Paul. 'Let's go.'

Jack nodded and Charles went up to the bow and got ready to cut the mooring cable with an axe. They had prepared for a quick getaway and this was by far the fastest way of getting clear.

Jack hit the engine start button and prayed. The engine churned over for a second and then caught with a satisfying growl and without further instruction, Charles swung the axe and severed the cable. He came aft and confirmed that the bow was clear. Jack pushed the throttle fully forward and turned Jacaranda towards the open sea.

Just as Charles was about to re-enter the cockpit his eye was caught by something in the water astern of them and very close.

'Jack, hard to starboard,' he shouted in something of a panic because what he had seen was the bow wave of an approaching ship and it was only a few yards away. Jack did as instructed instinctively, spinning the wheel fully to starboard and then looking astern and upwards as the bowsprit and the rest of a French warship rushed past them. The bow wave lifted Jacaranda and slewed her around and he had to fight the wheel to keep them clear. Only a few feet away, the tumblehome of a large frigate rushed past them. There was no time to react and luckily the same applied to the French crew. They were clearly at quarters. All the guns were run out and they could actually see the faces of some of the surprised crew staring out of the gun ports at them as they rushed past. Thinking fast, Jack slammed the throttle shut and the Frigate was suddenly clear but not before they heard alarmed shouts from her quarterdeck.

'Bugger, bugger,' exclaimed Jack. 'Shit, that was close and now we don't get to sneak away and get a head start.'

It was steadily getting lighter and they all saw the Frigate start to alter course.

'Come on Charles, what's she going to do? You're the expert.'

'Well, if it was me and the whole landing seemed to be going wrong and then I stumbled upon a strange vessel, even one this small, I think I might be inclined to shoot first and ask questions later.'

'Damn, right what do we do?' even as he spoke Jack slammed the throttle open again and turned away from the warship.

'What you're doing old chap. Get the hell out of it and run for Guadeloupe. Oh and keep a bloody good look out for the other frigate.'

'Bloody hell, good point. Right everyone keep your eyes skinned. There's another one of these buggers around somewhere.'

Jack started to feel a little easier as it became clear that they were pulling away from the enemy ship as she cumbersomely wore around. 'I think we'd better get some sails on her guys. He's going to be wondering what on earth is going on soon enough. Let's not pique his curiosity too much.'

It only took a few minutes to hoist the mainsail and a working jib. At least Jacaranda looked like a sailing ship now. It was lucky Jack had decided to hoist the sails because just as they were starting to relax again, Paul who had been looking over the side in the gathering light called to Jack. 'Hey old chap, I hate to be a spoilsport but should that exhaust be smoking like that?'

As he said it, the shrill scream of the engine warning system started and was almost immediately followed by a banging grinding noise from below somewhere as the engine ground to a halt.

'Jesus, that sounded pretty catastrophic,' said an anguished Jack. 'Charles come and take the wheel and keep us away from that frog. I'd better go below and see what's happened.'

It only took a moment to see the damage and Jack came straight back up. 'Well I'm sorry to say but the technical term for that engine begins in F and ends in Ucked. There's a con rod sticking through the crankcase I'm afraid. It's totally dead. What was that you said Paul, about plans and the enemy's first shot?'

Paul didn't answer he was on the coach roof tugging at their gun. 'Jack come here and give me hand, we need to mount this at the stern.'

The two of them struggled with the heavy weight of the gun and managed to reposition it so that Paul could fire it over Jacaranda's transom. In the distance, they could see the frigate had completed her turn and was setting of in pursuit.

'You know, it's lucky she didn't decide to fire her broadside at us as she wore round, she was well in range,' observed Charles as he studied the French ship now starting to become much clearer in the rapidly brightening daylight.

'Why do you think she didn't?' asked Jack as he continued to steer Jacaranda onto the best course for evasion.

'Probably because we were stern to and too small a target and of course we caught them a bit by surprise.'

'You can say that again. Shit what was that?' A flash from the front of the frigate was almost immediately followed by a rumbling roar and a large splash of water several hundred yards to port.'

'Jack, they're shooting at us,' shouted Emma with a note of hysteria in her voice.

'It's OK,' said Charles reassuringly. 'They may have the range but their chances of hitting us are tiny. We're too small a target.'

'Maybe,' said Paul from behind them. 'But we need to get away and without an engine it could be difficult, especially as we seem to be heading out into the Atlantic not towards Guadeloupe.'

'Sorry,' replied Jack. 'But with this wind if I turn that way, she'll probably be on a better point of sail and could catch us.'

'Well, let's see what I can do about that,' said Paul. 'What we need is twenty first century technology to help us out.'

Turning to his gun he selected a clip of high explosive rounds and inserted it into the weapon. He then pressed a release button on the side of the rounded bulk and what could only be a sight of some sort sprang up into place.

'I see you've been RTFIing,' said Jack as he saw Paul's preparations. This got him a puzzled look. 'Reading The Fucking Instructions,' he explained.

Paul grinned back. 'Oh yes old son and I know what this thing can do. The only problem might be that these rounds need something solid to hit to make them go off. If they only hit wood they'll probably go straight through that bloody ship and out the other side. However, I know how to solve that problem.'

As he spoke, the frigate fired her other bow chaser. The result was no better this time. Paul laughed derisively and lay down looking through the sight.

On the frigate Pique, the ships Master Gunner was preparing the starboard long nine pounder to fire again. The First Lieutenant was standing by him and not helping by continually exhorting him and his crew to greater efforts. *'Didn't the bloody man realise the chances of actually hitting a small sloop at this distance were tiny and anyway the damned thing was pulling away and would soon be totally out of range,'* he thought grimly.

No one saw the little red dot appear on the side of the gun. Even if they had, it wouldn't have meant anything. However, half a second later, a one inch, high explosive round, travelling at two thousand metres per second, hit the base of the gun carriage. It carried right through the wood of carriage until it impacted the metal of the gun barrel, where it detonated. The carriage disintegrated immediately but the thick iron of the cannon's barrel withstood the blast. Unfortunately the charge of gunpowder inside the barrel was set off and the gun fired. With no carriage to restrain it, the massive iron barrel flew backwards, straight through the First Lieutenant, turning him into a mass of gore in an instant. It then continued down the gun deck causing mayhem as it went, until it impacted one of the cannons half way down the ship and came to a smoking rest. The Master Gunner wasn't hit but the blast shredded the front of his torso. His last conscious thought was a puzzled satisfaction that at last that bloody officer had stopped shouting at him. Then the world turned black.

On the upper deck there was stunned silence for a second and then before anyone could react further the bottom of the foremast simply disappeared in a cloud of metal shards and splinters. Suddenly sheared from its base, the remains of the mast dropped to the deck before the whole assembly tilted to port and toppled over the side in a clattering tangle of rigging. The main mast took the strain for a second before exactly the same thing happened. The base inexplicably exploded before the remaining crew's startled eyes.

On Jacaranda there was a cheer as the two masts fell and the frigate slewed around out of control. Clearly she was no longer a threat.

'Bloody hell Paul, how did you do that? You only fired three times.' asked an amazed Jack.

Paul grinned back. 'These rounds actually steer themselves to a degree. All I have to do is keep the sights on the target and the rounds correct their trajectory. I aimed at the base of the masts because they always have large iron bands around them at that point. Just the thing to ensure that the rounds would go off.'

'Well she's not a threat anymore and no doubt the Royal Navy will have a new prize in due course,' observed Charles.

'Yes but how many people were killed?' asked Melissa with concern.

Charles put his arm around her and kissed her forehead. 'Always the humanitarian my love and the answer is probably very few. I don't think you could disable a frigate so effectively without some bloodshed but just remember they were trying to kill us. They fired first.'

'Good point,' said Jack. 'But we now have another problem, look over there.'

Several miles to the north the other frigate, the Thetis was under full sail making a fine sight as the early morning sun illuminated her massive spread of canvas. But she wasn't a threat to Jacaranda she was heading north, clearing the area and heading back towards Guadeloupe.

On the deck of Thetis, Victor Hugues was beyond rage. No one had dared to come near him since his shouting match with the Captain. He had seen the results of the betrayal by that bastard La Croix when the leading lights on shore all went out at the same time. Now it was daylight, the wrecks of his transports could be seen. Two were fast aground on a reef and the other two were entangled together. Not one had all their masts standing. He had briefly considered going ashore anyway to rally the survivors. Most of the troops would probably have been able to make it to the beach but then he realised that if he had been betrayed then the bloody British were probably waiting in ambush anyway. And then inexplicably his other frigate had been dismasted while chasing some piddling little local boat. Quite what her Captain had been thinking he couldn't even guess at. When the Captain of Thetis had exhorted him to go to their aid, he exploded in anger, telling the man that they could go to hell for all he cared. Even through the red mist he knew he must get back to Guadeloupe as soon as he could. He had enough troops left there to maintain order, just. His plans might have come to nothing but he was damned if was going to take any further hurt. And there was that pretty young wife who he could at least wreak some vengeance on. For the first time in hours he actually smiled.

Chapter 36

The look of anguish on Paul's face said it all. Their carefully laid plan, to use the diversion of the attack on the Martinique to slip away and rescue Francine, lay in tatters.

Jack put a hand on his shoulder. 'It's not over yet mate, this is a quick boat and faster than that garbage scow up ahead. We can still get to your wife first and I think I might be able to get us some diesel power as well.'

'Eh? I thought you said the engine had thrown a rod. You're not going to repair that this century.'

'Of course not but I've got the other engine which I might just be able to persuade into action. It was only a lack of oil that meant I could only run the one. Let me get below and see. Why don't you come and help? Charles and the girls can sail the boat pretty well without us. Can't you?' he asked, looking at them all.

Charles nodded, conscious that Jack was trying to keep Paul busy and his mind off what might happen. Smithy offered to help as well, so the three of them went down to the engine room.

It was obvious what had happened as soon as they entered the cramped space. The side of the engine was a broken splintered mess. Black oil was splattered over the walls and floor.

'Right,' said Jack, 'we need to retrieve as much oil out of the old engine as we can. Smithy, go and see if you can find an old sheet or something to strain it through, we'll see how much we can recover.'

An hour later they had managed to transfer as much of the oil as they could from the blown engine. It wasn't enough.

'OK, what we need to do now is try to recover some of the old stuff which I kept in these cans over here. It's horribly contaminated with sea water though.'

Smithy had an idea. 'Maybe if we heated it up we could boil off some of the water, would that work?'

'Worth a try. You and Paul start on a sample and I'll just check up top and see what's going on. We don't need much good oil to give us enough.'

As Jack poked his head up into the cockpit, Charles had just returned from the foredeck where he had hoisted their biggest foresail. Jacaranda was responding well and a gurgling wake was surging from below her counter and streaming astern in a crisp white line.

'Any idea how fast we're going?' asked Jack.

Emma answered. 'She only starts making that noise when we're over eight knots so I would think nine or so Jack. It's just a shame we have no instruments left.'

'And what about that bugger over there?' he asked looking ahead at the frigate who was also making a good speed.

'Well he's not gaining but we're not catching him either. If we could get closer we could get Paul to have a go at him with his rifle but he's well out of range at the moment,' replied Charles. 'Still, with this wind, we should easily make Guadeloupe in daylight, which is a definite bonus.'

'Good point. If we can get the engine going we might be able to make time on him as we go behind Marie Galante although the island is too low to give too much of a wind shadow.'

They settled down into the chase. If wasn't for the gravity of the situation Jack would have been loving it. A blue sky and clear blue sea, accompanied by a fifteen knot trade wind made for perfect sailing conditions. Jacaranda, despite her eighteenth century modifications, was flying. It wasn't long before Smithy poked his head up with a rather messy looking saucepan in his hands.

'Jack, have a look. When we heat this up some goes into lumps but we do seem to get some clear oil. What do you reckon?'

Jack looked at the mess in the saucepan. 'The first thing I think is that Emma is going to murder you for destroying her saucepan. But yes if we strain that lot off the top it looks useable and anyway what else can we do. Go for it.'

'Jack, have you any idea why your engine went bang like that?' asked Charles. 'I only ask because it would be good to know if the same will happen to the other one.'

'Good question, all I can think of is that the strain we put on them during the hurricane and then water contaminating the oil damaged something inside like the oil pump. I have no way of checking the other engine, so we're in the lap of the gods I'm afraid. However, if we get this one working, I'm going to treat it with kid gloves, believe me.'

An hour later, Paul called Jack down to the engine room. He showed him the dipstick which was now registering just above the minimum level.

'What say we give it a go Jack? I've checked the raw water system and even put a new impeller in.'

'I guess we've got nothing to lose. Why don't you do the honours? There's a start switch and auxiliary throttle just there.' Jack pointed to the side of the engine.

Paul set the throttle and pressed the start switch. The engine started turning over but clearly didn't want to fire.

'Hold on,' said Jack and he opened a fuel bleed valve and then told Paul to try again. As the engine turned over air bubbles came out of the bleed for a few seconds and then it turned into a jet of pure fuel. Jack shut the valve and the engine roared into life.

The three of them grinned at each other like small children. Jack then shot up to the helm position and checked the oil pressure gauge which was showing a healthy reading and looked over the side and to his final relief saw a clear exhaust with no smoke but a with healthy trail of cooling water spitting out.

The day wore on and the chase continued. The breeze was so good that despite their efforts to recover the engine, actually using it didn't seem to add to their speed. Jack decided to keep it in reserve. At one point they saw the frigate spill the wind from her sails but she very quickly regained her course and speed. No one could account for her actions but whatever she was up to it didn't help them catch her up significantly.

Smithy and Paul came in for a severe ticking off from Emma when she discovered what they had done to her galley and several large pots and pans. Comments about 'bloody men not being ever allowed near her galley again' only raised smiles all round. However, despite all their efforts to trim Jacaranda for more speed, they didn't seem to be gaining any distance on their quarry. That all changed in the middle of the afternoon.

Charles had been steering and was looking up at the masthead wind vane. 'Jack, I'm having to get harder on the wind to maintain course but the wind hasn't shifted drastically. I think the current is building.'

Jack looked all around. Dominica was disappearing astern and Guadeloupe was clearly in sight. The moon was up and he did a quick mental calculation. 'Well with that big moon up there, we are on spring tides and we're now getting the first of six hours of the ebb which is going to add to the normal east west current. Do you think that heading up into it will mean we can't make Point a Pitre?'

'No but it's going to a problem for our frigate friend over there. He's already as close to the wind as he can get and the current will be stronger in an hour or so,' and with a note of optimism he continued. 'We should easily be able to out sail him now Jack. To get to Point a Pitre, he's going to have to tack up wind. We should be able to get in hours before him.' He gave Paul an encouraging slap on the back and Paul even managed a smile in return.

Sure enough, as the minutes ticked by the Frigate started sagging down to leeward. What was even better was that he couldn't tack back upwind because Marie Gallant was in the way. It would take several hours before they cleared the island by which time Jacaranda would be well away.

However, Charles then pointed out that as they sailed past they could easily get within cannon range. Marie Gallant was now limiting their own ability to get further to windward and so they watched the large warship with trepidation as they started to haul past. Paul went to his rifle which had been lashed down securely and turned it around to face the new threat.

'Just in case, you understand, I don't need to use it now that we should get there first by some margin but you never know,' he said grimly.

No one argued.

Just as they were drawing ahead, someone on the frigate must have finally decided that the cheeky little sloop was in fact an enemy. Suddenly, smoke wreathed the ship and the concussive boom of cannon fire was heard. They all instinctively ducked, not that it would have made any difference if any of the shot had struck home. Luckily, none did although one cannon ball made a neat hole through the working jib.

'Right Paul, you've got about three minutes to give them something to think about,' said Charles. Of course if that was a British ship, it would be less than two. History is quite clear who was the best at gunnery in this age.' He added slightly smugly.

Paul needed no second bidding and was already lying down and sighting the massive rifle on its tripod.

'Not going to be so easy now,' he said grimly. 'Last time we were in light winds with the deck level. With this big swell, life this is going to much more difficult.'

He started looking through the sight and the realised something else. 'Sorry guys but with her heeled over like that I can't see the base of any of the masts. Charles where else are there large lumps of metal I can aim at?'

Charles thought for a second. 'Can you see the rudder Paul? It will be held on by large iron brackets.'

Paul looked carefully. 'Sorry Charles but we're too far ahead. I can't see her stern at all. That leaves the anchors or the gun ports.'

'Go for the gun ports Paul. Whatever you achieve will surprise them and hopefully put them off their aim.'

Paul grunted acknowledgement and concentrated on his own aim. He fired several shots with no discernible effect. 'Christ it's hard to keep the sights on target,' he exclaimed. 'If it's not him rolling it's us. This damned gun was never intended to be used like this.'

The frigate was rolling hard across the beam swell and showing her weed strewn copper hull. Paul had an idea.

'Charles how thick is that copper?'

'If the French use the same as us, then about half an inch. They only started using it recently after they discovered how the Royal Navy was able to out sail them at the battle of the Saintes'

'Right that should do nicely. That's a nice big target.'

Pauls next shot was aimed at the hull as it crested a wave. The effect was discernible to all of them even at long range. A large portion of the hull exploded outwards and a gaping hole several feet square appeared. It disappeared as the ship rolled back. Paul repeated the trick again and then suddenly the frigate spun into wind and stopped. Shooting at the little sloop was clearly no longer a priority.

'Bloody hell Paul,' exclaimed Jack. 'I can see she's lower in the water already.'

Indeed, it was soon apparent to everyone that the frigate was slowly foundering. Suddenly streams of water appeared from the side as the desperate crew got their pumps working.

'Will they be alright?' asked Melissa.

'Who gives a toss?' asked Paul.

'I do. Come on they're only doing their job.'

'They should be alright Melissa,' said Charles. 'There is every chance they can plug the holes, especially now they have their pumps going. They should have ship's boats enough to get most of the crew off if they have to and it's not that far to land. Anyway there is nothing we can do. I don't think they would take kindly to us offering assistance. They may not know how we did it but they will certainly know we were responsible.'

Jacaranda swiftly pulled away but they were all relieved to see that the frigate didn't seem to be actually sinking. However, it was also clear that she was no longer a threat.

Jack took a couple of quick bearings of land with a small compass and disappeared below. When he came back he looked pleased. 'It's about fourteen more miles to go. We should be there in a couple of hours. Paul, any ideas about where to go?'

Paul considered the question carefully. 'I strongly suggest we don't go into the main anchorage. We should be able to claim we're just a trading vessel but if we have to leave in a hurry things could get dodgy. Their third frigate will almost certainly be moored in the harbour for a start. Apparently she's not seaworthy anymore but she still has her cannon on board. Anyway, we shouldn't keep repeating this habit of shooting them up,' he said with a lopsided grin. 'No, there's a creek before the main anchorage. Jack will know it. In the future it's where they build the new marina. If we anchor there, as many of the smaller ships do, we will have a good escape route.'

Victor Hugues smiled grimly to himself in satisfaction as he stepped ashore. Getting the frigate Captain to drop him off in the ship's cutter had been the right thing to do once the man had explained that with the turning of the tide they would be unlikely to make Point a Pitre that day. The frigate had luffed into wind and they had launched quickly and sped away. The little boat had been wet but fast and quite able to maintain a direct course for the town, unlike its big, ungainly, square rigged, parent. His plans were in a mess but he still had this island and there was a pretty little woman who would pay for her husband's betrayal.

Chapter 37

Pascal and Marie Dubert together with Francine La Croix were just sitting down to dinner when the door flew open with a crash.

Victor stood in the doorway. 'Betrayed,' he shouted at them all. 'Betrayed by your pernicious husband madam,' he continued, with spittle flying off his lips as he pointed at Francine. 'He may have escaped my wrath but believe me, you will not.'

Pascal had pushed his chair back and stood up at Victor's unannounced entrance. 'I have no idea what you're talking about Victor but how dare you enter my house in this fashion?'

'How dare I? I dare because this is my bloody island and I rule here. I don't need you permission to arrest a spy.'

'She is no spy Sir,' interjected Marie. 'How can you say that? She's been here with me all the time.'

'And hostage to her husband's good behaviour, you stupid woman, surely you worked that out? Everyone else has. And now the invasion of Martinique has failed because her damned husband lured my ships into a trap. All my transports and soldiers are lost because of his duplicity.'

Pascal was totally taken aback by the announcement. 'What, the whole fleet? How could that happen?'

'It seems our good madam's husband here set the leading lights to wreck them on the reefs, not guide them in as promised. As soon as the first one went aground all the lights were extinguished and the rest foundered as well. I have no doubt that the British were waiting for my men who will now all be prisoners, those that haven't drowned, that is. Do you honestly believe this bastard La Croix did not discuss his plans with his wife? Did she warn you or me? She is just as guilty as he is. Now hand her over. I have arranged some stocks for her in the town square. She can entertain my remaining troops for the night before she meets madam guillotine tomorrow morning.'

Francine had withdrawn as far away from Victor as she could. She was shaking and looked terrified. Pascal had seen her reaction. He had come to like this shy young girl since she had arrived and been a guest in his house. Suddenly, his own rage came to a head.

'No! Absolutely not. You might like to remember that you are not the only commissioner on the island. In fact until you arrived, I was the commissioner here. You may be right about Jacques but you definitely do not have the right or the power to order such a disgusting thing.'

Victor took a step back at the vehemence in Pascal's response. Nobody had ever spoken to him like that in recent times. Unfortunately, he had to acknowledge the truth behind Pascal's statement. Paris had been quite insistent on two commissioners ruling the island. It was only because the idiot Michel had died that he felt justified in taking sole charge. He had completely forgotten that technically, Pascal had the same rank. Until now the man had seemed content to stay in the background. He considered what to do.

'Very well, but she cannot stay here. I will take her to the jail where she can spend her last night.'

Marie then proved that she was made of sterner stuff than Victor had imagined. 'In that case, I will accompany her Sir. I can then make sure she is not abused in any way.' She stared defiantly at Victor.

Realising he had been outflanked he gave a curt nod and called for the two soldiers who had been waiting outside to escort the two women away. Marie led a trembling, sobbing, Francine through the door.

Victor turned to Pascal. 'If you want to play at being a commissioner Pascal, you will sit with me to oversee her execution. Tomorrow, at dawn.' And he turned and strode angrily out.

The sun was just beginning to set when Jacaranda came to anchor in the little creek. As soon as she was secure, Paul and Charles went ashore in the little wooden dinghy they kept on the foredeck. It had been agreed that there was no need for them all to go and retrieve Francine. Hopefully they would return in a couple of hours and could be on their way back to Martinique at day break.

The four of them had shared a simple meal and were waiting quietly in the cockpit when they heard the splash of oars. Jack looked in the direction of the noise and was relieved to see the outline of three bodies. His relief turned to surprise when a strange man came on board after Paul and Charles. When he saw the look on Paul's face he realised something was very wrong indeed. They all went below.

'Jack, Smithy, Emma, Melissa this is Pascal Dubert, my contact here. He and his wife have been looking after Francine while I was away.'

'Well, where is she then?' asked Emma.

'I'm afraid that Victor Hugues got here first and arrested her. He took the frigate's cutter and arrived several hours before us. That must have been when we saw the frigate spill her wind for a few minutes this morning. We didn't see the cutter because it was on her far side.'

'So what is he going to do with Francine?' asked Melissa.

Pascal answered. 'She goes to her death tomorrow morning at dawn. She shares your guilt Jacques. The guillotine is already in place in the town square.'

Jack looked at the newcomer. 'Why are you helping us Sir? I'm sure you know what happened on Martinique only this morning. Surely we are enemies?'

Pascal looked pained. 'You are correct Monsieur but I have to balance my allegiance to my revolution and its principles and my allegiance to my friends. Hugues is not a true revolutionary. He serves himself. So, in this case shall I. The man is a brutal monster at times. I have come to know Francine La Croix very well over the last weeks and she does not deserve what Hugues is planning. I can help only a little. Indeed I will be one of the two people sitting in supervision no matter how much it pains me. There is no way I can possibly intervene, you understand?'

Paul and Jack both nodded. Pascal continued. 'I can explain where she is being held and how she is being guarded but no more. After that, I must leave things to you.'

'That's alright,' said Paul. 'We understand.'

The two of them spoke privately for another half an hour and then Paul took Pascal ashore before returning. When they were all back below Jack spoke first. 'Right, Paul and Charles, you're the military types. What on earth do we do?'

'How many SA 80s do we have Jack?' asked Paul grimly.

Jack frowned, he knew where this was going but he had to answer. 'We've got five of them and about a thousand rounds of ammunition. Also, there are five nine millimetre pistols, two boxes of hand grenades, some Semtex and detonators. I guess we could blow quite a lot of people up and then shoot the survivors.'

Charles broke in. 'I've seen those weapons Paul. Although I've no real idea of how effective they could really be. But there are six of us here and despite what I know my wife is about to say,' and he gave Melissa a warning look, 'the girls cannot be involved. In reality that means four of us, of whom only one person, you, knows how to fight with them.'

Paul replied. 'Let me stop you there Charles. For goodness sake, why do you all think I want to walk in guns and grenades blazing? I can do subtle as well you know. But one thing you must understand, I don't leave this island without Francine.'

They all hear the steel of determination in Paul's voice. Jack answered for them. 'We understand Paul and we've all agreed to help. So come on it's your shout.'

'Pascal has told me where she is being held and one complication is that his wife is also with her. Apparently, she volunteered to ensure that Victor didn't decide to take out more revenge on her overnight. God that man's a bastard. Anyway, they are in the town jail which unfortunately for us is right in the middle of the town and the building is part of the military garrison headquarters. Apparently, there are still five hundred or so troops based there. Our friend Victor didn't want to lose control of this island while trying to take ours.'

'So, what you're saying is that a direct assault on the jail is going to be problematical?' asked Charles.

Paul laughed. 'I think a better word would be suicidal. Even with modern weapons. You might remember that one of the problems last time we used modern guns in the past was that no one recognised them for what they were. Consequently, we would need mass slaughter to make our point. I can't think of any other way than to wait until they bring her out. We can position ourselves around the square and then use the rifles and maybe a few grenades to scatter everyone and rescue her.'

'Bloody hell, that sounds risky Paul,' said Jack frowning. 'Surely we can do something before that?'

'What?' Paul almost shouted. 'She's surrounded by hundreds of troops. On top of that, Pascal is terrified his wife will also get caught up in anything we try. I promised him she wouldn't be harmed, OK?'

'Paul, Jack, I've kept out of this so far.' Smithy was looking anguished. 'Please don't doubt me. I will help as much as I can. I can use a rifle believe it or not but one thing is very important. You must not shoot Victor Hugues. Whatever happens, he must survive tomorrow.'

'Why Smithy? He's the bastard who's already committed dozens of atrocities by all accounts. What do you think he'll continue to do?' Paul was looking really angry.

'Just hear me out Paul, this is too important. Please?'

'Go on.'

'The history is quite clear. Hugues stays in command on Guadeloupe and commissions a number of Privateers to terrorise the whole area. It causes a great deal of trouble for several years.'

'Sounds like a good reason for blowing his brains out then,' said Paul grimly.

'No, you don't understand. It eventually brings America into the war on the British side against him and the French. Hugues eventually gets recalled and gets his just deserts back in France but we just can't risk such large change in history especially between what will become the next superpowers.'

'So much for butterflies farting then,' said Paul.

'I know but surely we can rescue Francine anyway?' asked Smithy. 'Not having a go at Hugues shouldn't affect that.'

'I suppose so,' responded Paul looking even more worried. 'OK Smithy, you've made your point. I just hope you were right when you say you can use a rifle because I do have a plan and you're part of it.'

Smithy just nodded.

'Right everyone, I need to give you a crash course in modern weapons. The boys get the rifles but girls I've got a little task for you two as well. It will be away from the main action but may make all the difference. Now, this will take a while and we haven't got much time.'

Chapter 38

Paul lay on his stomach waiting. The tension was getting to him. He was having to actively force himself to stay calm. The comfort of the SA80 rifle against his cheek was the only thing that kept his heart rate down. He kept telling himself that with it his plan had every chance of success. He looked down into the town square from his vantage point in the little bell tower of the church. It was still dark but wouldn't be for much longer. He knew that at several other points around the square the other men were getting ready as well, although in their cases the weapons were concealed under their coats ready for use only after he had initiated the rescue. The girls were also out there somewhere, some distance away but nevertheless with an essential role to play. He just prayed that he had thought things through correctly and that just for once things would go even slightly according to plan. He was going to be disappointed.

Victor Hugues was snoring loudly. His servant had been told to rouse him before dawn but he couldn't get him to wake up. The empty wine bottles lying around the bed were testimony to the reason. The servant didn't dare touch the man. Last time he had, Victor had lashed out instinctively and caught him quite a blow in the testicles. The servant wasn't going to risk that again. He then tracked down his assistant, who just shrugged and told him to wait until Victor woke up. Everyone was aware that Victor needed to be there for the execution at dawn. The one he had so hastily arranged the previous night. However, everyone also accepted that it would now have to wait until he awoke. A message was sent to the jail to that effect. Two hours later an angry and very hungover Victor screamed for his servant and the day finally got underway.

'What the bloody hell is going on?' whispered Jack through the corner of his mouth. 'It's been ages since dawn. Did the Frenchman get it all wrong?'

'I've no idea,' responded Charles. 'Hopefully it's just some form of administrative delay. What's worrying me more is all these people appearing. The word is obviously out now. It's really going to complicate things.'

'Well, we can still do our bit. I just hope Paul and the girls have the patience to wait it out.'

'Well, what did you see?' asked Melissa.

'Nothing,' replied Emma. 'The square is filling up with people but there's no sign of any activity. There must be some delay. Anyway, we'd better get back in position. I'm going back to the dock. You'd better get back as well.'

'Right. fingers crossed, at least all these people must think something is going to happen soon.'

Francine La Croix was in a state of catatonic, supernatural calm. The terror of the previous evening had faded into the distance. She felt almost as if she was floating. She knew if she allowed her fears to overwhelm her she would totally break down. She just shut everything out. She had even given up on the idea that Jacques would somehow be able to rescue her. No, he was miles away in Martinique and could offer no help. Her one regret was that neither of them would get to see the child growing inside her. She hadn't even noticed that the light had been brightening for several hours before the door opened and two soldiers grabbed her by the arms pulling her roughly to her feet. Marie Dubert, who had been with her all night just sat down and sobbed.

Victor had a seething headache. *'So he was a little late. He ruled here didn't he?'* he thought testily as he sat down in his chair next to Pascal, who gave him a withering stare but wisely said nothing. Just then the doors to the Marie opened and soldiers brought out the prisoners.

'What is going on Victor? I thought this was just for the La Croix girl?'

'Hah, why waste a good execution session on one pathetic female. I've got twenty more Aristos here from Basse Terre. They can all suffer my justice at the same time. Now who'll feel the kiss of the blade first I wonder?'

Paul felt he was going mad but there was absolutely nothing he could do. He saw Francine brought out with a gaggle of other prisoners, about twenty in all. They were hours late and the bloody square was now teeming with people. He looked down the telescopic sight of his rifle and with alarm realised he couldn't see the guillotine properly any more. There was a press of local people in the way. He would bloody well shoot through them if he had to but if he couldn't see his target then he wouldn't achieve the desired result. He tried moving and managed to get one side of the guillotine in sight. It would have to be enough.

Suddenly, Victor Hugues appeared on the far side and sat down next to Pascal. They seemed to confer for a moment and then Hugues stood up and started speaking. He was too far away for Paul to make out what he was saying but the baying reaction of the crowd made his meaning quite clear. For a second Paul had a crystal sharp picture of the man in his rifle's sight. All it would take would be a little pressure of his finger and the bastard's head would be splattered all over the wall behind him. He started to tense and then forced himself to relax. It wasn't because of Smithy. It was simply not part of the plan and shooting Hugues could easily jeopardise everything..

Something had been said because two soldiers brought Francine forward. Victor said something and the soldiers started to force her on her knees. She didn't resist. The crowd surged forward and suddenly his view was completely blocked. Frantically he stood up but it was almost too late. The wooden stock was already in place and the executioner was about to reach for the handle to release the blade.

Time stood still for a second and then the executioners head literally exploded. He fell backwards on to the sand, which was already covered with his blood and brains.

'Oh thank you, thank you, whoever it was who fired that shot.'

The crowd panicked as more shots rang out. Paul suddenly had the clear view of the guillotine that he needed. He sighted more carefully than he had ever done in his life and squeezed the trigger three times and then ran down the stairs praying he would be in time.

His first shot would have been enough. It hit the wooden wedge holding the stocks in place and shattered the whole locking mechanism. He next two actually missed as there was nothing left to hit. By the time it took him to get to the guillotine, Jack and Charles were already there helping Francine to her feet. She took one look at Paul and all her reserve broke. She flung herself on him crying and laughing at the same time.

'No time Paul, we've got to get out of here now,' yelled Charles over the frightened screams of the crowd. People were running in all directions not helped by the continual firing of a weapon which must have convinced them that they were under attack by a large force of some sort.

Suddenly there was a loud explosion from the dock area, almost immediately followed by one from the rear of the barracks. If he didn't know better, Charles would have thought it was a full scale attack. The explosions kept coming and suddenly the square was empty except for the shackled prisoners who couldn't run because of their chains. Jack ran over to them, pulled out a pistol and fired at the chain which flew apart. 'Run for your lives,' he shouted. They needed no second bidding.

'Come on Jack,' shouted Paul who was already on the far side of the square.

'One last thing,' he yelled back. Reaching into his small backpack he retrieved a hand grenade and pulled out the pin. He carefully placed it at the base of the Guillotine and then ran as fast as he could as the priming handle released. He had almost made it to the others when it exploded. They all turned to watch as the hated device flew apart. Surprisingly, the metal blade stayed intact and was fired up its track and exited spinning in the air end over end. The silver blade catching the sunlight as it flew.

'Oh shit, it's heading this way,' said Jack. Who nevertheless remained riveted to the spot in fascination as it wickered past them and dug into the doorframe of a house with a solid thunk.

'They'll not be using that again,' said Charles as he tugged it free. 'My souvenir I think.'

'Come on you silly sods,' called Smithy who had broken cover from behind a garden fence. 'I've used up all my ammunition and we really need to get the hell out of here.'

An hour later, Jacaranda was heading out of the anchorage under engine power. Francine was down below being checked out by Melissa, who had managed to prize Paul's hand out hers, only with the promise that it wouldn't take long and he wouldn't be far away.

In the cockpit everyone was sharing a bottle of brandy. As Paul put his glass to his lips, he realised just how badly his hand was shaking as the reaction set in. Nevertheless, he raised his glass to them all.

'What can I say my friends? A toast to you all, especially to whoever it was who fired that first shot.'

Smithy looked embarrassed. 'I'm afraid that was me Paul. It seemed the right thing to do even though you threatened us with blue murder if any of us fired before you.'

Paul clapped him on the back. 'Well you and Nelson both my friend. Thank God for people who can think for themselves. By the way, did anyone see what happened to that bastard Hugues?'

Smithy answered. 'He ran away at my first shot, the bloody coward. At least some of the soldiers made an attempt to see what was going on. And despite what I said last night, yes I was sorely tempted to take a shot at him. Luckily he legged it too fast. Why is it bullies always seen to be cowards as well?'

Paul grinned back. 'Yes, I too had him in sights to for a second. I wonder if he will ever know just how lucky he was today?'

Melissa came up followed by Francine. 'She's fine Paul and it looks like the baby is too.' And she turned to Francine and introduced her properly to everyone.

'Thank you too girls,' Paul responded, when the introductions were over and Francine was sat by him holding his hand once again. 'Those explosions really had the effect I wanted. It must have soundedd like a whole army attacking.'

Melissa laughed. 'Well Paul, it's something I've always wanted to do. How often do you get the chance to chuck hand grenades all over the place?'

Francine was looking puzzled. Paul caught her look, 'what's the matter my dear?'

'Why is everyone calling you Paul?'

Chapter 39

Jack looked over at Smithy. He seemed pensive. 'What's up Smithy, you look like you're sucking a lemon?'

'Oh, sorry Jack, it's just that we seem to be heading out to sea. Isn't Gosier over there to the left?'

'Oh I see, sorry I should have explained. We need to get off shore a bit. Firstly, because there are quite a lot of reefs off this bit of coast and also because if you look over there you will see a fort and I want to be out of cannon range. Don't worry, Devil Ship reef is next on the passage plan.'

Smithy looked relieved. 'Thanks mate, how long do you reckon before we get there?'

'Oh not long, less than hour.'

'Right, I'll just go down and check out the magnetometer.'

'Fine but don't be surprised if you hear a lot of noise up here. I'm going to get the sails on her to disguise the fact that we're motoring. I know the wind's quite light today but we shouldn't give the locals too much to wonder about.'

'What about the soldiers at the town?'

'They're going to running around with their trousers on fire back in Point a Pitre for a while yet. No, we should be left alone where we're going.'

Half an hour later Jack was regretting his last remark. With all sails set but hardly drawing as the wind was so light, they rounded the western point of Gosier Bay.

'Oh shit, that's definitely going to complicate things just a tad,' exclaimed Jack.

'You're not wrong there,' replied Charles. 'I guess we didn't see her before because her topmasts are down and they've got her over at such an angle.'

Up against the shore at the far end of the bay, the frigate Thetis had been beached and careened. Her damaged starboard hull was clear of the water and clustered around it were members of the crew clearly repairing Paul's damage from the previous day.

'Well, at least they all survived,' said Melissa.

'I suppose so and they certainly can't fire their guns at us with her over at that angle,' added Charles.

It was suddenly clear that they had been spotted. A flurry of activity started up on the beach.

'So, what do we do Jack?' asked Smithy worriedly.

'Carry on, at least for the moment. The reef is just over there. I don't see what they can do to interfere, at least for the moment.'

'Yes well, if you don't mind I might just go and get my little rifle back up. Just in case, you understand,' said Paul.

'Fine but let's try not to use it this time,' responded Jack. 'I'm getting a little fed up with shooting at people.'

Jacaranda slipped across the bay staying well clear of the careened frigate and approached the reef at the far end. The water was crystal clear and flat calm but they could all see the swell piling up on the far side and the odd wave still managing to crash over the rocks.

'Sorry Jack but our French friends clearly want some revenge. They've obviously recognised us,' called Charles pointing astern.

Creeping out from the shore, were two boats with banked oars either side. Mounted in the bows of one was clearly a cannon.

'How long until they're in range Charles?' asked Jack anxiously.

'Not long, five minutes no more.'

'Damn, well we're clearly not going to have time to search the reef.'

'Paul, can't you stop them with your rifle?' asked Smithy

There was a chorus of 'No' from the girls and Jack who summed it up for all of them. 'I am not going to be responsible for killing anyone when I can simply out run them.'

'But Jack,' said Smithy. 'You of all people, know what this means.'

'Yes but I won't be responsible for indulging your desires by cold blooded murder. Whatever you might discover, it's not worth that.'

Smithy could hear the steel in Jack's tone and part of him agreed anyway. Shooting that man back in the town had affected him more than he thought it would.

'Alright but can you at least get me reasonably close to the reef, please?'

'Certainly, it's on our way out anyway.'

As Jacaranda approached the shallow water, Jack turned her towards the open sea and they slowly skirted the edge of the reef. All the while he was keeping an eye on the pursuing cutters but it was clear they were making little headway against Jacaranda's diesel powered progress.

Smithy turned on his detector expecting little as they were still quite a distance away from the main reef. To his and everyone else's surprise, the buzzer immediately went off.

'Well there's something there alright, can anybody see anything?' Smithy asked anxiously as he peered towards the reef.

Despite everyone looking intently, the reef seemed to be just that; rocks coral and sand. There was definitely nothing that looked like a wreck or even the remains of one.

Sadly, as they came to the end, Smithy turned off the machine. 'It's a shame I couldn't have at least rigged up some form of signal meter. It would have allowed me to see where the signal was strongest and get a better idea of where the main mass was.'

He turned to Jack clearly about to formulate a question.

Jack answered before he could speak. 'No Smithy, we can't go back. They would be waiting for us. Anyway it doesn't matter does it?'

'Eh? How do you work that out?'

'Well, if we were picking up the main generators of Poseidon on you detector then a mass of metal that large is bound to still be there when we get back to our time isn't it? It will have been underwater so should be as pristine as you want.'

'You've got a point there. I'm pretty sure that this wasn't an area we looked at when we surveyed, so yes, good thinking Jack.'

Jacaranda headed away from Guadeloupe, leaving two boat loads and a town of angry Frenchmen well astern.

Two weeks later, it was another departure. The party the night before had been a celebration and a form of wake. Emma knew she was never going to see Charles and Melissa again and she was finding that a little difficult. She also realised she was going to miss Paul and his delightful wife. However, Smithy made it clear that the longer they tarried the more difficult it might be to get home and so here they were on the small jetty below Paul's estate about to say their goodbyes.

'Are you sure you don't want to come with us Paul? Or any of the rest of you for that matter?' Jack asked looking at his friends. 'You would all be very welcome and Smithy says it should be no problem.'

Melissa just hugged Charles and smiled.

Paul looked thoughtful. 'I might miss cars and television and all that stuff now that I remember it all. But I also remember my recent years here with Francine and to use the old cliché, they really have been the happiest years of my life. Francine and I have talked about it. You won't be surprised to know that we both agree that staying here and raising our family is what we want to do. So sorry Jack, no deal.' Francine just put her arms round Paul's waist and nodded agreement.

'Well, that's about it then I guess. The British seem to have been pretty grateful. Not surprising really as they got three transports, a frigate and almost a thousand prisoners out of the deal. So it looks like you will be in good favour Paul.'

'Yes and he's agreed to keep an eye on our estate in Antigua for us as well,' said Charles. We can go home with a clear conscience.'

'Yes, as long as we get just few of those antibiotics you promised.'

'Of course,' smiled Melissa.

Suddenly there was nothing more to say and with hugs, handshakes and not a few tears all round, Jack, Emma and Smithy climbed into their dinghy and rowed out to Jacaranda in the bay.

The others stayed on the beach and watched as the anchor was pulled up and Jacaranda slowly motored out past the reefs and into open sea. The last they saw of her was her white sails disappearing over the horizon to the east.

When they were alone Charles turned to Melissa. 'What was that bit of paper that Jack slipped to you when he thought no one was watching?'

Melissa looked sheepish and handed it to Charles. On it was a date and time and the location: 'Ministry of Defence Main Building, front steps'.

Jack was looking worried, so was Emma, Smithy was looking even more so.

'That was our fourth try Smithy,' said Jack. 'If we don't find the rift soon we might as well go back and become sugar planters.'

'Bear with me Jack. It was never going to be that simple. Our navigation estimate always started from only a rough position. Let's try this heading now. We should be there pretty soon by my calculations.'

Emma looked at Jack and handed him something. Smithy saw the exchange and sighed. 'If it will make you any happier, don't let me stop you, you bloody superstitious primitives.' His grin belied his words.

Jack opened his hand and looked at the little bone shark. The sunlight glinted in its eyes and suddenly the world lurched.

Epilogue

The hire car drove passed the ivy covered gates and down the ornamental drive. As it parked at the front of the house, Jack and Emma got out and surveyed the building.

'I didn't expect to be stopping here Jack. What on earth are you up to?'

'Oh just a bit of nostalgia. We were going past the house to get to the airport after all.'

'You're up to something you sneaky sod, come on out with it.'

'Maybe, in a minute,' he said. 'Give me a hand with little Charles.'

As they were getting the pushchair out of the car, the front door opened and the owner greeted them like long lost friends. Once the little boy was firmly strapped in he ushered them inside.

'Sorry but once again I need to disappear but feel free to look around and just lock up and pop the key in the letter box at the lodge when you're done.' And he left them alone in the echoing hall.

'You've been planning this haven't you? We were clearly expected.'

Jack just made a non-committal grunt and headed for the stairs.

They had been in England for three weeks finishing off their debriefing with Smithy at area 52 and were now on their way back to St Lucia. Their arrival back in the present had been almost an anti-climax. With no radios left functional on board they couldn't contact anyone. Luckily, they had returned to their original position and so with no other ideas in mind, were heading back to Rodney Bay when a British frigate found them. Once the news of their return got round things happened very fast. Jacaranda was hoisted back onto the repair ship and all the disguise was stripped off. She was then taken back to St Lucia where, as promised, the government paid for a full refit and restoration to her original condition.

Smithy shot off to Guadeloupe to surreptitiously survey the reef, which looked very much the same, except that this time there was absolutely no trace of any metal or wreckage of any sort. Try as they might nothing remained. The only conclusion that could be drawn was that some enterprising local, sometime in the past had discovered the remains and salvaged it for his own unknown purpose. To say Smithy was totally devastated was a no exaggeration. However, by the time they all returned to England he was putting it behind him and enthusiastically thinking of alternative methods to unlock his secret.

Jack climbed the stairs whilst lifting the pushchair with his son in it. He stopped in front of the portrait.

'Well that hasn't changed,' he mused. 'I did wonder if they might try to leave another message of some sort.'

'Jack Vincent, if you don't come clean about what you're up to very soon, you'll regret it.'

'OK,' said Jack. 'What's that on the landing up there in that wooden case?'

'Oh God, it's that bloody guillotine blade isn't it? I'd forgotten it was here. Well don't ask me to look at it again.'

'Ah but you might just want to. Remember these?' and he held out one of the pocket watch detectors that they had all been given. 'We never got round to using them but I kept mine and it still works, at least I think it does.'

'So what?'

'Try this thought. I know that reef. I've often taken customers there snorkelling and never seen any sign of wreckage. Just like we didn't when we were there in the past.'

'So what set the detector off then?'

'Well, I've a theory about that. Suppose we already had some of the metal on board Jacaranda? Even a small amount would have set it off.'

Comprehension dawned on Emma's face.

'Go on then, try it.'

Jack went up the remaining few steps and turned on his detector holding it close to the case with the guillotine blade inside. It started warbling immediately.

'What are we going to do Jack?'

'Absolutely nothing.'

Author's notes

Truth can often be stranger than fiction. Some years ago I was in the Caribbean and both French islands were on strike. It was the start of the recession of 2009 but no one really knew why the islands were so upset. However, the attitude in Guadeloupe was very different to that of Martinique. When I asked why, I got the answer, 'hey man the guillotine never made it to Martinique.' When I researched this remark, I found out it was true. In fact the blade does not reside in 'Hinchfield Hall' rather it is in the National Maritime Museum in Greenwich. Quite how it got there is a bit of a mystery. It is attributed to Captain Scott of HMS Rose and was donated many years after its liberation by a Scott family member. However, the Rose was wrecked off Jamaica only weeks after Victor Hugues arrived in Guadeloupe so it would seem extremely unlikely that Scott himself actually liberated it. Whatever the truth, it has informed the basis of my story and allowed me to let Jacaranda sail into the past once more.

Hugues and the timeline of the capture and recapture of the islands remains faithful to the truth. The French Islands did indeed ask for British support but not expect invasion! Getting 24 pounders up an impossible hill, the Zebra storming the fort when the Three Decker Asia, turned away all happened as described, I merely added another ship, the Polaris. Hugues's recapture of Guadeloupe using liberated slaves which he then re-enslaved was also true and he was indeed the bastard I paint. His subsequent piratical actions were one of the reasons for the Americans to eventually join in the war against France on our side.

It is a fascinating story of an area of the world that is chock block full of fascinating stories. St Lucia changed hands seventeen times in two hundred years. The other islands weren't far behind.

The Guadeloupe Guillotine

6434655R00138

Printed in Great Britain
by Amazon.co.uk, Ltd.,
Marston Gate.